SMALL SPACES

"*Small Spaces* is a beautifully crafted psychological thriller. I couldn't put it down."

FLEUR FERRIS, AUTHOR OF *RISK*, BLACK, WRECK AND FOUND

"This gripping debut messes with your head and makes you doubt your own senses. With *Small Spaces*, Sarah Epstein smashes it out of the park."

ELLIE MARNEY, AUTHOR OF THE EVERY SERIES

"*Small Spaces* is a deliciously creepy YA thriller that reeled me in, made my heart race and kept me guessing to the very end."

RACHAEL CRAW, AUTHOR OF THE SPARK SERIES

SMALL SPACES

SARAH EPSTEIN

WALKER
BOOKS

First published in Great Britain 2018 by Walker Books Ltd
87 Vauxhall Walk, London SE11 5HJ

This edition published 2018

2 4 6 8 10 9 7 5 3 1

This book has been typeset in Fairfield LH

Printed and bound in Great Britain by
CPI Group (UK) Ltd, Croydon CR0 4YY

British Library Cataloguing in Publication Data:
A catalogue record of this book is available
from the British Library

ISBN 978-1-4063-8703-2

www.walker.co.uk

MIX
Paper from
responsible sources
FSC® C020471

For Tony, Hugo and Harvey.

1

NOW

A lot of people have a fear of small spaces.

Elevators, photo booths, changing rooms in clothing stores. Hedge mazes, enclosed water slides, narrow staircases, walk-in wardrobes. I mean, I get it – I avoid those things too. I can't even lie in a bathtub without thrashing like a netted salmon. But sometimes I think the small space I fear most is the one inside my own head.

"You're freaking out, aren't you?" says my best friend Sadie. She's been in enough of these situations with me to recognise the fidgety hands and repetitive swallowing. She's more than familiar with my foot-to-foot shuffle as my eyes hunt down anything resembling an exit. In the eight years I've known Sadie she's talked me down off the ledge at least a hundred times. She's my own personal claustrophobia negotiator whether she wants the gig or not.

"I'm not freaking out."

Sadie snorts, suppressing a smile. "Mmmkay. You're gasping like a goldfish there, champ. Deep breaths." She keeps her eyes on the shop's display counter, at the twenty flavours of ice cream underneath. "Hold it together for thirty more seconds, you got me?"

New negotiation tactic: mild threats, apparently.

I close my eyes and work on slowing my breathing. The last thing I want is to hyperventilate somewhere as public as the Seaspray Kiosk. It was practically empty when Sadie insisted we come inside, until a large group of Port Bellamy High girls followed shortly after us. The tang of body odour and coconut oil seeps into the available oxygen like black ink into paper towel.

"I'll have you know," I manage through clenched teeth, "I'm as chilled as your precious mint choc-chip."

Sliding me a dubious look, Sadie struggles to hold her ground as more bodies press in behind us. She's shielding me from them, carving out a small arc of free space, enduring catty elbows and dirty glares for her trouble. Above me, blowflies snap and crackle as they meet their fate inside the insect zapper, and I try to ignore the warm air sliding around my ankles from beneath the Coke fridge by the wall.

Just breathe, Tash.

Hold your shit together.

Mind over matter.

But if we're relying on my mind as a touchstone, we're really in trouble.

"You and your damn crush," I mutter, and we both glance

8

at the redhead behind the counter. *Alice*, her name badge tells us. She's willowy and timid-looking with a crumpled apron and flyaway hair, the polar opposite of my strong-shouldered and self-assured best friend of Māori descent. "You know she's probably into guys, right?"

Sadie turns to me in mock surprise. "Natasha Carmody, you are *cold*, woman. Don't be such a spoilsport."

I want to be a good wingwoman, I just wish Alice worked somewhere twenty times larger. The Seaspray is a weather-beaten shack at the end of Port Bellamy Pier, where the boardwalk meets the breakwall. Once well-maintained and a drawcard for tourists, it's now perched here like a discarded toy, salt-chewed and clinging to memories of its heyday. Which, when you think about it, pretty much sums up our entire town. Travel websites call Port Bellamy a hidden gem of the New South Wales mid north coast, with its sandy beaches in close proximity to sprawling national parks. But likening it to a precious jewel is far too generous. A rough diamond more like, with flaws you can spot without squinting.

"Our turn next," Sadie assures me above the din of our classmates, a cluster of Year Twelve girls we've known, and barely spoken to, since primary school. Alice hands change to the girl next to us and finally turns our way. Sadie manages an overeager "Hi!" before Rachael Tan elbows her way to the front.

"Raspberry sorbet in a cup," she says, tapping the glass with a glittery fingernail. "Make sure you fill it to the top this time. Be nice to get my money's worth for once."

Sadie turns to Rachael, shaking her head in disbelief.

"Yeah, hi? Earth to Rachael? Way to cut in line."

Rachael barely looks at us, and it's difficult to imagine how the three of us were inseparable when she first moved here from Melbourne. We invited Rachael to sit with us at lunch because we thought it must be tough moving to a new school, especially when her twin brother was immediately embraced by the IT club crowd. And while Rachael readily accepted Sadie's chatty confidence, it felt like she merely tolerated my clumsy attempts at conversation. I remember eleven-year-old me feeling so grateful that this pretty girl, with her trendy clothes and plane trips to her grandparents in Korea, forgave me for being so dumpy and small-town.

"I've been waiting forever," Rachael says now, tucking a strand of black hair behind her ear. "It's my turn."

"Ahh, no?" Sadie folds her arms. "You weren't even here when we came inside."

Rachael takes a long moment to look Sadie up and down, from her faded Sex Pistols T-shirt to her surgically attached purple Chucks. Alice is already serving somebody else and I'm more than ready to cut our losses and get out of here.

But Sadie, being Sadie, is just warming up.

"Mmm, sorry. What was that?" she says, cupping her ear. "Sounds like somebody owes us an apology."

A groan escapes me because I know how this is going to end. I mean, don't we get enough of this at school? There are only a few days left of summer holidays and I'd planned on slipping into my final school year undetected. If I want to prove to my parents I'm capable of looking after myself, I need this year to be incident-free.

Yet, I spend all my time with the most confrontational person on the east coast. Clearly, I haven't thought this through.

Rachael's friends press in closer, surrounding us like seagulls at a picnic, waiting for Rachael to throw them a scrap they can scrabble and squawk over. "Oh, I'm sorry," she says, "that was rude of me. I didn't realise there's an express line for dykes and whackjobs."

And there it is.

"Great," I mutter to Sadie. "Can we leave now, Dee?"

The word *whackjob* slips under my skin and sets it alight. I wince at the word *dyke* too, though I know Sadie couldn't care less. She's learned to ignore this town's small-minded gibes about everything from her skin colour to her rainbow pride T-shirts. She's like Teflon and always has been. I'm a sponge.

"Come on, Rachael," Sadie says, leaning in and arching an eyebrow. "I think we all know why you invited me to so many sleepovers."

She winks like she's flirting but there's no humour in it. Sadie's distracting the seagulls away from me by offering herself up as a hot chip. Rachael's not taking the bait. She smiles coolly and drums her fingernails on the counter.

"Well, gee, if we're talking sleepovers–" she glances over her shoulder, ensuring her audience is captive, "–then maybe Tash can explain to us all why she peed in her sleeping bag like a two year old."

Titters ripple across Rachael's posse and the shop's humidity wraps around my throat and clings there. Mrs Tan made Rachael promise she'd never breathe a word about my little accident five years ago. It seems promises have expiry dates when Rachael's short on ammunition.

"And the way she talked in her sleep," Rachael says, addressing Sadie but looking at me. "Calling out for her little imaginary friend."

Shut up, Rachael. Shutupshutupshutup.

"Oh, Sparrow," she whines. "Help me, Sparrow! I'm so afwaid of the daaaark."

She scrunches her fists like a helpless toddler, and I want to grab them and ram them into her face.

I never said those things in my sleep. I know I didn't.

Did I?

Sparrow is the last person I'd ask for help. I never wanted him to exist in the first place.

Did I?

I didn't.

I don't.

Never again.

"You're so full of it, Rachael," Sadie says, reaching for my hand. She tugs me towards the exit, ramming her shoulder into those too slow to move. We burst outside through the plastic ribbon curtain, the sea breeze grabbing fistfuls of our hair.

Wriggling free of Sadie's grip, I stride down the pier towards the beach.

"Tash," she calls. "Aww, c'mon. Wait up."

I bristle at her voice, at the boats in the marina with their ropes clanging against steel masts. Somewhere, a fisherman has his tinny radio up too loud. The sky is tainted with the brown haze of bushfire smoke from a national park twenty kilometres away. It encroaches from the west like an omen.

Be prepared. Something bad is coming.

Sadie catches up to me where the boardwalk meets the shore.

"Hey, you're okay, right?" she says to my back. "You're out of there now. I'll never drag you in there again."

She thinks this is about my claustrophobia. I whirl around to face her. "We could have just let Rachael order her damn sorbet."

Her mouth drops open. "No, we couldn't. You can't let people walk all over you. You can't say nothing and let them get away with it. Life doesn't work that way."

It does for me. The more forgettable I am, the better. The stigma that's followed me around since childhood is finally waning. Without panic attacks and psychiatric appointments I've become bland and unimportant, another forgettable face in the school corridor cattle drive. Sadie can be brash and provocative and have people talking behind her back, but it's the last thing I want for myself.

"The slumber party, Dee. Did you have to bring that up in front of Rachael?"

She holds up her hands, apologetic. "I wasn't thinking. If I could take it back, I would."

"Yeah, well, you can't. And now I get to kick off my final year with a bedwetting rumour circulating the quad."

I avoid mentioning Sparrow, and Sadie knows better than to bring him up.

"Come on, Tashie. You know I'd never deliberately draw attention to that stuff."

My sandal bows as I stub it on the boards, my aqua toenails looking like I'm trying too hard. "I know ..."

"Carmody–" Sadie looks at me sternly, "–who's got your back?"

Huffing, I glance at the horizon where broody clouds are gathering out at sea.

"Carmody ...?"

I sigh and mumble a begrudging, "You."

"Huh? You'll have to speak up. I couldn't hear you over all the sulking."

"*You've* got my back."

"Damn straight, sister." She hooks an arm around my shoulders and bumps me to her hip. "I've also got your front, your sides, those weird knobbly knees and that big complicated head of yours too."

This time it's my turn to snort. "Great. My own best friend thinks I'm a head case. What hope do I have of changing anyone else's mind?"

Sadie waves a dismissive hand. "Let them think what they want. Those douches at school made their minds up about us years ago. It's your parents we've gotta convince, right?"

Exactly. The only chance I have at applying for a photography degree at a Sydney or Melbourne university is if I can convince my parents I'm capable of looking after myself. It would mean moving out of home and living on campus – not exactly something my mum will be doing cartwheels over. I mean, the woman doesn't even trust me to load a dishwasher properly. She thinks I can't hear her restacking it after I've gone to bed.

"Listen," Sadie says. "My mum's got us another waitressing gig if you want it. A couple of hours and fifty bucks cash in hand?" She wiggles her eyebrows, wanting to make things right.

There's no denying the money comes in handy for professional photo printing, and I need to save for a smart-looking folio to display my work for university interviews. Plus, it's hard saying no to Sadie's mum, Kiri, who's worked so hard to establish her catering business as a single mum with no help from family back in New Zealand.

I slump against a wooden bollard painted to look like a swarthy seaman. "When and where?"

Sadie's shoulders drop an inch, relieved I'm letting it go. As blunt as she can be, I know it rattles her when she upsets me.

"Next Saturday on Banksia Avenue," she says.

I release a low whistle. Banksia Avenue is where all the old brick bungalows are being knocked down and replaced by modern homes with concrete rendering. Most of them have glossy timber gates and high walls lined with palm trees, not to mention views of the ocean.

"Fancypants," Sadie agrees. "Some big welcome-back party for a family returning to the port."

"You mean they actually got out of here and they're *choosing* to return?"

"I know, right?" Sadie tugs her wavy dark-brown hair into a topknot and wrestles an elastic around it. "Not renting either.

They bought that two-storey house with the kooky porthole window. Mum says she's catering for a hundred people."

"Popular family."

We wait to cross Marine Drive as cars inch out of the beach car park, reluctant to leave the warm afternoon behind. Across the road, daytrippers linger outside the fish and chip shop, loose T-shirts over damp swimmers and sandy feet in rubber thongs.

"And I suppose Rachael's wangled an invite," I say, "just to make us really earn our money?"

"Probably," Sadie admits. We turn at the milk bar and head up the hill away from the shops. "Has there ever been a party in Port Bellamy that she hasn't got herself invited to? And anyway, Rachael's mum sold this family the house, so the Tans will be the official welcoming committee."

We cut up through Banksia Avenue and I see that Sadie's right: a real estate sign with a life-size photo of Francine Tan in a blue blazer is attached to the wall at number eight. The cream-coloured home, with its sleek plantation shutters and sandstone driveway, has sat empty for almost eight months. Now there are wicker chairs on the deck and matching topiary trees on either side of the front door.

My attention drifts along the driveway where it stretches past the house to a large double garage at the rear. Something ripples in the back of my mind, lurking under memory's surface like a scent you recognise and can't quite put your finger on.

Up on the cream house's second level, a shadow moves across the round porthole window. A sheer curtain hitches up, then quickly falls back again.

Back again.

Back again?

"Who did you say lives here?"

"I didn't," Sadie says. "I saw the booking on Mum's wall calendar." She squints in a bid to recall. "Beachy-sounding name from memory. Waters or Sailor or something?"

The world suddenly speeds up, then slams on its brakes. My next word is like balancing on tiptoe. "Fisher …?"

"Yeah! Fisher. That's it. You know 'em?"

My mouth goes dry and I don't trust myself to speak. I manage a vague shrug, but my mind is bolting.

"All right, I'd better motor," Sadie says. "Promised Mum I'd help her make seafood fritters." She moves towards the corner where we need to part ways until she realises I'm not following. She takes a hesitant step back, fingering her studded belt nervously. "So, we're okay, right? You still look kind of upset."

"Yeah," I croak, "we're cool."

"Hug it out?"

She comes at me with a hopeful smile and open arms, hooking me around the shoulders the way I hug my little brother when he lets me. I peer across the road to number eight, Banksia Avenue. There's no movement at the window now, but I know she's in there somewhere.

Mallory Fisher.

The girl he took instead of me.

2

THEN

The Mid Coast Times | Archives
Section: News
Date: 13 January 2008

GREENWILLOW, NSW – A missing child alert has been issued for six-year-old Mallory Fisher.

Local authorities say Mallory went missing from Greenwillow on the New South Wales mid north coast on Saturday, 12 January. She attended the Greenwillow Carnival on Summit Road with her parents, Daniel and Annabel Fisher, of Port Bellamy. Mallory became separated from her eight-year-old brother, Morgan, outside the public amenities building at the southern end of the carnival site shortly after 2 pm.

A search of the site was conducted by Mallory's parents

and carnival staff before police were called at approximately 2.45 pm. The search was extended on Saturday evening into surrounding rural properties and nearby bushland.

Mallory is described as an outgoing and inquisitive kindergartner who may have wandered off and become disorientated. She was last seen wearing a yellow and white chequered sundress, a pink short-sleeved cardigan and white canvas shoes. She is approximately 112 cm tall and is described as Caucasian with shoulder-length blonde hair and blue eyes.

If you have any information about Mallory Fisher's whereabouts, contact Crime Stoppers on 1800 333 000.

3

NOW

If you google images of Mallory Fisher, the same three pictures turn up over and over again: her kindergarten photo, a snapshot with her brother at a campground and a cropped section of a blurry family Christmas photo. The first two were released to the press by her parents and graced the short-lived circulation of MISSING posters. The Christmas photo was probably supplied by some well-meaning relative who'd been doorstepped by a pushy reporter.

Perhaps if she hadn't been found alive there would be dozens more. Mallory as a baby, Mallory's sixth birthday party, Mallory riding the Greenwillow carousel. There may have been photographic renderings of how she'd look older – as a ten year old, as a tween, as a pretty teenager. Her age-progressed image might be circulating Facebook as we speak.

Instead Mallory Fisher stumbled out of a hiking trail,

filthy and dehydrated, her scalp bleeding in raw patches where her blonde hair had been torn out in chunks. Mallory Fisher disappeared for seven days and when she resurfaced, the once-chatty six year old never spoke another word. The MISSING posters came down and the Fishers left Port Bellamy, seemingly for good.

The general consensus among locals is that Mallory had been abducted, most likely from Old Meadow Lane, the first road she'd come upon after wandering away from the carnival. *A crime of opportunity* people called it – someone had taken Mallory on a whim, then got scared or bored or grew a conscience, eventually dumping her in Barrington Tops National Park to fend for herself. Newspapers reported that suspects had been questioned but no arrests were ever made. Leads were followed up and eliminated, and unreliable witness statements were debunked.

Including mine.

It makes me cringe when I think about what I told the police I saw that day. It had all seemed so real at the time.

"Who's that?"

I slam the laptop closed and Mallory's images are swallowed up in one jarring bite. My brother Tim peers around my bedroom doorway, craning to see what had my attention.

"Hey. What's doin', Timber?"

He slumps against the doorframe and picks at an old paint drip. "Mum wants her laptop back. And you're not allowed to call me that."

"Call you what, Tim*ber*?"

21

"Stop it," he says with a flash of nine-year-old surliness. "Mum says you're not allowed to call me that any more."

"Yeah, well, Mum says I'm not allowed to do pretty much anything. So maybe you can cut me some slack in the nickname department."

Tim considers this for a moment, then shrugs his approval. He can't work out why the name is suddenly banned either. When he was a baby learning how to walk, he'd plop onto his backside and I'd call out *"Timberrr!"* like he was a tree falling in a forest. He'd giggle every time, so the nickname stuck. It was perfectly acceptable until two weeks ago when Tim tried his new skateboard for the first time.

"Don't call out *Timber* whenever he falls over, Natasha," Mum scolded. "You're drawing attention to his failings. It will scar him psychologically."

Which basically translates as: "One child in this family with issues is plenty, thanks very much."

Not issues, Dr Ingrid would remind her. *Challenges*.

"What were you looking at?" Tim asks, glancing past me at the laptop. I roll my chair in front of it and his eyebrows dip in suspicion. "Who was–?"

"Hey, what are Mum and Dad bickering about?" I usher him back into the hallway, slipping the laptop under my arm. Our long-haired tabby, Mouse, springs off my bed and pads after us.

"Dunno," Tim says, his hand going for the computer. I'm too quick for him and hold it above my head. "They were okay before Dad's phone call."

We pause at the top of the stairs. "What phone call?"

"I answered it – she asked for Dad. She said it was Aunty Ally." Tim glances up, all big blue eyes and tiny freckles. He has a narrow, refined face like Mum, nothing like my pudgy cheeks and deep dimples. "Do we have an Aunty Ally?"

"Yeah–" I chew the inside of my lip, "–we do."

His eyebrows lift. "Are you sure? I've never heard of her. Is she, like, really old? Like a granny? Or a rich person?"

I chuckle quietly, keeping one ear trained on the voices below. No wonder my parents are arguing. It's what happens when Ally drops into their lives, like a grenade in a goldfish pond.

We tiptoe halfway downstairs and plop ourselves on the listening step. From here you can watch TV, eavesdrop on the kitchen and spy on the front yard, all without being seen.

"Aunty Ally's four years younger than Dad," I whisper to Tim. "So she's not old. And definitely not rich."

"Dad's sort of old."

"He's forty-nine, T."

"He's got grey hair," Tim whispers, indignant. "No one else in my class has a dad with grey hair. No one else's dad is nearly *fifty*." He shakes his head like he can't believe this escaped my notice.

"Well, you were a surprise, you know that. Mum and Dad thought their baby-making days were over. Maybe Dad was so shocked it turned his hair grey."

I bug my eyes at Tim and his mouth drops open. He touches light fingertips to his sun-kissed hair. "Can that happen? How scared do you have to be?"

He tickles Mouse's ears absently as his mind wanders,

and I wish I could crawl inside his head and see the scenarios playing out in his mind. A broken Xbox, the angry dog next door, Mum smothering his hair with goop to eradicate head lice. Sweet, innocent nine-year-old stuff – the sort of thing kids' fears *should* be made of.

Mum's voice drifts into the hallway below.

"You said she was in Byron Bay until February. Christ, Richard! There goes our element of surprise."

"It doesn't matter," Dad replies. "Showing her a real estate appraisal won't sway her in the least. She won't budge."

"I know she won't budge, *Richard*." She mutters Dad's name like it's a dirty word. "The whole point of getting the property valuation done while she was away was so the estate agent could get through the door. Francine Tan said your sister threw a bucket of water at her!"

Beside me Tim slaps a hand across his mouth to stifle a giggle. He's probably thinking whoever this old and penniless aunt is, she sounds quirky enough to be cool! And I suppose Ally *is* cool in her bohemian art-hippy kind of way. Last time I saw her she'd shaved her head and planned to paint a huge wall mural down the middle of her house. Only problem is, Willow Creek House is technically not just hers – it belongs to both Ally *and* my dad. Grandma left them the old Colonial Georgian farmhouse when she passed away ten years ago, and Dad's been wanting to sell it ever since.

"She's on her way over," Dad mumbles. "Let's try to sit down and discuss it rationally."

"What? She's coming *here*?"

"She was in the Hunter Valley this morning, so she's calling in on her way home."

Tim blinks at me, his mouth a small *o*. It's never occurred to me that we don't talk about Ally in front of him. The odd few Christmases Ally's dropped in here, Tim's been too young to remember it. One year Ally got so drunk she kicked the Christmas tree over and passed out in her car. Another time, she called Dad a condescending bastard and threw a drink in his face. Needless to say, Mum's stopped inviting her over.

Within minutes there's the low rumble of Ally's Ford F100 in our driveway. The brakes screech as the old truck judders to a halt and promptly backfires. Dad will be cringing – he loves that brown ute with its chrome grille and 1970s pinstriping. It must be tormenting to see it in such bad shape. It belonged to Gran, and since Dad used it to make deliveries for her antiques business, it was a no-brainer he'd inherit it. Then Ally reappeared from some backpacking trip or other and claimed it for herself.

Dad opens the door while his sister is marching up the garden path, and she walks inside without hesitation.

"Richard," she says curtly, fluffing her wavy chestnut hair with both hands. It's halfway down her back now, bringing home how many years have passed since I last saw her. Her figure is slender in an earthy-toned sundress, arms crowded with beads and leather bracelets.

"Bring one of your boyfriends to intimidate me?" Dad says, nodding at the truck. "That loser PJ? Or maybe Klaus the German meathead?" He lets the screen door clatter closed and I duck my head to peer through the window. I spy the outline of someone smoking in the truck's cab.

"Oh, sure, Rich," Ally says, "that's *so* my style. Like I need a man to fight my battles for me. Are you *that* threatened by a woman asserting herself?"

"I don't know. Are you going to throw a bucket of water at me?"

"I don't know. Will I *need* to?"

There's a subtle playfulness to their exchange that reminds me they shared the same house growing up, the same mealtimes and favourite TV shows. If there wasn't so much resentment between them, they'd probably be as thick as thieves. But if I've learned anything it's that the closer you are to someone, the deeper their criticisms cut. Their distrust of you feels like panic; their disappointment in you, like poison.

"Hello, Ally." Mum's voice is tight. "What can we do for you?" No invitation to sit down. No offer of coffee.

"Well, it's more about what you can *stop* doing, Elaine. Like sending snooty little bitches up to my house with keys to let themselves in."

Beside me Tim fights to hide his pleasure at the swearword. I frown a warning and press a finger to my lips.

"Francine Tan is a real estate agent," Mum says carefully, as though explaining to a small child. "We thought you were up at Byron and we wanted to–"

"I'm well aware of what you wanted to do," Ally says. "Which is why I'm here for my other set of keys. Hand them over."

"*Your* keys?" Mum says.

"That's my private space," Ally continues. "No one is welcome in my house without my permission."

"Why? What have you got to hide?"

There's a pause after Mum's question, riddled with pins and wrapped in barbed wire. I think of my summer at Ally's nine years ago, the off-limits rooms and locked doors, the damp steps down into the cellar like the black throat of a beast intent on swallowing me whole. I can almost smell the chalky decay of the window frames, almost hear the clicks and snaps of the old house cracking its joints. If I let myself, I could probably feel the sensation of my socks snagging on nail heads in the floorboards as I'm dragged from one room to another.

My thudding pulse warns me not to let myself.

"Give me the keys, Rich," Ally says.

"You're not having my set. I own half the house, remember?"

"And you're determined to sell it out from under me."

Dad sighs. "We're not trying to force you out. You know I've been wanting to sell my half for years. You can't afford to buy me out so we need to talk about this."

"What was all that crap about getting it heritage-listed if you just want to sell it?"

"I've been approached by Gloucester Shire Council," Dad says. "They're keen to buy it and have some good ideas about how the building could be used."

"It *is* being used. By me!"

"It's crumbling around you and neither of us are in

a position to restore it," Dad says. "We need to sell it to someone who can."

"It's been standing since 1820, Rich. It's hardly going to topple over tomorrow."

"Look, I've given you a decade—"

"So what's the rush now all of a sudden?"

"Tash is starting university next year," Dad says. "There'll be fees to pay, and we'll also try to help her out with a car when the time comes."

My brother glances up at me and I give him a shrug. I had no idea Mum and Dad want to help pay my uni tuition. I just figured I'd get a part-time waitressing job and defer my fees like everybody else. I guess that'll be the case anyway since my parents won't be anticipating the cost of student housing somewhere like Sydney or Melbourne. They're expecting a Newcastle campus I can commute to from here. A way of keeping me close at hand.

A way of monitoring.

"How is Tash?" Ally says, her voice shifting from defensive to curious. My body goes rigid and Tim elbows me in the ribs. "She's what? Sixteen now?"

"Seventeen," Dad says.

Another awkward pause, this time laden with the obvious politeness of what everybody's not saying.

"And she's … okay?"

"She's fine," Mum snaps. "So is your nephew too, if you're interested."

"Of course I'm interested. You're the ones who won't bring him up to Willow Creek. He'd love it there with the bush at the back door and running around with Benny."

Tim touches my arm. I whisper "Her dog" and he smiles with delight.

"What about Tash?" Ally says. "Is she still taking photos? She might like a change of scenery to help get her creativity flowing. She's welcome anytime up at the family home."

"*This* is her family home," Mum says. "And I don't think that's a very good idea."

"Oh, come on, Elaine. You're not still coddling her? She's practically a woman now."

"Will you keep your voice down!" Mum hisses. "Please keep your opinions to yourself. You have no idea what you're talking about when it comes to that girl."

That girl.

I'm usually only *that girl* when Mum is complaining to Dad behind closed doors about not knowing what to do with me.

"Why don't you ask Tash what *she* wants?" Ally says. "Maybe she'd like a couple of weeks' break from your criticism and judgement. God knows I would."

Mum makes an exasperated noise and mumbles something under her breath. Beside me Tim's smile has slipped as he tries to decipher what any of this means.

I feel a strange mix of gratitude and suspicion at Ally's words. I want to believe there's some kind of kinship between us, an understanding of how it feels to be kept at arm's length from your family. It's like she understands how it is for me and yet ... she barely knows me.

"*Okay*," Dad says. "I think we're done here. I'll email you regarding the house."

"What about my keys?"

"They're *my* keys," he says. "The real estate agent still has them."

"I want them back, Rich. And no more drop-ins to fix leaky showerheads. I know you're just doing that to spy on me."

Dad shakes his head as he marches into the hall. He stands with one hand on his hip, the other gesturing towards the door like a bouncer escorting a troublemaker from a nightclub. He looks worn-out in his faded tracksuit, his salt-and-pepper hair in need of a trim.

In contrast, Ally sweeps through the hallway in a rush of tinkling beads and swishing skirt, her hair whipping behind her like fury. "I'd like to say it's been a pleasure, big bro, but that would be a stretch."

"No?" He feigns shock. "Ya think?"

If I squint they could be teenagers.

Mouse decides the open door is an invitation to bolt for the front yard. She springs from Tim's lap, scratching a claw across his knee and causing him to cry out. Dad and Ally turn at once to discover us perched on the stairs, and Dad slides a guilty look towards the kitchen as though their mentions of me are lingering like the whiff of burnt toast.

Ally's eyes lock with mine. I'm suspended in a look of solidarity. It's like she knows–

"It will be our little secret, Tash"

–exactly what I'm thinking.

Tim moves to stand and I slip a protective arm around his shoulders, scooping him back to my side. I'm not sure why

I do it. I'm not sure why I need him to remain untouched by Ally and Willow Creek. After all, it was *me* who created problems there.

Mum strides into the hall and my aunt's connection with me severs. As Ally slips out of the house, the screen door thwacking shut behind her, Mum discovers Tim and me watching from our vantage point. She'll no doubt gloss over what just happened, or perhaps chastise us for eavesdropping.

In the end she does neither. She simply holds out her hand. "Laptop, please."

I lean over the banister and hand it to her, realising too late that I forgot to clear Mallory Fisher's pictures from the web browser.

4

THEN

4 MARCH 2008
TRANSCRIPT FROM THE OFFICE OF DR INGRID BALLANTINE, PHD
CHILD AND ADOLESCENT PSYCHIATRY,
NEWCASTLE CHILDREN'S CLINIC
PATIENT: NATASHA CARMODY, 8 YEARS OLD

IB: Hi, Natasha. It's good to see you again. I met you a couple of weeks ago with your mum. Do you remember?

NC: Yes.

IB: I'm Dr Ballantine. But you can call me Ingrid if you like.

NC: Okay.

IB: Your mum has gone into the next room to have a cup of coffee so we can have a chat, just the two of us. Is that okay?

NC: Yeah ...

IB: How old are you, Natasha?

NC: Eight. I'll be nine soon.

IB: I see. Do you think you might have a cake or a party for your birthday?

NC: Umm, I don't think so. I haven't been very good.

IB: Oh? You think you haven't been very good?

NC: Mum thinks that.

IB: Does she?

NC: Yes.

IB: What makes you say that?

NC: Because I ... I wet the bed.

IB: Sometimes that happens.

NC: It happens a lot.

IB: It does?

NC: Yes. I can't help it. And Mum says, "Enough now. This really has to stop."

IB: Does that upset you?

NC: Yes, because I don't do it on purpose.

IB: It happens while you're sleeping?

NC: Sometimes.

IB: And the other times? Does it happen sometimes when you're awake?

NC: ...

IB: Why do you think that might be?

NC: I try to hold onto it because I don't want to go to the toilet.

IB: Because you're tired?

NC: Because I'm scared.

IB: What are you scared of, Natasha?

NC: He sometimes comes in the dark.

IB: Who does?

NC: ...

IB: Does somebody come to visit you in the dark?

NC: Not for a while. But he might come back. He told me he's always watching. If I get out of bed to go to the toilet he might be waiting in my room.

IB: Who might be?

NC: ...

IB: Is it someone you're afraid of?

NC: I wasn't at first.

IB: Where did you first see him?

NC: At Aunty Ally's.

IB: You went to visit your Aunty Ally?

NC: Mum and Dad sent me there while Tim was being born. I think it was for two weeks. It felt like a really long time.

IB: Had you stayed away from home before without Mum and Dad?

NC: No.

IB: You missed them?

NC: I didn't want them to be with Tim. I wanted them to be with *me*.

IB: I understand. Did you feel a bit left out?

NC: I was all alone. I didn't have anyone to talk to.

IB: What about Aunty Ally?

NC: She was busy. I wasn't allowed in the rooms she was working in. And she went out on deliveries and stuff.

IB: I see. So you really needed a friend? Someone to talk to?

NC: I wanted Mum and Dad.

IB: And then a new friend came, did he?

NC: I didn't ask him to come.

IB: Is this a boy you're talking about?

NC: No.

IB: A grown-up?

NC: No.

IB: Is he a toddler?

NC: ...

IB: Is he a baby like your brother Tim?

NC: ...

IB: An animal?

NC: I don't know what he is.

5

NOW

Port Bellamy High School sits only two streets back from the bluff but offers not one single view of the ocean. It's comprised of three severe brick buildings, the oldest of them built over a century ago. Even with a backdrop of cloudless sky and the school's generous playing fields, the whole vibe still screams *institution*. I feel myself literally slowing down as I get closer, until the last few metres feel like I'm trudging through mud.

I text Sadie my third message for the morning just inside the school's wrought-iron entry gates.

Where you at, kiwi?

She replies lightning-fast: *On my way, kanga. Three minutes. Maybe five, tops.*

First day back at school and she's already running late, though I shouldn't be surprised considering Sadie's only punctual around thirty per cent of the time.

I'll wait for you at the gum tree, I text back, *so we can go to rollcall together.*

And so I don't have to face the school corridors alone. I'm not embarrassed to admit I miss Sadie like a limb when she's not around. In Year Eight she went through a phase of wagging school every second Friday when her mum had hospitality classes at TAFE. I commiserated when she got caught, but secretly I was thrilled.

My phone chimes again.

What's the rumour mill doing? Any cracks about you needing Pull-Ups?

I snort at Sadie's text and find my eyes sweeping the grounds for Rachael Tan.

So far so good, I reply. *But hey, the day is young.*

Seeking shade under the large gum tree on the edge of the car park, I drop my bag near my feet just as a black SUV pulls into the car space in front of me. A tall sandy-haired man climbs out. When he removes his sunglasses, my stomach somersaults in recognition.

Daniel Fisher, my former orthodontist.

And father of Mallory and Morgan.

My pulse trips over itself as I watch the other doors of the vehicle. Morgan and Mallory could be *right there* on the other side of that dark glass. I squint in a futile bid to see beyond the window tint, like I need to prepare myself somehow. In all of my sessions with Dr Ingrid we never explored the possibility of this happening. We never talked about how coming face to face with the Fishers might make me regress.

I'm not that girl any more, I remind myself. That lonely eight year old who made up stories. That girl who told police she watched Mallory being taken from the carnival by an imaginary monster.

I can't be that girl again or I'll never leave this town, never go to university, never have a future. I can't let my mind slip back into swamps I've managed to claw my way out of.

Before I have a chance to recall any of Dr Ingrid's reassuring mantras, the SUV's passenger door pops open. A lanky teenager steps out, scratching his neck awkwardly as he looks around. He's a few inches taller than me, his dark hair a messy quiff reined in at the ears and neck with a mum-imposed trim. He wears a leather cuff watch around one wrist, the other hand slung casually from the belt loop of his skinny jeans.

Morgan, my brain thumps. *Morgan Fisher*.

I flush from head to toe like I've been caught spying on somebody in their underwear.

Retreating behind the low branches of the gum tree, I watch Morgan and his father cross the car park towards the school office.

Morgan wouldn't recognise me anyway, and even if he did it would no doubt be a disappointment. My haircut is safe, my freckles are obvious and the only hip piece of clothing I own is a vintage *E.T.* T-shirt I found in an op shop. And I don't even wear it in public because I'm not cool enough to pull it off.

"Dude." Sadie appears at my side, making me jump. "Might have to get you a bib to go with those Pull-Ups."

She slides her sunglasses onto her forehead as she watches

the Fishers slip inside the school office.

"Please," I splutter, folding my arms. "Not even a drop of drool."

"Why the hell not? His look's on point, especially his hair."

I narrow my eyes at Sadie and she widens her own in response.

"For reals," she says. "I totally want to get my own cut like that. Come on."

She grabs my arm and drags me towards the door the Fishers disappeared through.

"Wait." I attempt to dig my heels in. "You're going to ask him for hair-styling tips *now*?"

Sadie smirks and rummages inside her schoolbag. She pulls out a flyer for her mum's business, *So Delish Catering*. "Good idea. But no. I need to get this to Smiley Janice to put into the school newsletter. She owes Mum a favour."

She links her arm through mine, giving me a play-by-play of who she saw on the way to school, and I feign interest with the occasional smile, all the while thinking about the two members of the Fisher family in that office and how we're heading straight for them.

You know the drill. Just be cool. It was years ago and the Fishers know nothing about what you told the police.

Plus, I was a kid. People forgive kids for making up stuff, right? Even serious stuff? Even if it was for attention?

I chew my thumbnail and avoid looking at my reflection in the glass door.

"Oh, and this is for you," Sadie says, releasing my arm to dig around in her bag again. She tosses me something black and floppy in clear plastic. My eye catches the embroidered *So Delish* logo with its spiralled koru symbol. "We're wearing the black shirts on Saturday. Mum wasn't sure if you have one."

Tucking the polo shirt into my bag, I trail behind Sadie as she strides into the office and up to the reception counter. Smiley Janice, our sour-faced school receptionist, is on a phone call and holds up a stern finger for us to wait. From the corner of my eye I sense someone sitting on the boxy couch beneath the window. I know it's Morgan – his father is across the hall in the principal's office.

Janice hangs up the phone without looking at us and marches into an adjoining room. Sadie rolls her eyes at me and slouches with her back against the counter. She juts her chin in greeting at someone over my shoulder.

Not just someone. Morgan.

"Hey," she says.

"Hey."

I know I should turn around too – it looks weird if I don't – but I keep staring across the counter at Janice's collection of potted mini succulents.

"So, new kid, eh?" Sadie says.

"What gave it away?" His voice is deeper than I expected. Wherever Morgan's been, he hit puberty and grew two feet. He might have pimples. He might even *shave*.

"Well, for starters," Sadie says, "no one around here can maintain that kind of elevation on their hair. It's the sea air – it's too moist and salty. If you were local, you'd've given up by now. I give you two more weeks of styling, max."

"Uh-huh." I hear a smile in his voice. "Go on."

"Secondly, you're pale. Like, sleeping-in-a-coffin pale. Prefer bookstores over beaches, amirite? Total city kid."

He chuckles at this. "Kind of. What else you got?"

"Thirdly, this school has, like, less than six hundred students. And I've never seen your mug before in my life. I'm guessing you're a Port Bellamy newbie."

"Not exactly, no."

Sadie shifts, her interest piqued. I keep staring at those ridiculous terracotta pots all lined up in a row.

"I was born here and moved away when I was eight," Morgan explains. "We've been living in Brisbane and my parents decided to move back here to their home town."

"Okay, wait," Sadie says, clicking her fingers and jerking upright. "Are you a *Fisher*?"

The change in mood is palpable. I can't help glancing over my shoulder to see Morgan's reaction. His cheekbones are stained pink, his thick eyebrows set way, way low.

"Yeah ..." he says, the word wrapped in apprehension.

"My mum's catering your party on Saturday night. Tash and I are waitressing." Sadie whacks my shoulder by way of introduction. It leaves me no choice but to smile awkwardly and nod hello.

Morgan glances at me for the first time, his frown clearing like maybe he remembers me. Like maybe he remembers sitting opposite me in Miss Suresh's Year Two class, how he'd catch me looking at him and he'd cross his eyes at me and we'd giggle into the pages of our books. Like maybe he remembers the day I shared my lunch with him and he drew me a picture of a monkey holding a flag that read *Tash is kind*.

"Tash Carmody," he says, grinning as my name comes to him. One of his front teeth is adorably crooked. How does that happen when your dad's an orthodontist? "Wow. It's been a few years."

"Mm-hm. It has."

"Still live over on Melaleuca Road? Near the old boat sheds?"

He remembers.

"Yep," I offer cautiously. "Lived there my whole life."

He smiles broadly at this, long dimples curling from his cheeks to his chin. "I lived two streets away on Boronia Avenue."

"Number eleven," I blurt.

"Yeah." He laughs lightly, impressed by my memory. His gaze is more attentive now, his round green eyes no longer including Sadie in our conversation. "So, the last time I saw you was ... Man, when would that've been?"

My body temperature soars from warm to blistering.

"Umm ...?" I crush my eyebrows together as though trying to recall, as though that day isn't branded across my psyche like a tender puckered scar. The shimmer in Morgan's eyes dulls and I can tell a response won't be necessary. His mouth slackens and I know he's remembered.

The last time we saw each other Morgan was sitting in the back of a police car.

His legs were dangling from the open rear door, his eyes bloodshot as though he'd been crying. It was five o'clock and the Greenwillow Carnival was closing. His sister had been missing for nearly three hours and the evening search team was being briefed by police beside the carousel. The magnificent horses continued their graceful gallop, braying heads catching the lights as hollow organ music gave the impression nothing was wrong.

But it was *all* wrong.

It was wrong the carnival carried on as normal for hours after it swallowed up a little girl.

I hadn't known what to do with myself as the Fishers' initial panic gave way to helplessness. I skirted around the edges of Mallory's parents and the search team, not sure if I should tell them what I saw. When Ally finally materialised to take me home, she turned up at our agreed meeting place looking frantic. She'd heard second-hand news in the car park.

"I thought it was you," she'd whispered, gripping my shoulders. "They said a girl had gone missing and I thought it must be *you*."

She crouched in front of me, crushing me in a hug that was too close and stifling, her blouse reeking of that sweet, smoky scent she always had. Over her shoulder, Morgan sat all alone in the back of that blue-and-white police car. I freed myself from Ally and wandered over to where Morgan sat, offering him a half-hearted smile. "See you at school?"

He'd looked up at me then, blinking back fear and guilt. "I don't know how I lost her."

My mind has held that image of Morgan for nine years, retracing it over and over as though with a pencil, enhancing the roundness of his bewildered eyes, the smudge of shadows around his downturned mouth. I let my aunt pull me away from him, my resistance weakened by my own need to get as far away from the carnival as possible.

I thought I'd see him again.

I thought I'd have the chance to reassure him: *Morgan, it's not your fault. It's mine.*

"So, you starting today?" Sadie asks now.

Morgan blinks at her. "Uh, no. A couple of weeks."

"Year Twelve?" Sadie asks. He nods. "Cool. We'll see you in class then. Hey, got any cute sisters I should know about?"

A crack snakes through Morgan's composure. He shoots me an unsettled look and my stomach squirms.

"She's only fifteen," he says stiffly. "Plus, she's not even going here."

Sadie glances at me, eyebrows raised. "Dude, it's okay. I'm joking."

"She's homeschooled," Morgan says, "and not into girls, as far as I know."

"She doesn't talk to you about that stuff, eh?"

Morgan's cheeks burn hotter still. "Actually, my sister doesn't speak at all."

Sadie's about to respond when a few things happen at once: the school bell rings, Smiley Janice reappears and Mr Fisher pokes his head out of the principal's office to beckon Morgan over.

"See you Saturday," Sadie says to Morgan. "We'll be the ones trying not to drop food on your mum's rug."

"Yeah," he mumbles. "Nice to meet you." He glances at me and something in his eyes relents. "See you soon, Tash."

"Okay, Morgan. Bye."

I ignore the looks Sadie's giving me as she deals with Janice, the way she's bursting to tease me or press for more details. It's only when we're scurrying late to rollcall that she can't contain herself any longer. "Do we have a little crusharoo, Tashie Tashkins?"

I slide her a *don't-even-start* look and she breaks into a victorious grin as we part ways at the end of the corridor. There's no hiding anything from Sadie. She knows all of my secrets.

Well, nearly all of them.

*

On my way home from school I pick up Tim from Port Bellamy Primary, and I'm grateful to turn my mind to the inner workings of a nine-year-old boy. By the time we reach our house I feel refuelled with Tim's energy, somehow managing to push all thoughts of the Fishers to the back of my head. But when Mum ushers Tim into his bedroom without an afternoon snack, I know my distraction was short-lived.

"Natasha," she says. "I need to talk to you about something."

As soon as we're alone, Mum spins the laptop around on the kitchen counter. I'm confronted with dozens of images of Mallory Fisher.

"You left this Google search open the other day when I asked for my computer back."

I shrug and drop my gaze to her shoulder. "Yeah, I know."

"Do you want to explain why?" Her voice rises. "I mean, we're well past this, aren't we?"

She folds her arms and quickly drops them again, resting one hand awkwardly on the benchtop. *Body language is important*, Dr Ingrid would say. *You need to appear open and receptive.*

"Yes, of course we're past it." I nod earnestly and Mum's shoulders relax an inch. "It's nothing like ... well, you know, like *that*."

She spins the laptop back to her and lowers the lid. It's a slow deliberate movement as she carefully constructs what she'll say next.

"It's just, Sadie's mum wants me for a waitressing gig," I say. "I found out it's a welcome-back party for the Fishers. Did you know they're back in town?"

Mum's mouth drops open slightly. "Uh ... no, I hadn't heard about that."

"It got me thinking, that's all. I've had Mallory on my mind. No big deal."

Mum watches me speak as though lies are hiding in the gaps between words. It takes me back to when I was eight and everything I told her was met with a flash of concern that all was not right with me.

"Mallory Fisher coming back to Port Bellamy," she says, delicately. "It's important that you don't make this all about you."

"Mum! Of course not. I'd never say anything." I step towards her and detect the tiniest flinch. "I'm not a kid any more."

"The Fishers will want the past left in the past. It's the best thing for you too."

"I don't even think about any of it," I lie. "I'm seventeen, Mum. All that Sparrow stuff–" she flinches again, more obvious this time, "–all that stuff is gone. You don't have to worry."

She gives me a long look that tells me she's never stopped.

"Look, I don't think this waitressing job is a good idea," she says, reaching for the phone. She starts scrolling through the saved numbers. "I'll call Kiri and explai–"

"No, don't!"

Sadie can't find out like this; she doesn't know about my connection to the Fishers. I've told her everything else, just not that part.

The truth is, I want to see her. *Mallory*. I need to see her up close after all these years. To be able to look her in the eyes and …

And what?

I don't know.

Yes, you do.

"I can't leave Kiri and Sadie in the lurch like that," I say. "They'll never find someone else on such short notice."

"It's best if–"

"Mum, really." I keep my voice light but firm. "This won't be an issue. You can trust me on this. Everything's going to be fine."

There's a rare glimpse of weakness in Mum's eyes. This year is about proving I've grown up, and waitressing at the Fishers' is a good place to start. It will show my parents that troubled phase of my life is over and all those sessions with Dr Ingrid actually worked.

"Let me show you I can do this," I implore. "There'll be no trouble. I promise."

Mum releases a long breath and returns the phone to its base. Her hand hovers over it for a moment before quickly moving to a nearby notepad.

"Well, anyway," she says, switching gears. "Your aunt called to speak to you."

She tears the top sheet off the pad and wiggles it at me. Ally's name and number are scrawled across it in blue pen.

I blink at Mum. "What does *she* want?"

One fleeting look last week and now Ally's keen to reconnect after all these years of silence? Maybe she was serious about that invitation to her house, but would I seriously consider going back there? The last time was the summer Tim was born, and that was only because Mum and Dad were desperate. I think they even paid Ally to babysit me for those two weeks – that's how little relationship we actually have.

"No idea," Mum says, feigning disinterest. "You don't have to call her back if you don't want to. In fact, it's probably best if you don't."

She trails past me into the family room, plucking Tim's dirty socks from the armchair. When she glances back at me, I make an obvious point of scrunching up the note.

I wait until she's well inside the laundry before slipping the balled-up paper into my pocket.

6

THEN

"It's just that I don't know what you mean, Tash."

Aunty Ally slides the glass milk jug across the table towards me and I try really hard not to crinkle my nose. My aunty doesn't drink regular cow's milk — it has to be this soy stuff that looks off-white and tastes sort of off-white too. I pour some over my muesli and watch as raisins bob to the surface, then push one under again with the tip of my spoon.

"Explain it again," Aunty Ally says, shoving her own cereal bowl to one side. She puts a cigarette between her lips and flicks a green plastic lighter until a small flame appears.

"Which part?" I say.

"From when you woke up in the dark. Let's see if we can't figure this out."

Figure it out? It's not a puzzle. Somebody was in my bedroom last night. I don't know why I have to say it all over again.

It might have been the thunder that woke me up, or maybe a door blowing closed upstairs. The wind was squealing through the old house's cracks like the brakes on Aunty Ally's ute. I remember opening my eyes and blinking at the wallpaper – old-fashioned aeroplanes and hot air balloons. For a second I couldn't remember where I was. It was my dad's bedroom when he was a kid, and that's why I chose it when my aunty said I could sleep anywhere. I don't like the other rooms. This house is cold and nobody laughs here.

The big room didn't scare me as much as the night before because I'd figured out what made the tall bendy shadows. I knew where the lumps in the mattress were, and if I curled my body just right I couldn't even feel them. And to help me fall asleep I could dig my hand under the pillow and find the satin label poking out of the pillowcase. Rubbing it between my fingers almost felt like home.

But I'm not at home.

I've never come here without Mum and Dad before.

I don't really know Aunty Ally.

He made a small sound; that's why I turned over. He was so super still that at first I couldn't even see him in the dark. I blinked a few times to make my eyes see better, and that's when I noticed a dark shape in front of the window, like a black hole blocking the sparkly raindrops on the glass.

There was a big flash of lightning and the room went bright. And there he was, crouched on the window seat facing the bed. He was wearing a hood pulled down low so I couldn't see his face, and his knees were tucked up to his chest like a cat getting ready to pounce. When the lightning flashed again, I saw his bare feet covered in bits of grass. His bony toes were curled over the edge of the window seat like the roots of that tree I tripped on out near the driveway. He looked like one of those stone statues you see on the side of old buildings. Always frozen. Always watching.

"Who are you?" I whispered. If he answered then I couldn't be dreaming.

His head flicked in my direction, tilting to one side like a curious little bird. It reminded me of the sparrows that sit on the fence at home. Mum lets me feed them breadcrumbs if I'm gentle so I don't spook them.

I was very careful not to spook my visitor. He was much, much bigger than a sparrow.

"What's under your hood?" I asked him. He didn't take it off to show me. Instead he moved a hand up to his face and held his pointy finger to his mouth.

"Sssshhhhh."

His hand trembled like he was holding in a giggle. Even in the dark I could see his shoulders wiggling around.

"Is this a game?" I asked, hoping I was right. There'd been no one to play with since I got here. Aunty Ally told me children should make their own fun.

"Yes," he replied. His voice was scratchy like he needed a cough drop. He smelled like wet socks drying on the oil heater.

"Close your eyes and count to fifty," he said. "No cheating."

"I'd never cheat!"

To prove it, I quickly rolled onto my back and covered my eyes to start counting. I'm not sure what number I got up to because the counting made me sleepy. Maybe thirty-five?

Forty? I wasn't sure what would happen once I reached fifty and now I'll never find out. I started dreaming about my aunty's labrador, Benny, and when I woke up it was morning. My visitor was gone.

"Tash?" Aunty Ally says now, the cigarette dangling between her lips. She leans forwards and waves a hand in front of my face like she's wiping invisible glass. "Whoa. Where'd you go, kiddo?"

"Nowhere. I'm right here."

"Your parents know you space out like that?"

"I–I wasn't doing anything." I put my spoon down because I'm not hungry any more. "I was just thinking about my dream."

My aunty watches me as she reaches behind her for a coffee mug on the kitchen bench. She places it on the table next to her green lighter and flicks her cigarette ash into it. "So, now you're saying it was all a dream?"

"No, the dream came after, when he told me to start counting. We were playing a game. I don't know what it was."

She drops her cigarette into the coffee mug. "Do you have bad dreams a lot, Tash?"

"No, I hardly ever dream. And it was a fun dream. I was playing with Benny."

Aunty Ally's voice sounds calm but her eyes don't blink, like maybe she's getting a little bit cross with me. "I mean the part of your dream when you saw someone in your bedroom."

"I didn't dream that part."

Her fingernails tink against the coffee mug over and over again. "Your eyes can play tricks on you in the dark."

"No," I say loudly. Mum says raising my voice is rude, except she isn't here. Neither is Dad. "He was right there beside the bed. He spoke to me. I heard him. I could smell him."

My aunty's mouth tightens and she runs a hand over her short, fuzzy hair.

"It's my fault," she says. "I let you go to bed way too late. And with all the thunder and lightning? I'm not surprised you had a nightmare."

"It wasn't—"

"It was a nightmare, Tash," she says. "You can trust me on that. I came to your room, remember? You called out for me."

I frown at my soggy muesli. I don't remember doing that.

"You must have looked right at him then," I say. "He was crouched on the window seat beside my bed. He was right there!"

Aunty Ally reaches across the table and cups my cheek in her hand.

"Tash, honey, I didn't see anyone."

7

NOW

As I trudge up Banksia Avenue, I can't shake the feeling
that something's clinging to me like a shadow. I have to turn
around once or twice just to check Mum isn't hovering nearby
in her car. She's made a point all week of not mentioning
the Fishers' party until this afternoon when she offered to
drive me over here. I lied and said Sadie was picking me up
from the corner, afraid Mum would find an excuse to invite
herself inside and keep tabs on me all night.

I double-check Sadie's most recent text.

Follow driveway to the back door. We're just setting up.

My eyes find the Fishers' home near the top of the hill,
its upper level painted with hazy evening sunlight. It's been
a warm afternoon, but now long shadows drape languidly
across the road, a cool night promised in their murky depths.
A light breeze dusts the fine hairs along the back of my neck,

and I shiver a little in my black polo shirt. My watch tells me I'm–

Wait.

What was–?

A footstep?

I glance over my shoulder at the street rolling out behind me, at the patchwork of paved driveways and trimmed lawns. A boat trailer here, a caravan there, a handful of pink galahs picking their way through a patch of dandelions.

Wiping my hands across the thighs of my pants, I feel foolish for being so jumpy.

Too much talk about the Fishers. Too much thinking about the past.

I resume walking, a little faster now, my black leather shoes slapping against the bitumen. The white *So Delish* van is parked three driveways away, the gates of number eight thrown open like welcoming arms. The party doesn't start for thirty minutes, so Sadie and her mum will be getting down to the last minute–

There! Again!

I whirl around, my gaze sweeping left and right. Banksia Avenue mocks me with its robust walls and boxy hedges like an expert game of statues.

Don't think about games.

Don't think about him.

"Who's there?" I call, causing one of the galahs to take flight. I feel conspicuous and silly, but I can't deny that prickly sensation of being watched. As I turn to keep going, my eye catches movement. Two houses down are a pair of stacked stone columns flanking a driveway. A shadow moves behind one of them.

Shit.

Panic roils in my stomach.

I spin and sprint flat out towards the Fishers' house. When I reach the *So Delish* van, I skid around the side of it, placing it between me and the road like a shield. I press my back against the hard metal, clamp my lips together and listen.

The only sound I hear is the frenzied swish of blood in my own ears.

You're being paranoid.

You really think you're being followed?

I wait until my pulse slows before peeling myself off the van. This is ridiculous. *I'm* ridiculous. I need the distraction of work to stop my mind from sliding into dangerous territory.

No more than three steps further, a thick clump of azalea bushes quiver below the Fishers' front window.

For a second I think I imagined it, then the branches rustle again. I want to write it off as a cat or a possum, but even in the dimming light I can distinguish the outline of somebody crouched against the house.

He's come back.

Impossible.

Is it?

Hot saliva fills the back of my mouth.

Backing up to the letterbox, I seek out a garden stake or rock in the flowerbed. I snatch up a broken tree branch, sharp on both ends and maybe threatening enough if held the right way.

I creep towards the house again, stick raised. A mix of fear and anger roars up from my belly and into my throat.

"Come out!" I growl. "Come out and face me!"

The bushes shake violently as someone stumbles out of the garden bed. I jerk backwards, clutching my stick like a baton. Then—

He's too big, logic tells me. *It's not him.*

Of course it's not him, genius. He was imaginary.

A young guy straightens in front of me, his tall frame unfurling like a flag.

"Keep your hair on," he grumbles. "Just wanted a few photos."

He holds up both hands in surrender, one clutching a DSLR camera not unlike my own. He can't be more than twenty-five, his cheeks peppered with purple acne scars. He wears a satchel draped across his middle with a staff security tag hanging off it. The circular logo of *The Mid Coast Times* catches my eye.

"What the hell?" I say. "You're a reporter?"

"Photographer," he says. "Unless you'd like to give me a little info about the soiree here tonight? Do you know Mallory Fisher? Does she remember anything about her disappearance?"

"*Hey!*"

The photographer and I jump at a third voice from behind us on the deck. We turn to find Morgan glowering at us, an unlit bamboo torch in each hand.

"You okay, Tash?" he says, dropping his voice to a gentler tone. I nod, lowering my stick behind my back as Morgan turns his attention to the photographer. "Take a hike, vulture. I'm about two seconds away from calling the cops."

"No statement then?" the guy asks, but he's already walking. "Mallory Fisher's homecoming is big news. There'll be a story in Monday's issue either way."

"If there's a photo," Morgan calls after him, "we'll sue you for trespassing."

The photographer forces a laugh as he moves quickly down the hill. When I glance over at the deck again, Morgan is placing the torches to one side. He looks unintentionally nautical in a striped navy T-shirt and tan pants, his lofty crop of hair still defying the moist sea air.

"Wow," he says, breaking into a grin. "You were really going to bludgeon him with that twig, huh?"

My cheeks grow hot as I quickly toss it into the garden.

"He was around here the day we moved in as well," Morgan says. "Although, that day he hid in his car across the street. He must be getting desperate for a scoop if he's resorted to peeping in windows."

"That's creepy," I say. "He's trying to get pictures of Mallory?"

"I guess we're asking for it, coming back to the town we lived in when she disappeared."

"What? No! She should feel safe here. This is her home."

Morgan angles his head, inspecting me closely like he did on Monday at school. "Maybe you could be her bodyguard, come at the paparazzi all twigs-a-blazin'."

I gulp out a laugh and Morgan grins again. I'm not sure how it's happened – we seem to have picked up from our

Year Two days of smiling at each other across our desks. It feels safe and comfortable. And also weirdly thrilling.

"So, how does it feel to be back?" I ask.

Morgan glances towards the horizon, considering this. "I'd like to say it feels like we never left. But it's actually a lot more awkward than I thought it would be."

"Why's that?"

"People are tiptoeing around us now, the ones who knew us before. They're making friendly chitchat and asking polite questions, but you can see it in their eyes – they want answers about the past. They watch you a little bit too closely like they're looking for clues, you know?"

I do know. I know precisely. "As though you're hiding something from them."

"Exactly. I don't feel like I've had a genuine conversation with anyone since we got here. Well, except maybe for this one." He smiles and a silly wave of dizziness rushes over me.

"Happy to hang out and talk anytime you want," I say.

"Okay, cool. I might hold you to that. None of the kids I knew before have bothered following me back on Instagram, so I'm kinda dreading starting school. I hate being the new kid as it is. Now I get to be the new *old* kid that everyone feels uncomfortable around."

"Not me," I say. "Look me up on Insta. I promise I'll follow you back."

Morgan chuckles lightly. "Okay. You've promised now, so don't leave me hanging."

"I won't," I say, smiling at my shoes. I thumb towards the driveway. "Look, I'd better get to work."

"Me too." He scoops up the torches, half-turning towards the front steps.

We both wait a beat longer before parting ways, and I wonder if he feels it too: a flutter, a tiny ripple of possibility.

Then I catch myself.

I'm far too good at imagining things that don't exist.

*

The first hour of the party is a blur of serving trays and champagne glasses. I don't cross paths with Morgan in my many circuits of the house. I haven't seen Mallory either, and I keep looking at the staircase as though she'll make a grand entrance any moment. Although, I imagine parties are probably not your scene when you don't actually talk.

Mr and Mrs Fisher are in their element reuniting with old friends and meeting new ones. Francine Tan keeps clutching Mrs Fisher by the arm and dragging her to meet some local council member or other. Morgan's mother looks radiant in a rose-patterned cocktail dress with matching red lipstick, and his father is equally dapper in a buttoned shirt and blazer, his sandy locks flopping in his eyes like some kind of ageing screen idol.

The thing about waitressing is just how much you can eavesdrop without looking suspicious. Handing around a tray of pastizzi informed me Mr Fisher's reopening his orthodontic practice in Newcastle next week. Collecting empty wineglasses, I overheard that Morgan is creatively inclined, though he doesn't have a clue what he wants to do after finishing school. And serving cups of punch enlightened me about Mrs Fisher's hope to visit the family's holiday house in Greenwillow in March.

My hand wobbled at the mention of Greenwillow, but I managed to keep the punch from sloshing all over the table.

There's a small lull in the serving as we wait for Kiri's kumara patties to heat, so Sadie and I take the opportunity for a short break in the kitchen. Kiri fusses over a plate of sandwiches at the island counter, glancing up briefly to give us a wink.

"Mum's loving this," Sadie says, handing me a glass of water. She tugs at the collar of her polo shirt and I catch a glimpse of her All Blacks rugby T-shirt underneath. "All those potential clients out there with more money than sense."

Across the kitchen Kiri hums, her quick hands in several places at once, always ready with a warm smile or an encouraging word. As well as Kiri's heart-shaped face and deep brown eyes, Sadie has definitely inherited her mum's generosity and fighting spirit. It's been a decade since Sadie's dad convinced them to leave Auckland for a new life in Australia, before draining their bank account and running off to Bali with a bookkeeper from his office. Kiri was left to pick up the pieces and start all over again in a brand-new country. She built *So Delish* from the ground up with little funding and bucketloads of tenacity.

She garnishes the sandwich platter with a sprinkling of tiny blue flowers.

"They're edible," she says in response to our raised eyebrows. Sadie makes a crack about how her mum will be

61

tossing grasshoppers on there next. Kiri simply pokes out her tongue as she shoves the platter into her daughter's hands.

"This one's for you, Tash," Kiri says, as Sadie disappears into the dining room. She hands me a small tray with a few sandwiches, a lemon tart and a bottle of mineral water. "It's for Annabel's daughter, Mallory. Poor wee thing's not a fan of parties."

Kiri isn't aware I know exactly who Mallory is. Sadie and her mum arrived in town a year after Mallory disappeared from the carnival. The Fishers had already packed up and moved away.

"Er, you want me to–?"

"Take it up to her room. Yes please, petal." Kiri sprinkles some flowers over this plate too. "Annabel says it's upstairs, last door on the left. Go through this other door here for a shortcut to the stairs." She points out a sliding door at the rear of the kitchen I'd wrongly guessed led to a butler's pantry.

I take the tray reluctantly. "Maybe Sadie could ..."

"I love my girl," Kiri says, squeezing my elbow, "but she's not exactly discreet. She'd probably talk the poor girl's ear off. Better you do it, eh?"

I smile feebly as Kiri thanks me and returns to the oven. *Okay*, I remind myself. *You wanted to see Mallory face to face? Here's your chance.*

As I follow the short hallway to the stairs, my hands are slick against the underside of the tray. With each step of the staircase my pulse gallops, whipped along by nerves.

Will Mallory remember me?

Can I trust myself not to pummel her with questions?

The last door on the upstairs landing is the only one closed. An EDM song pours out of a doorway on the right, and I spot Morgan and Christopher Tan – Rachael's twin brother – lying across his bed playing video games. Christopher notices me walking by and nods hello, nudging his black-rimmed glasses to the top of his nose. To my irritation, Rachael is squeezed up on Morgan's other side. She glances up as I pass, her eyes taking in my uniform and tray, prompting a smirk.

Tamping down a flare of jealousy (I mean, really? How long has she known Morgan for? She's practically sitting in his lap!), I try to concentrate on the job at hand. I raise my fist to Mallory's door and let it hover there, seriously tempted to leave the tray on the hall runner and skulk away. A roar of laughter floats up from downstairs and I'm momentarily distracted. My knuckles deliver two short raps on the door before I realise what I've done.

There's movement on the other side. The click of a lock. The door opens a crack and a sliver of girl is silhouetted against golden lamplight. She's smaller than I expected and I find myself looking down at her. Half her face is covered by dirty-blonde hair, the other half hidden behind the door.

One eye peers up at me through her hair, piercing-blue and wary.

"Here's some food," I offer. She glances at the tray and back up at my face. "I'm one of the catering staff. I can just leave it out here if you like."

I move to place it on the floor just as Mallory opens the door wider, gesturing at an antique desk positioned near the porthole window. A few empty moving boxes are piled up beside it, a length of bubble wrap draped to the floor.

Her room is lined with pine bookcases crammed full of colourful spines, some books shelved vertically and others stacked in haphazard piles. The walls are plastered with posters of fantasy worlds and rambling secret gardens, her pinboard dotted with postcards of far-flung galaxies and medieval castles. A hand-carved box shelf sits above the bed, filled with a menagerie of stuffed dragons, owls and foxes. A sky of fairy lights on the ceiling gives the room its otherworldly glow.

"God, I love your bedroom," I say, drinking it all in, this haven from the outside world. I quickly remember my role here tonight and step back into the hall. "Sorry. I'll leave you to it."

Mallory tugs at the sleeves of her oversized shirt as she watches me. I try not to be obvious about snatching glimpses of her face. There's little hint of the grinning kindergartner from her MISSING posters all those years ago. Her skin is dull and waxy now, her hair lank. She curls her shoulders defensively as though warding off some kind of threat.

But it's her eyes that seize hold of me, crystal clear and evaluating. There are questions there, and a sea of answers too. It sparks an urge in me to shake her, demand to know how she disappeared. Did she wander off? Was she taken?

Did I really imagine him, Mallory?

Please tell me my mind isn't that sick!

Instead I mumble "See you later", lingering briefly for a response until I realise, of course, I won't be getting one.

When I return to the kitchen, I find Sadie on her hands

and knees mopping up a spill.

"Minor catastrophe," she says. "Mum dropped a jar of mayo. She's racing down to 7-Eleven to get another one."

I grab a stack of cocktail napkins and crouch beside Sadie. She picks out the glass as I swab the creamy goop into a runny pile. I pretend to come at her face with a globby napkinful, and she jerks away, landing on her backside. We erupt into giggles.

"Oh, crap," she says, scrambling to her feet. "Mum wanted me to get these kumara patties out while they're still hot."

"I'll finish this up," I tell her. "Just direct me to a mop and bucket."

"Maybe the laundry? That's where I found a dustpan," Sadie says, nodding towards a doorway off the back of the kitchen. She hesitates. "It's kinda tight in there though. I can do it when I get back."

I trail over to the laundry doorway. It's a narrow, windowless room lined with cupboards below the benchtop and above. My limbs stiffen, a slightly woozy sensation fizzing at the base of my skull.

"I'll be quick," I assure Sadie, though I'm really just reassuring myself. "In and out. It'll only take a sec."

I flick at the light switch until Sadie calls out, "Bulb's blown. Just wait for me, eh?"

This is absurd. I feel like a little kid too scared to go down a slippery dip. Balling my hands into fists, I stride into the laundry and yank open cupboard doors.

"On a mission, are we?" Sadie says, mildly amused. "In that case, try those top cupboards for some floor cleaner.

There's a small stepladder by the back door if you can't reach the high shelves."

I move towards the wooden chair propping the door open.

"Don't use that!" Sadie blurts. I pull my hand away like the chair is electrified. "The door closes by itself and the handle's dodgy. Found that out the hard way."

She lifts the platter and hovers for a moment longer before heading back out to the party. I search as quickly as I can, trying to ignore the cupboards encroaching on my personal space.

There's definitely enough oxygen.

There's absolutely no reason to panic.

I manage to locate a mop inside a skinny cupboard and prop it up beside me. As I reach for one of the high cupboards, the tiny room is plunged into shadows. The silhouette of a body is framed in the doorway, blocking the light.

No.

Backing up quickly, I knock into the wall. The mop clatters to the floor and it sets my heart racing.

Not him. Not here.

My right hand flails for the benchtop as the figure approaches.

Get out get out get out.

"What have you lost?" he says, the side of his face now illuminated by the kitchen.

Morgan.

I slump against the wall and release a shaky breath.

"J–just a bucket," I say. "Um, maybe some floor cleaner?" I turn and grope around on the floor for the mop.

"No problem," he says. "Here to help."

I don't realise what Morgan's doing until the swathe of light across the floor begins to shrink. I turn to find he's dragged the chair over to the counter. The last thing I see is Morgan placing a foot on the seat before the door clunks shut, plunging us both into darkness.

"Oops. Hang on," Morgan says. I hear the door rattle, the useless *click click click* of the light switch.

"The bulb's blown," I croak. "Try the doorhandle again?"

"Just can't seem to—"

The door rattles again and Morgan grunts like he's tugging on the handle. I blink rapidly, willing my eyes to adjust. All I can make out are the shadows of Morgan's feet disrupting the strip of light along the base of the door.

The temperature of the tiny room is climbing. Or my skin is. The air around us tastes dank and warm.

My air.

"Are you okay?" Morgan says. "Your breathing sounds funny. Are you asthmatic?"

I fight to keep my voice level. "I need to get out."

Pacing back and forth in the corner, my knees knock into cupboards like pinballs.

"It's all right," Morgan says. "I've just gotta …" The door rattles again and the handle makes a clunking noise. Something metallic pings across the tiles between our feet. "Okay, that's not good. Hey, you're not claustrophobic, are you?"

There's a smile in his voice, a hopeful stab at humour. I can't answer him. Instead, I sink to my knees—

"Do you want to play a game?"

—the darkness pressing in. It fills my nostrils, oozing thickly down my throat.

"Please," I gasp.

I can't breathe.

"Tash?" I sense Morgan moving towards me. "Where are you?"

I bring my knees to my chest, wrap my arms around my shins.

Be small. Breathe small.

Morgan's hands find my shoulders and—

"You're not playing it right. Stop struggling."

—my body jerks, my arm knocking some part of him away.

"Whoa, Tash," he says. "What's wrong?"

I pant tiny, minuscule breaths.

Don't run out of air.

"You're hyperventilating." Morgan's hand finds my shoulder. This time I let it stay there. "You've got to slow your breathing down. Deep breaths. Listen – like me."

He takes a long breath in through his nose, releases it low and steady through his mouth. His hand finds my other shoulder and he coaches me through another five breaths before we hear a clatter in the kitchen beyond. He squeezes my shoulders a final time before sliding across the floor to pound against the door.

"Hello?" he says. "We're kinda stuck in here. *Hello?*"

I concentrate on breathing – slow and deep, long and steady – and my chest flutters with relief when I hear Sadie swear on the other side of the door. Next second there's a loud thump and the door pops open. Sadie tumbles into the laundry in a blast of bright light.

"What are you doing to her?" she says, when she spots me balled up in the corner.

She shoves past Morgan and drops to her knees, her arms gathering me up and pulling me close.

"Nothing!" Morgan says, wide-eyed. He backs into the kitchen to give us more room. "I moved the chair and we got locked in. Tash just panicked. I was trying to help."

Sadie helps me to my feet. "You and your small spaces, eh, kid?"

My face must look grave because Sadie's good-natured teasing stops there. Morgan moves to the sink and returns with a glass of water.

"The Sparrow thing again?" Sadie murmurs.

I nod sheepishly.

"What's the Sparrow thing?" Morgan asks, his gaze bouncing between us.

Sadie narrows her eyes at him. "Hey, this is *your* house – how do you not know that door jams?"

Doubt stirs in the pit of my stomach. Sadie's right. Why would Morgan move that chair?

"I forgot," he says, turning to me. "We've only lived here for three weeks. I'm sorry, I just forgot."

Sadie scowls as she takes the water glass from him. She offers it to me but I shake my head. "I'm fine," I tell her, my voice sounding a bit stronger than I feel. Sadie looks about as convinced as if I'd insisted my head is a watermelon. I glance at Morgan. "You don't need to be sorry. It was an accident."

Sadie peers over her shoulder at him. "I've got this." Her voice is skating a fine line between efficient and rude. For the sake of her mum's business she forces a smile, adding, "We're all good here. Please go and enjoy your party."

Morgan's eyes find mine and I nod to reassure him. He sighs heavily and trails back into the dining room. Once Sadie's satisfied we're alone, she drags a stool out from under the breakfast bar and thrusts the water glass into my hands.

"Sit down," she says. "Drink this. No bloody arguments."

I give her an army salute and she flicks me on the earlobe before marching over to the laundry. Within seconds she's yanking open cupboard doors in search of a bucket. I slide onto the stool and bring the water glass to my lips, my gaze drifting across the island bench to the sliding door in the back corner of the kitchen.

Mallory is standing in the doorway.

I startle, sucking in a breath and inhaling water. My chest explodes as I double over coughing. Sadie pokes her head out of the laundry. "You *serious*, Carmody? What now?"

"It's okay," I choke out, gesturing towards Mallory. Sadie glances at the corner and frowns. "She just–"

Words escape me when I see what Sadie is looking at.

Absolutely nothing.

Mallory's disappeared like she was never there at all.

8

THEN

11 MARCH 2008
TRANSCRIPT FROM THE OFFICE OF DR INGRID BALLANTINE, PHD
CHILD AND ADOLESCENT PSYCHIATRY,
NEWCASTLE CHILDREN'S CLINIC
PATIENT: NATASHA CARMODY, 8 YEARS OLD

IB: Do you want to talk about Tim?

NC: Okay.

IB: Your mum and dad must be busy now with a new baby. He's
so small and can't do anything for himself, can he? So your mum
and dad need to look after him. Babies can be a lot of work.

NC: Yeah.

IB: And he'll grow up a little more each day, won't he? Your mum
and dad need to take care of him as well as you. How do you feel
about that?

NC: Good. If they don't take care of him he'll starve to death.

IB: That's true. Your mum and dad will have to divide up their time to take care of both of you as you grow up.

NC: I know.

IB: You used to have your mum and dad all to yourself, didn't you? You probably have to wait sometimes now while they do things for Tim.

NC: Mm-hmm. And Mum's always tired. She never wants to do crafts or make muffins with me any more.

IB: Does that upset you?

NC: We used to do things together. Plus Tim cries a lot. He wakes us all up at night because he's really loud. But sometimes I don't mind.

IB: If he wakes you up? Why's that?

NC: I have bad dreams. He saves me from them.

IB: Tim saves you?

NC: I get stuck in bad dreams sometimes and I can't get out of them. Tim's crying wakes me up.

IB: What are your bad dreams about?

NC: I can't remember them all.

IB: Can you remember any?

NC: Yes. I was trapped inside a box and it was dark. I couldn't breathe.

IB: Were you afraid?

NC: Yes! I thumped on the sides of the box with my hands, and I pushed and kicked. I didn't have any space! It was hard under my knees and I knocked my head on the sides. The top of the box was – right here – against my back.

IB: All right. Why don't you sit down and move back onto the couch again? Just get nice and comfy there – that's the way. I see that dream makes you feel worried.

NC: And no one helps me. Even when I call out for Mum and Dad, they don't come.

IB: I see.

NC: Mum says she's tired from getting up for Tim so much and she really needs to sleep. She says I need to stop calling out for her. She says I'm doing it for attention.

IB: Your mum said that?

NC: To Dad. I heard her. She says I'm acting out.

IB: Do you know what "acting out" means?

NC: Not really. I know what "attention" means. It's when you want everyone to look at you and fuss over you and stuff.

IB: Do you think you do or say things sometimes to get attention from your mum and dad?

NC: Maybe sometimes.

IB: What kind of things might you do to get attention?

NC: I say, "Excuse me, Mum" so I can ask her a question.

IB: Do you tell her when something bad has happened? So she can listen to you and give you a hug?

NC: I do, but she doesn't give me a hug. She says I need to stop making things up.

IB: Do you sometimes make things up?

NC: I'm not sure …

IB: You're not?

NC: No, because some things happened that were real and no one believed me, and now I think they might not have been real. I didn't make them up, though.

IB: You mentioned earlier that if your mum didn't look after Tim he might starve to death. That's quite a grown-up expression, isn't it? "Starve to death"? Where have you heard that said before? Did you hear your mum say it?

NC: No. He said it to me.

IB: Your dad?

NC: No, *he* did.

IB: Your visitor at Aunty Ally's?

NC: Yes. He said mean stuff sometimes.

IB: What kind of mean stuff did he say?

NC: He told me if I didn't do what he said he'd lock me in a box and no one would find me and I'd starve to death.

IB: That doesn't seem nice at all. Why do you think he said something like that?

NC: Because he wanted me to do things.

IB: What sort of things, Natasha?

NC: I'm not supposed to tell you.

IB: Why not?

NC: He didn't want any grown-ups finding out.

9

NOW

News of my panic attack at the Fishers' party made it all over school less than thirty-six hours after it happened. Now it's like every weird little public breakdown I've ever had has bobbed to the surface in everyone's minds. A guy in Monday's rollcall muttered "Drama queen" behind my back and the week went downhill from there. In Tuesday's PE class, Rachael's fangirls made exaggerated whimpering noises when I left the netball court with a twisted ankle. And by Friday a group of smirking Year Eight boys asked me point-blank if I'm that "crazy chick who's scared of the dark".

Even now, a full week after the laundry incident, my face still burns at the memory. I shouldn't be surprised that Rachael kickstarted the rumour mill again. Gossip is her currency at school; the crueller she is with it, the more powerful the reminder that people had better stay on her good side. She doesn't get top marks like her brother, and she's not gifted with social eloquence like her mum. She plays to her strengths and her talent is manipulation.

So while I expect it of Rachael, I can't help feeling a twinge of betrayal at Morgan for sharing with her what happened in his laundry.

He didn't have to tell her – he didn't have to tell anyone – even if he doesn't know Rachael very well yet or how she'd exploit it. It's like I have this silly notion that because we shared a sandwich once in Year Two, Morgan has some kind of allegiance to me.

"You gonna eat that?" Tim says, leaning across the kitchen table.

I glance at my plate to find his fingers pinching my last pancake. We normally eat cereal at opposite ends of the couch on Saturday mornings, but today I insisted on a sit-down breakfast. Two weeks into school and I already feel like I don't see enough of his grubby little face.

"Not now it has boy germs all over it," I tell him and nudge my plate in his direction. He's already dangling the pancake in midair. His grin is all mischief and maple syrup, and I feel a sudden swell of affection for him.

"Aww, what a shame," he says as he tips his head back to lower the pancake into his mouth. A strawberry slides off his chin and slops down the front of his T-shirt. He side-eyes me making *mmm* and *yummm* noises, so I dip my fingers into my water glass and flick them at his face.

"Really, Natasha," Mum says, striding into the kitchen. She dumps two shopping bags on the benchtop. "I have trouble determining which one is the child. I mean, *honestly*."

She *tsks* at the water droplets all over the table, prompting her to seek out a disaster zone in the sink. Her eyes hunt for a dirty frypan or flour and milk spread from one end of the benchtop to the other. I won't pretend I don't feel smug when she finds everything pristine. I almost imagine an approving eyebrow arch, a small noise in the back of her throat to show she's impressed.

Instead, she yanks open the dishwasher and mumbles, "Well, this will all have to be restacked."

My chair screeches as I stand to collect our plates. Tim gives me a secret eye roll and I attempt to smile back.

"We need to go shopping for shoes today," Mum says, while she unpacks the groceries. Jars and tins knock together in the cupboard as she corrals them into rows. "You both need new sneakers. We'll drive over to Watergardens as soon as Tim's changed his T-shirt."

"I was going to head down to the old mill to take photos," I tell her. I feel like I haven't photographed anything in months even though it's really only been a couple of weeks. "The light's no good in the middle of the day."

"This is the only chance I *have*, Natasha. I have to go to Gayle Simpson's this afternoon to organise the school fundraiser. God knows when I'll have time to sew Tim's scout badges onto his uniform before tonight's barbecue."

"Why don't I take Tim shoe shopping?" I suggest. "I can do it this afternoon while you're over at the Simpsons' place. That way you can sew the badges on now and I can head down to the mill."

Tim nods eagerly at this. If it's just the two of us, we can go to the churros place and he can spend some of his pocket money at the arcade. We can have some actual fun.

Mum doesn't even pretend to consider. "No. We'll go now. Change your T-shirt, Tim. I'll meet you both out the front."

My brother groans loudly and drags himself to the stairs as though his limbs are made of lead. I snatch up my bag and shrug it over my shoulder as sulkily as I can. Mum doesn't register our protests. She's bent over something on the front doorstep.

"What is ...?" She straightens quickly and backs up a step. "Ugh."

"What's wrong?" I move to the doorway and peer over her shoulder. A small grey and brown object is sitting in the centre of the doormat.

"Bloody cat," Mum mutters, jiggling her keys nervously. "Do me a favour and get rid of it before Tim sees. It might upset him."

She takes an exaggerated step over the doormat like she's traversing a crocodile tank, and I can finally see what she was looking at.

A tiny dead sparrow.

Who's she kidding? Tim's a nine-year-old boy – icky things like this are what he lives for. The only person who gets squeamish about this type of stuff is Mum. It's her phobia, I suppose, having to handle dead things, or worse, having to kill something with her own two hands. Dad finds it funny how Mum will crawl up the back of the couch and call for help rather than whack a cockroach with a shoe. Even more amusing to Dad is how *I* can manage to dispatch spiders and dead mice, yet I can't ride through a car wash or spend longer than three minutes in a toilet cubicle.

But it's not like we pick and choose what to be afraid of.

It's like our fears pick us.

I crouch in front of the sparrow, nudging it with my finger in case it's merely stunned. Tim clomps down the staircase behind me, so I straighten to a stand and block the dead bird from his view.

"Mum's favourite," I say dryly, nodding at his black Darth Vader T-shirt. "You know she'll make you come back inside to change."

He gives me a cheeky grin. "There's not enough time." I snigger as he wanders over to the car.

Once the coast is clear, I dash back into the kitchen for a plastic bag, returning to the doormat with it over one hand like a glove. I gingerly pick up the sparrow, distracted by how its head flops unnaturally to one side. I flick my wrist left and right, and the sparrow's head lolls like its neck is made of rubber.

Can a cat do that? Twist a bird's neck until it breaks?

As soon as the thought surfaces I realise what should have been obvious as soon as I spotted it over Mum's shoulder: the bird doesn't have a scratch on it. Not a spot of blood, not a feather out of place, no evidence at all it met with Mouse's teeth or claws.

And as I place it in the wheelie bin among a graveyard of garbage bags, something even more unnerving registers.

Its body is still warm.

An hour later I'm still thinking about it as we wander around Watergardens. I've almost convinced myself that sparrow flew into our screen door and shattered its body. Birds fly into windows all the time so it's not a stretch to think this one might have misjudged its flight path too. But a niggling thought fuels my paranoia: is it merely coincidence a dead sparrow appears on my doorstep only two weeks after Rachael broadcast my imaginary friend's name to her clique at the Seaspray? Those girls would do anything to please her. Rachael could be trolling me without even getting her manicured hands dirty.

Mum drags us from store to store like a woman on a mission. Tim soon grows frustrated about being ordered which shoes to try on without being given a choice.

"No one wears these," he complains about a pair of fluorescent sneakers. His growing resentment about being babied results in a flat *No* to three more pairs I know he'd dearly love to own. Mum's oblivious to the tug-of-war of independence going on, and in some ways I blame myself. At Tim's age I was behaving helplessly, unpredictably. Mum had no choice but to take control.

However, Tim's not needy and erratic like I was. He's level-headed and reliable. He's given Mum no cause to think he can't be trusted. I pull Mum aside while Tim's sulking by the sports socks.

"How about I take him up to the food court for something to eat?" I say. "You do the other things on your list and we'll meet you in an hour." I don't mention that I'll take Tim back to the sports store after lunch to pick out his own shoes. I still have fifty bucks from last Saturday's catering gig in my purse.

Mum doesn't argue. She actually concedes with a grateful sigh. It makes me feel good that I've found a way to help her out. And, more importantly, she's going to trust me to do it.

Tim becomes animated again as soon as Mum's gone. We hit the arcade before lunch, playing pinball and air hockey until we're out of coins. As we make our way up to the food court, I'm so caught up in Tim's game of Spot-the-Secret-Superhero I almost walk into someone at the pick-up counter of Caffeined.

It takes me a second to realise he's walked into my path on purpose.

"Uh, hey, Tash."

I swerve around him, taking in his round green eyes and tousled bed hair. Morgan gives me an awkward wave.

"Oh, hi." I stop abruptly and Tim wanders ahead before he realises I'm no longer beside him.

"How are you?" Morgan says, rocking on his heels. "You know, it occurred to me we should have swapped phone numbers last Saturday. I haven't been able to call and check in with how you're doing after ... Well, you know, after the party."

His words tumble out so quickly I'm not sure I heard him correctly. "You want my number?"

"Well, yeah. If that's cool? Except now you're looking at me like it's weird."

"No, it's just—" I glance over my shoulder to find Tim peering into the display case of the bakery next door. I lower my voice. "Sometimes I get a little haywire, I guess you could say."

Morgan smiles, leaning in conspiratorially. "We've all got a few defects though, right? I mean, faulty is my favourite kind of people."

Eyeing him for a moment, I'm unsure of how to reply. He might be referring to his sister, and I don't know if I should acknowledge that or if it would come across as rude. He catches my look and his face reddens. My brain only now catches up.

Wait. *I'm* his favourite kind of people?

"I'm sorry," he says, reading my stunned look as offence. "I don't mean that you're – I mean, you're not *defective*. I'm just mucking around."

If only he knew how accurate he really is.

"Can we erase all of that and start again?" he asks sheepishly.

I laugh. "Consider it done."

Morgan fills me in on his week of shopping for his schoolbooks and uniform, the online cartooning course he's just signed up for, how he wiggled out of unpacking boxes at home by helping his Dad paint the walls of the orthodontic practice.

"God, sorry. I've barely taken a breath," he says. "I think I'm a bit wired."

"You really need that coffee?"

"Probably not." He smiles. "I only had a few hours' sleep

though. Late-night gaming with Chris Tan."

"Oh, right. So you guys are friends?"

"Yeah, it seems so. He's a pretty cool guy. Different to my mates in Brisbane."

"Different how?"

"Chris is pretty switched on and he's got a lot of similar interests with the tech and creative stuff," he says. "Most of my Brissy mates were either revheads or footy fanatics. We moved houses and schools a lot, so I just tried to fit in wherever I could."

"I didn't realise you'd moved around so much."

"It's Mum – she gets restless," he says. "I think the whole time we lived up there she just wanted to be back here in Port Bellamy."

"It must be hard changing schools so often."

"Yeah. I learned to develop hobbies that didn't require me to be in one place for any length of time," he says. "Like drawing and stop motion animation. My parents have paid for me to do a lot of online courses."

"I've done a couple of those myself for photography."

"Really? I'd love to see some of your work sometime."

"You can check out my Instagram. Only if you promise to scroll past any goofy selfies with Sadie."

Morgan chuckles. "And who's this?" he says, peering round me at Tim who's been amusing himself with the bakery's free samples. "Cool T-shirt."

I'm just about to call Tim over to introduce him when Morgan's name is called by the cafe's barista.

"Guess that's you," I say.

"Yeah." He glances over his shoulder but doesn't move. I feel that little flutter of anticipation again, like I did in his front yard last Saturday. The barista repeats his name, louder this time. "Okay, I'd better go and get that."

"So I'll see you at school on Monday then?"

"You will indeed," he says, jogging over to retrieve his coffee.

*

In the food court Tim orders a greasy burger with the lot, plus extra fried onions and pickles. It's inevitable half of it will end up in his lap. I make a mental note to grab more serviettes from the sushi place when I go over there to buy my lunch.

"Don't leave the table, okay?" I tell Tim, uncapping his bottle of water for him. He's busy licking a trail of tomato sauce from his wrist. "I'm just going to grab some sushi from that place over there. Wait here for me, okay? Tim? Are you listening?"

"Mm-hmm," he grunts. His gaze is dancing over store signage and spinning mobiles.

People swarm around the food outlets like angry bees and it takes some effort to push my way through. When I finally reach the sushi shop I can still spot Tim through the crowd. The line for sushi is five people deep so I let my gaze wander to a nearby bookshop, then onto a homewares store with some plastic flamingos Sadie would think are cool. My attention is drifting over the crowded walkway when it snags.

A figure is standing in front of the escalators.

Watching me.

He could almost be just another scruffy dark hoodie in the crowd. A little strange to wear the hood up indoors, although teenagers do it all the time. He'd be completely unremarkable standing outside the music store, or even passing by me in the arcade.

But in a stream of shoppers pouring off the escalator, he's a jagged rock disrupting the flow. People trickle past him, around him, accommodating his presence without actually seeing him.

I see him.

Like I've zoomed in with a camera lens and everything else has blurred into the background.

His hands are shoved into the pockets of baggy jeans, his hoodie swimming on a scrawny frame. His head is tilted to one side, watchful. Calculating. The shadow from his hood erases the top half of his face, and his lips peel back in the rotten sneer I know all too well from my nightmares.

"Do you want to play a game?"

I crush my eyelids shut.

Stop this, Tash. It's not him.

I suck in a deep breath, release it. When I open my eyes, he's gone.

I glance across to our table in the food court. Tim's still happily shoving burger into his face. Pressing the balls of my hands into my temples, I rotate them in rough circles until pain throbs behind my eyes.

Why is this happening again?

Over at the escalators it's business as usual: people tussling with shopping trolleys, teenagers texting, dads piggybacking toddlers. I try to keep my attention on the sushi menu board, willing myself not to look over my shoulder. Instinct gnaws at my common sense, though, and I can't help combing the crowded walkways in a macabre game of *Where's Wally?*. I feel myself drifting away from the sushi line, too distracted to care that my spot fills quickly in my absence.

My eyes dart from one gleaming shop window to the next, from this person to that one. Seeking, scouring, hunting.

And then I spot him.

Eight stores down, peeking out from behind a column.

My heart slams against my ribs.

How? I got rid of him! How the hell can he be here?

This has to be some kind of prank, and I'm already moving to find out.

He takes off in a light run when he sees me coming. I battle against the flow of foot traffic, knocking into shoulders and muttering apologies, trying to keep a lock on the black hoodie as he bobs and ducks out of my crosshairs. The crowd becomes more congested when we reach the forecourt area. Scanning left and right, I scrutinise every dark piece of clothing. None of them his. None of them him.

Hot tears prick at my eyes and I growl in frustration. After all of my sessions with Dr Ingrid, I can't believe I'm back here wondering what's real and what isn't.

Feeling ridiculous, I haul myself back up to the food court, my appetite lost to the festering worry in the pit of my stomach. My watch tells me it's almost time to meet Mum, time to shake this off and plaster a smile across my face. Be normal.

As I weave my way back towards our table, I think I must've got turned around somehow.

This can't be right.

I glance behind me to reorientate myself with the sushi shop. This is definitely the section where I left Tim.

Tripping and stumbling over chairs, I fight my way through to our table, a fist of panic seizing my chest. Tim's half-eaten burger is lying dishevelled on its waxy wrapping paper. His bottle of water is on its side vomiting its contents all over the floor, and Tim—

Tim's gone.

10

THEN

The Mid Coast Times | Archives
Section: News
Date: 19 January 2008

PORT BELLAMY, NSW – Six-year-old girl missing for seven days found alive.

Police confirmed that Mallory Fisher, who disappeared from the Greenwillow Carnival last Saturday, was found yesterday near a hiking trail more than forty kilometres from where she went missing. At around 4 pm she was spotted by hikers as she attempted to climb out of a dry creek bed in Barrington Tops National Park.

Brandon Elliott, a nineteen-year-old university student hiking with his parents in the area, claimed he heard a "mewling noise" he believed to be an injured animal. When he peered into the creek bed below he saw a small girl trying to pull herself up a steep dirt bank. He could not confirm if she was wearing the yellow sundress she disappeared in because she was "so filthy", although he did confirm she had no shoes or cardigan. Elliott also claimed she was covered in scratches and "looked like she'd yanked some hair out. She was pretty messed up."

Mallory was mildly hypothermic and suffering from dehydration and multiple abrasions. She was taken to John Hunter Hospital in Newcastle where, according to her father, Daniel Fisher, she is in a stable condition but "confused and exhausted".

It is unclear how long Mallory was wandering in Barrington Tops National Park. Police believe she may have been held in a prior location. Her general state of health indicated it is unlikely she was outside for the full duration of her disappearance. Inspector Owen Morris also stated, "There's evidence she has interacted with another person or persons due to the nature of her injuries." Inspector Morris would not speculate if a possible abductor was still at large. He did confirm a dog squad is undertaking a search of the surrounding area.

"Now that Mallory has been located safe and well, we will concentrate our efforts on the investigation of her disappearance and the circumstances of how she came to be found in this location," Inspector Morris said.

He confirmed his team were hoping to speak to Mallory today, but their focus first and foremost is on the child's wellbeing. "As you can appreciate, Mallory needs to recover from her injuries and her exposure to the elements. We need to make sure she is in good health before we can question her further."

Police are encouraging anyone to come forward who may have information that will assist in their investigation.

11

NOW

Not again.

Not again not again.

I circle the table uselessly.

"Tim?" I call across the food court. I spin around. *"Tim?"*

Nearby eaters offer me curious glances; beyond those few tables my cries are absorbed into the drone of shopping centre commotion.

Why did I leave Tim alone? Why the hell did I run off chasing shadows?

Because Sparrow wanted you to. You left Tim exposed so he could swoop in and take him, just like he took Mallory.

Dragging fingers across my scalp, I scrunch my eyes closed. No.

Sparrow was a fabrication, Dr Ingrid says, created by a lonely girl craving attention. Sparrow didn't climb into my bedroom at Ally's house, or lock me in a box, or steal Mallory from the Greenwillow Carnival. It doesn't matter how I *think* I remember those events, I know now I made them up.

"Excuse me," I say to an elderly lady on a nearby table. "Did you see a little boy sitting here? Blond hair. Black Darth Vader T-shirt?"

"Oh, sure, hun." She places her coffee cup down and peers over the rim of her glasses. "He spilled his food all over the place, and his friend came and took him away."

Lead weight presses into my chest. "His friend?"

"That's right, hun. Went in that direction." She points towards the opposite end of the food court. "Boy was happy to go with 'im. Guy seemed real friendly."

Yeah, because that's what he does. He tricks you into doing what he wants.

I crush my eyelids shut. "*Stop*," I hiss under my breath. When I open my eyes the lady is watching me. I mumble my thanks and bump around dizzy-headed, searching one end of the food court to the other. By the time I've retraced my steps all the way back to the arcade, I know it's hopeless. I'm going to have to call my mother.

She picks up on the third ring. "Have you two finished eating? I'm about five minutes away."

"Mum, I've lost Tim," I blurt. "He was at the table and I went to get food and I came back and he's gone and I looked everywhere and I don't know where he's *gone*."

"Natasha, slow down. What's this about Tim? Where is he?"

"That's what I'm saying! I left him eating at the table

and when I came back he wasn't there." I feel woozy and disconnected. There's a real risk I might throw up right here outside Kmart.

There's no response at the other end, and for a moment I think maybe the phone line has cut out.

"Mum? Are you there?"

Her words are frosty when she answers. "Are you telling me you left Tim by himself?"

This is my fault – *my fault* – and we both know it.

"Just for a minute," I lie. "Just while I lined up for sushi."

Mum's already talking over the top of me, because it doesn't matter where I was. I wasn't with Tim. I wasn't looking after my brother, end of story.

"I'm walking to the concierge desk on level one," Mum says. "We'll put a call-out over the shopping centre's sound system. Meet me there. *Now.*"

As a testament to my mother's efficiency, a message is broadcast before I'm even off the escalator.

"Tim Carmody, your mother is waiting for you at the concierge desk on level one. Tim Carmody, please meet your mother at Concierge on level one."

Just "your mother". Not your sister, the one who carelessly lost you.

Dread soaks through me as I drag myself the last few metres to where Mum's standing. She's speaking to two security guards with walkie-talkies, and when she spots me she gestures impatiently for me to join them. The men in black uniforms are coordinating a search. The sense of *deja vu* is staggering.

Reiterating my story, I leave out the chunk about me chasing after a hooded imaginary friend. I mention the elderly lady in the food court, how she saw Tim leaving with somebody.

"Did she give a description?" asks one of the guards. "What did this guy look like?"

"I–I didn't ask her," I say, my naivety dawning on me. I didn't ask her because I already know exactly what Sparrow looks like. Except he's not real. So how could it possibly be Sparrow that she saw?

Beside me my mother heaves a sigh, and the security team hurries away. I sink onto a wooden seat and rest my elbows on my legs to stop them trembling. I can't look Mum in the face, and she's not interested in me anyway. She pesters the woman at Concierge for another announcement, peppering her with questions about how soon we should involve the police.

Music blares from a nearby clothing store and a clutch of giggling tweens skip past me without a care in the world. I drop my head into my hands and stare at my shoes.

What was I thinking leaving Tim alone? Even if I hadn't spaced out again, even if I hadn't imagined seeing Sparrow, why did I think it was okay to leave a nine year old alone in a packed food court when there are so many weirdos in the world?

I glance over at my mum, her face stony with worry. Her eyes are drawn to mine and I sense a momentary connection, an opportunity for me to support her. I scramble to my feet and move to her side, my hand hovering beside her elbow.

Her phone vibrates in her handbag and she dives for it, inadvertently knocking my hand aside. She leans into the concierge desk as she answers and it gives her an excuse to turn away from me. It feels like my whole life has been a view of Mum's shoulder, her folded arms and the jut of her chin.

Another ten minutes pass that feel like a lifetime. More announcements over the sound system. One of the security guards checks in with nothing to report. My mother juggles updates between phone calls to my father while I pace back and forth feeling useless.

Then I hear it: rapid footsteps, rubber slapping against polished concrete.

Tim's voice.

"Tash, I'm here. I'm right here!"

I spin around to find him hurrying down the concourse towards me. I barely notice the figure weaving through the crowd close behind. All that registers is Tim running for me with a mixture of guilt and relief on his face … and Mum intercepting him before he reaches me.

"Oh, thank god," she says, dragging him into a hug. "Where have you been? I've been worried *sick*."

Tim tries to untangle himself from her, annoyed at the fuss being made in public. He peers around Mum's shoulder, seeking me out.

"I made a big mess with my lunch," he tells me. "I needed to get cleaned up. We looked but we couldn't find you."

My stomach flutters at the mention of "we". Tim glances behind him and I follow his sight line to the lean figure loitering beside the concierge desk. Morgan gives me an awkward smile. Something flickers in the back of my mind that feels like suspicion.

"I'm so sorry," he says, his gaze bouncing between me and my mother. "We didn't mean to worry anyone."

For a second, both Mum and I struggle to articulate a response.

"Where did you take him?" Mum says. "Why?"

"My burger fell in my lap," Tim explains, pointing at a damp patch across the front of his shorts. There's faint residue of tomato sauce. "I tried to clean it up and then I knocked my water over too." His eyes find mine, his expression half shame, half accusatory. "I couldn't *find* you."

"I was lining up for sushi," I croak, feeling Mum's gaze on me again. "That place I pointed out to you, remember?"

"No, you weren't," Tim says, firmly. "We looked for you and you weren't there."

He glances at Morgan for backup and Mum arches an eyebrow. She has no idea who Morgan is. If she thought she had cause for concern already, just wait till she learns his name.

Morgan clears his throat and shuffles forwards. "I was wandering through the food court and saw him mopping up the mess on the table." He glances at me. "I recognised his T-shirt. You know, from earlier? He was wearing half his lunch in his lap and was pretty desperate to get cleaned up."

Tim kicks at the ground, embarrassed. Morgan winks at him.

"Hang on," Mum says. "Do you two know each other …?" She glares at me like she's missing the joke and isn't one bit happy about it.

"I'm a friend of Tash's," Morgan offers. He doesn't elaborate and I send him a silent message of thanks. He doesn't know that dropping the Fisher name in front of my mother right now would make things decidedly worse.

"Didn't you hear the announcements?" Mum asks, eyes narrowing. "Why wouldn't you bring him here the moment you heard he was missing?"

The thought crossed my mind as well.

"We were in the men's room," Tim announces. "I took my shorts off so we could wash them under the tap."

A tendon flexes in Mum's neck. "You took your *shorts off*?"

"No, no, no," Morgan says, waving his hands. "Tim was in the cubicle. He passed his shorts out underneath the door so I could wash them. Nobody saw."

He throws me a desperate glance as Mum gives him the once-over.

"I had the wet shorts under the hand dryer," Morgan adds. "We didn't hear a thing until the announcement five minutes ago." He glances at me again. "We were coming back to find you."

"At the sushi shop," Mum clarifies, her scepticism swinging back to me. "Where you were supposedly lining up the whole time."

Morgan slides me an apologetic look mingled with curiosity. I'm going to have to admit I wasn't where I said I was, and my reason for disappearing will sound absolutely ludicrous. And though Morgan will probably think I'm certifiable and Mum will have Dr Ingrid on speed-dial, the only person I'm worried about is Tim. I don't want him to think he can't trust me.

Sweat beads on my top lip as I try to think of how to word an excuse. "I don't know, I …"

Morgan watches me squirm, his gaze darting between me and my mother.

"Oh, wait," he says, clicking his fingers. "There are two sushi places, right? We must have looked for you at the wrong one."

"Er, yeah," I say. "Right."

"Well, it doesn't change the fact that you need to be more careful, Natasha," Mum says. "If you'd stayed at the table with Tim none of this would have happened. It's completely irresponsible."

She turns to inform the security staff they can call off the search. I quickly pull Tim into a hug and kiss the top of his head. "I'm so sorry, Timber. I shouldn't have left you alone. I promise it won't happen again, okay?"

He shrugs, already distracted by a nearby electronics store.

As my mother phones my dad, Morgan gently pulls me aside. Despite how wrung out I feel, a tingle dances along my arm where his fingers meet my skin.

"You all right?"

I muster a small smile. "Apart from my mother thinking I'm useless? Yeah, I'll live."

"Don't worry," he says. "I think I came out of this whole

thing looking a lot worse than you."

"Hey, Morgan, thanks." I don't specify what for but I hope he can sense it anyway. He lifts his chin and I can tell he knows he's helped me a lot more than merely by keeping Tim safe.

"You know, if you'd just given me your number," he teases, "none of this would have happened."

His words jolt me. An absurd thought flies in from left field: is Morgan saying he took Tim on purpose? To get my attention?

Morgan's eyes widen at my frown.

"I–I just mean I could have called you from the food court," he says. "And none of this–" he flails an arm in the direction of the concierge desk, "–would have happened."

I shake my ludicrous thought away. *Jesus, Tash. Get a grip.*

"Right," Mum says, marching over and taking Tim's hand. "Time to go." Tim wiggles his hand out of her grasp as she looks Morgan up and down one last time. "Thank you for your help ..." She tilts her head, an invitation for Morgan to introduce himself.

"Um, Morgan," he says, removing his hand from his pocket like he might offer to shake Mum's. She makes no return gesture so Morgan places it awkwardly on his hip.

"Right. Thank you, Morgan." Mum's face is a perfect mask of cordiality. She thanks the concierge staff and marches Tim towards the car park. I move to follow and Morgan falls into step beside me.

"Hey, if you ever want to talk about what happened today," he says, keeping his voice low, "I'm here and willing to listen."

He knows I wasn't at the sushi shop, and he knows I let him lie to my mother to cover for me. I know I owe him the truth, I just don't know how to explain it without sounding like a head case.

"It messes you up a bit," Morgan says, shoving his hands into his pockets again. "When your younger sibling goes missing on your watch."

This stops me in my tracks. Morgan takes another step before stopping too. He glances over his shoulder, his face so open and sincere I'm tempted to spill everything. Not only about today, about the past too.

Instead, I completely chicken out.

"Mallory doesn't blame you though, right?" I move half a step towards him. "I mean, it wasn't your fault she was lured away from that toilet block."

He frowns. "No one's ever blatantly come out and said they blame me, no." His frown deepens and it sets my pulse racing. "Why did you say Mallory was taken from the carnival's toilets? The police said she wandered off and someone probably snatched her from one of Greenwillow's back roads."

"Oh, I–" my stomach writhes, "–no, no, you're right. I'm getting mixed up. It was so long ago I'm getting things confused."

Morgan eyes me for a moment and it feels like he can see under my skin. For a split second there's a hardness to his stare, and I wonder if I have something to fear. He's going to press me for more details and I'll have to explain my delusion about my imaginary friend abducting his sister.

"Look, I have to go." I nod at my mother and Tim disappearing through the automatic doors. "I'd better not keep Mum waiting on top of everything else. Thanks again, and I'm sorry you had to get involved in my screw-up."

If there's lingering suspicion in Morgan's eyes, he blinks it away. "It's fine. Tell Tim it was cool hanging out with him for a little while. And listen, I hope your mum calms down and doesn't give you too much grief."

Maybe it's because he doesn't push for explanations, or the way he smiles at me with his crooked front teeth – Morgan makes me want to be more honest with myself. So why then do I lie to everyone that Dr Ingrid's therapy worked? Is it because I don't really agree with my diagnosis in the first place? Or am I just so desperate to be normal that I'm wishing Sparrow into flesh-and-blood existence, instead of the blight on my mental health he most likely is?

I know things aren't right with me – conjuring up Sparrow today is evidence of that. The worst thing I could do is drag anyone else into my mess, least of all the Fishers. I know I should talk to my parents. I know I need to arrange a session with Dr Ingrid now instead of waiting until June.

I also know I won't do any of those things.

Instead, I'll try to figure out how to get a mute girl to talk.

12

THEN

28 MARCH 2008
TRANSCRIPT FROM THE OFFICE OF DR INGRID BALLANTINE, PHD
CHILD AND ADOLESCENT PSYCHIATRY,
NEWCASTLE CHILDREN'S CLINIC
PATIENT: NATASHA CARMODY, 9 YEARS OLD

IB: You look a bit different to the last time I saw you, Natasha.

NC: I turned nine a couple of weeks ago. And also, I had a haircut.

IB: It looks very grown up. Did you celebrate your birthday with friends?

NC: Just Mum and Dad. And Tim.

IB: Did—

NC: I don't really have any friends right now.

IB: Don't you? You don't play with the kids from your class?

NC: I used to, but they don't want to play with me any more.

IB: Why's that, do you think?

NC: They call me Freak and stuff. One kid says I'm a schizo.

IB: A schizo? What do you think they mean by that?

NC: Mmm, not sure. I accidentally got locked inside the storage room and I got pretty scared. I cried and kicked the door and stuff and now they think I'm weird.

IB: A bit like that dream you told me about, where you were stuck in a box. Was it a bit scary like that?

NC: ...

IB: Do you sometimes feel lonely at school?

NC: Umm ... not really. I'm not sure.

IB: Do you feel like your teacher and classmates don't pay you much attention?

NC: I didn't do it on purpose. I accidentally kicked the doorstopper loose when Mrs Brooks asked me to get the paintbrushes.

IB: Okay ...

NC: She had to go all the way to the staffroom to get a key. I was stuck in there. I thought my air would run out. I was really scared and I kicked and cried. Some kids were laughing at me when she got the door open.

IB: Oh, I see.

NC: I thought maybe it was ... [muffled]

IB: Can you speak up for me, Natasha? I can't hear you very well when you bury your face in the cushion like that.

NC: ...

IB: You said, "maybe it was" ...?

NC: Him.

IB: One of the boys in your class?

NC: No, *him*.

IB: Your friend that comes to visit you?

NC: He's not my friend. He plays mean tricks, so I thought it might be him.

IB: Has he come to visit you at school before?

NC: No. Well, I thought I saw him once in the library, but I think it was just my imagination. When I ran up and down the aisles looking for him, there was no one there and I got in trouble from Mr Halliwell for running.

IB: Ah. So perhaps it was your imagination after all?

NC: Yeah.

IB: Do you think there might have been other times when you thought you saw something but it could have been your imagination?

NC: Umm ... maybe.

IB: Can you remember telling your mum and dad that you saw the little girl at the carnival being taken away?

NC: Yeah. That was real. It wasn't my imagination.

IB: Okay, let's think about that day then. Let's think about the little girl who went missing.

NC: Her name's Mallory Fisher.

IB: Yes, that's right. Mallory. Who did you see Mallory with?

NC: Morgan. That's her brother. He goes to my school, except now he doesn't. They've moved away.

IB: And that's who you saw Mallory with that day?

NC: I followed them to the toilets.

IB: Was your aunt with you? When you went to the toilets?

NC: No. She had something to do so she left me. I had to meet her at the ticket booth at closing time.

IB: You were all alone at the carnival?

NC: Mm-hmm.

IB: I remember you told me that sometimes when you felt lonely your friend would come to visit you. Do you remember telling me that?

NC: Yes. But he's not my friend. And he *was* there. I didn't ask him to come though.

IB: You seem to have a special connection with him. Do you think maybe he comes when you need him to?

NC: No! I don't need him. I don't even *like* him. He was really mean to me at the carnival. He played a trick on me and put me in a box. He trapped me inside!

IB: In a cardboard box?

NC: No, like a hard one.

IB: A trunk?

NC: Yeah!

IB: Like the one in your dream?

NC: This wasn't a dream. He really *did* it. He locked me inside.

IB: Your friend?

NC: *He is NOT my friend!*

13

NOW

I wait patiently for the sun to burn off the haze from my spot under Port Bellamy Pier. It's a peaceful morning, save for a hiss of wind through the beach grass and the distant hum of fishing dinghies heading out to sea. As the sun creeps higher, I bracket a few shots with my DSLR even though I have more than enough coastal images for my folio already. The dwindling likes on my Instagram pics tell me what I already know – it's all generic picture-postcard stuff. I doubt my folio will make the cut at university interviews unless I come up with something more personal.

It doesn't help that my heart's not in it this morning. Things are strained at home since the shopping centre incident, and Mum is barely speaking to me.

She's saying plenty to Dad, though.

"I thought she would have outgrown this unpredictable

106

behaviour," she said last night. I sat on the listening step as she and Dad cleaned up after dinner. "I really don't know, Rich. How's she going to move forward after high school if she can't be trusted with any kind of responsibility?"

"Maybe it's a long-term thing we're dealing with," Dad replied. "All we can do is take each day as it comes. It's obviously not as simple as her outgrowing it."

"So, *what* then? You think there's still a jealousy issue going on? You think she left Tim there alone on purpose just to see what would happen?"

I had to bite my lip at that comment. What kind of person do they think I am? How could Mum think I'd put Tim in harm's way "just to see what would happen"?

Keeping some distance between myself and Mum right now is the only way to prevent saying things I'm bound to regret. If we could get out of each other's faces for a few days, it would give us both a chance to calm down.

My phone's alarm chimes, letting me know the school's computer rooms will now be open. I've got a memory card full of images to back up for editing later this week. I slip on my socks and shoes, brushing the sand from my uniform. A tiny bulge inside my blazer pocket crinkles, and I dig my hand inside to remove a scrunched-up piece of paper.

Aunty Ally's phone number is scrawled across it in my mother's handwriting.

*

I turn the paper over and over in my fingers during the ten-minute walk to school, and by the time I'm on my way up to C Block, I know I need to call now before I lose my nerve.

Pausing on the deserted stairwell, I take a steadying breath before dialling my aunt's number. She answers after six rings with a fumble and a muffled swearword.

"Ally? It's Tash here. Your niece? From Port Bellamy?"

Silence stretches just long enough for me to hear her yawn.

"Tash? Oh, hey, honey," she says. Her voice is deeper over the phone, coarse and phlegmy. "It's good to hear from you. Wasn't sure if you got my message. You know, your mother ..."

Yeah, do I ever know my mother. "I'm sorry I'm only just getting around to calling you back."

"No worries. I remember being your age, so much happening all the time," she says. "So, listen. I was calling about the second weekend in March."

"Okay ...?"

"How would you feel about coming up here for a couple of days?"

After that visit when I was eight, I've had no desire to return to Willow Creek House, with its crack-riddled stucco like the caked-on face paint of a leering clown. I remember the way dampness clung to cushions like mouldering dead spots, the unsettling way shadows reached for me behind my back as the sun moved across the sky. And my questions about what really happened in that house have always terrified me. If I imagined it all, it means I was a disturbed child talking to myself, seeing things that didn't exist.

And if I didn't imagine it? Well, that's so much worse.

Then again, maybe revisiting Willow Creek might create some breathing space between me and my mother, show her I don't need her in my face all the time to cope. Being in that old house again could help me make sense of what happened there, what was real and what wasn't.

"Umm, okay," I tell Ally. "Why not? I can bring my camera."

"Perfect. The light around here is beautiful in the evenings. You probably can't remember that. It's been so long since you were last here."

It almost feels like I should apologise for the things I said and did that reflected on Ally's inability, in the eyes of my parents, to make me feel safe in her home. But I have to push all that childhood stuff aside. I'm seventeen now and everything is different. Ally and I both know I'm not that kid any more.

"You remember Benny, right?" Ally asks. "Poor old boy's getting on in years. Still thinks he's a puppy, mind you."

"Yeah, of course I remember Benny."

"So if I leave you alone with him for two nights, you won't have any issues?"

Swapping the phone to my other ear, I frown at the empty corridor. "You won't be there …?"

"No, sweetheart. I'll be at a yoga retreat, no dogs allowed."

I flush with embarrassment. Here I was thinking Ally was inviting me up there because she wanted to spend time with me. But is it really so bad? I *do* like dogs, and I'll get a house to myself for two whole parent-free days. If Mum and Dad see I can survive without them, surely that's got to score points when I pitch the idea about university.

"Benny's really no trouble," Ally says. "Sleeps most of the time anyway. A quick walk once a day and he's a happy old fool. Aren't you, buddy?" I hear the metallic *tink* of Benny's dog tag and imagine him stretched out on the bed beside her. "So what do you say? Wanna escape those nagging parents and do your own thing for a couple of days?"

Well, when she words it like that ...

"Yeah, okay," I hear myself saying. "Sounds good."

As soon as the words are out of my mouth I have to resist gobbling them up again. I feel dazed as Ally promises more details via text, as I hear myself agreeing to everything she says and cheerfully signing off. I try to tell myself that this doesn't change anything – I need this break from Mum, I need to prove my independence. It makes no difference whether Ally's there or not.

Except, of course it does.

Now I'll be at Willow Creek alone.

*

Most of lunchtime is spent trying to convince Sadie to join me on my weekend at Willow Creek. I try to dress it up like some kind of two-day girly pamper session even though that's not her thing at all and it's definitely not mine.

"Dude, my mum has two catering gigs lined up that weekend," Sadie says. "I'd get out of it if I could but I don't wanna leave her flying solo." She bites into her apple, winces, then lobs it into the nearest bin. It lands inside with a hollow thud.

I pick at my sandwich, my appetite suddenly dwindling. "I understand."

"Anyway, I thought you were creeped out by that place," Sadie says. "You sure you wanna go back there?"

"I was a little kid with a big imagination," I say, trying to assure myself at the same time. "How bad can it be? It's just an old house."

Sadie looks unconvinced. "How about this aunt, though? Why did she suddenly crawl out of the woodwork?"

"What do you mean?"

"No contact for years and now she's getting all chummy?" Sadie narrows her eyes. "What do you reckon she wants?"

"Dog-sitting," I say, laughing. "I think you can put your notepad away, Sherlock."

We eat in silence for a few moments, watching students milling around the quad.

"Hey," Sadie says, nudging me, "did you notice your stalker started school this week?"

"Who?"

"Skinny jeans."

I redden. "His name is Morgan. And by the way? Not a stalker."

"Okay. So what do you call following you and your brother around a shopping centre?"

"He wasn't following us. It was a coincidence that we even ran into him."

"A coincidence he turned up at the exact moment Tim decorated himself with a burger?"

I shove my sandwich back into its paper bag and fold

my arms. "What's your point, exactly?"

"Maybe he was watching you guys the whole time. Maybe he was waiting for an opportunity to swoop in and be the big hero."

"That would be bad because …?"

"Didn't say it was *bad*. It's just so friggin' transparent." Sadie digs around in her bag, her hand emerging with a banana.

"I really have no idea what point you're making."

Sadie rolls her eyes as she peels the banana, plucking away the stringy bits. "Come on, Carmody. For a bright girl you're slow on the uptake sometimes. He likes you."

I give her a blank-faced stare.

"He *like*-likes you," she says. "It's so obvious. He's always looking for a reason to talk to you or help you out."

"I've seen him on, like, three occasions, Dee."

"Yeah. And two of those he was all, 'I'm Mister Sir-help-a-lot at your service, m'lady.'"

I can't help sniggering. "Mister Sir? Wow. That's a serious title."

"Yeah, well, he's *seriously* obvious about it." Sadie leans back on the silver bench to rest against the warm brick wall. She bites into her banana, making her next words all gummed-up and sticky. "Just be careful, okay? I'm not sure I trust him yet."

"You don't even know him."

She points the stump of her banana at me. "Exactly."

I've only shared English with Morgan since he started, and I don't think he even realises we're in the same class. As soon as he walked into the room yesterday he was intercepted by Christopher Tan who seems to have found a kindred spirit in his obsession with zombie films and George RR Martin. He didn't see me slumped in the back row.

"So, I'll tell Mum you're not available second weekend of March," Sadie says, as the bell signals lunch is over. "She can call our neighbour Lilly if she needs another set of hands. Although Lilly's slower than dirt and just about as interesting."

Forcing a laugh, I feel my nerves twitch with the realisation I'm going to be all alone at Willow Creek. I have to remind myself this is a good opportunity. Maybe even a turning point.

As we part ways at the stairwell, Sadie backhands me lightly on the shoulder. "Watch out for that stalker, 'kay?"

I roll my eyes and give her a sarcastic double thumbs up.

As I head upstairs to B Block, Sadie's words turn out to be prophetic. Morgan's standing outside the art room with Rachael Tan when I get there.

"Hey, you," he says as I join them at the classroom door. "I was beginning to think you lied about going to this school."

"Well, here I am. I guess we don't have many classes together."

"Uh, hello?" Rachael says, flicking a curtain of black hair over her shoulder. "Aren't you both in my brother's English class?"

Morgan gives me a puzzled look and I screw my hands up into fists. I won't let Rachael make a fool out of me again. Not in front of Morgan.

"Are you still heading up to Greenwillow in March?" I ask him.

"Yeah. How'd you know about that?"

"Your mum mentioned something when I was at your party." I don't elaborate that I was eavesdropping on her conversation with a neighbour at the time. "I'm going to be staying at my aunt's house in Willow Creek on the second weekend of March."

"Really?" His face lights up. "That's awesome. We can hang out! You know, if you want to."

My whole body hums at the thought of it, at Morgan's shy smile, at the sight of Rachael grinding her jaw.

"Of course I want to. So … should we swap numbers?"

Morgan laughs as he pulls out his phone. "Who's been suggesting this for a while now?"

Our art teacher arrives in a flurry of coloured beads and green tea scent, clapping us into the classroom like she's rounding up sheep. I trail in after Morgan and see that Rachael's already chosen a spot. Each art table sits three across but Rachael's spread her stuff over two spaces, ensuring there's no room for me. Morgan doesn't notice this, however, and drags a stool over from a nearby table for me to squeeze in beside him.

Mrs Liotta explains our new art assignment, a mixed-media project based on our interpretation of *Dreamscapes*. We'll be divided into small groups and we're expected to work together in class as well as outside of school. I should be excited at the prospect of adding new work to my photography folio. Instead I'm completely distracted by how close Morgan is sitting, the way his bare knee accidentally brushes my thigh.

"To make this easy," says Mrs Liotta, peering over the top of her red-rimmed glasses, "let's just create groups of three based on the tables you're currently sitting at."

It's almost comical how Rachael and I shoot each other a panicked look at exactly the same time.

"No interpretation is wrong," Mrs Liotta continues, "and I encourage you to seek out different media. Most importantly, the three of you in each group must agree on a vision for your work. Each person's ideas need to be represented as part of a cohesive collaboration."

Rachael's hand is in the air before our teacher has even finished speaking.

"Yes, Miss Tan?"

"I'd like to request a change of partner," Rachael says quickly. "I think there will be a conflict of interest working with Tash."

Mrs Liotta tips her head to one side, her bright fuchsia lips twisting. "And by that I take it to mean there will be *conflict* because of your shared *interest* in our new student?"

The class erupts into sniggers. I can't bring myself to look at Morgan or Rachael, although I sense Morgan shifting uncomfortably on his stool. Rachael attempts a weak protest and Mrs Liotta cuts her off.

"I'm sure you'll find a way to work through any differences you have," she tells us.

"But I—"

"*Enough*, Miss Tan. I think you forget I taught your Year

Seven class when you and Miss Carmody were good friends. You'll just have to dig deep and find your common ground again. No switching groups."

Rachael and I exchange another look that tells me we're both one hundred per cent sure any common ground we once had has been torched and decimated. She turns away from us and buries her nose in her journal.

Morgan taps a pen against his project sheet. "Sooo, got any ideas about this?"

"Not yet. Maybe we can brainstorm?"

We spend the next twenty minutes talking about *Inception*, lucid dreaming and even *A Nightmare on Elm Street*, although Morgan has to explain the plot to me because I'm not into horror films.

"How'd things go with your mum on Sunday after the whole Watergardens thing?" Morgan asks. "Was she still mad at you when you got home?"

I glance at Rachael on Morgan's other side. She's still hunched over her notebook, but I keep my voice down just in case.

"She's barely said two words to me since then. I think it's safe to say I won't be winning Daughter of the Year."

"Seriously? That's harsh." Morgan musters a sympathetic smile. "I still feel kinda bad I got you in trouble."

"You didn't," I assure him. "It was my own fault. Truth is, I wasn't in that sushi line the whole time like I told my mum."

Why I'm admitting this is anybody's guess, considering how badly it reflects upon me as a big sister.

"Well, that much I know," Morgan says. "I figure you must

have a good reason for keeping it from her."

At this, Rachael's head turns slightly. Without looking at us she mutters, "Tash has never got along with her mum."

She doesn't really say it in a mean way, and it reminds me I used to confide in Rachael once upon a time. She used to listen back then, and even when she grew impatient with my ramblings she still offered helpful suggestions. These days she uses those confessions as weapons. I narrow my eyes now and wait for whatever she'll brandish to wound me.

"What?" Rachael says, when she catches my look. "It's true, isn't it? You told me she never had time for you and Tim's her favourite. No wonder you got all screwed up in the head."

Gripping the edge of my wooden stool, I strain to keep my voice level. "You have no idea what you're talking about."

Rachael huffs impatiently as though I'm ruining her point. She turns her attention to Morgan. "Did she mention she hears voices?"

Morgan throws us both an uneasy look. "I don't know what—"

"I don't hear voices, Rachael," I say, a bit too loudly. A few classmates at the table in front glance over their shoulders. "I wish you'd stop feeding that bull to anyone who shows the slightest interest in being my friend."

"Really?" Rachael straightens. "So what do you call talking to imaginary friends?"

Go to hell is on the tip of my tongue and I'm tempted to have it out with her here and now. However, I need to diffuse this quickly if I want any chance of hanging onto my pride.

"It's called being an immature little kid," I say. "A bit like you bringing this up over and over again even though *no one cares*."

Two guys on the next table snigger and Rachael's smug expression dissolves. She actually looks stung. It makes me regret biting back, even if it did feel powerful for a second, even though I know Sadie would be proud of me. I wish I'd just ignored Rachael and said nothing at all.

"Whatever," she mumbles, returning to her notebook. She freezes us out for the rest of the lesson and storms from the classroom as soon as the last bell rings.

Morgan and I pack up slowly as the classroom clears out, gathering up our scribbled notes and drawings. I fiddle with my bag longer than I need to, reluctant to head home.

"Hey, I'm sorry things got weird with Rachael," I say. "I'll make peace with her so our project doesn't suffer. She just gets to me sometimes."

Morgan spins on his stool to face me and his knee brushes my thigh again. I don't move my leg and neither does he. "You shouldn't be embarrassed about something that happened when you were a kid."

"I know."

"You can't let it define who you are now. I mean, you think I'm proud of what happened to Mallory? Why didn't I wait for her outside that toilet block until she'd been in and come out again? I regret it every day, but it was years ago, you know?"

I'm caught off guard by Morgan bringing up the carnival.

"How could anyone know what would happen to Mallory?" I say.

"Yeah, well, I'll never forget that look in my mum's eyes when I came back from the toilets without her. Disbelief, I s'pose. She just couldn't believe I'd been so careless."

"A bit like my mum with me at Watergardens," I admit. "Although I'm nine years older than you were. I have no excuse."

Morgan picks at a loose thread on his shorts. I can tell there's something he wants to broach. The question he asks is not one I'm expecting at all. "Do you have a boyfriend your mum doesn't know about?"

"*What?*" Heat blossoms from the neckline of my uniform.

"Did you sneak off to see him at Watergardens? Is that why you lied to your mum about where you were?"

I almost snort at the absurdity of it – me having a secret boyfriend! – and then feel flattered that Morgan doesn't think the idea is absurd at all.

"No," I say quietly. "No boyfriend."

"Okay, so who's Sparrow?"

I fumble with my pencil case and two Sharpies clatter to the floor. I focus all my attention on retrieving them. "Uh, sorry, what?"

"At my parents' party, your friend Sadie asked you about Sparrow after you were trapped in the laundry with me." Morgan ducks his head, coaxing me to look at him. "Did he hurt you? Is that why you were afraid of me?"

I reach out and touch his arm. "I wasn't afraid of you! It wasn't that at all."

Morgan's shoulders relax, his gaze falling on my hand. I remove it quickly and instantly wish I could put it back again.

"Sparrow is—" I try to think of how best to word this, "—that imaginary friend Rachael was talking about."

"Oh. Okay ..."

"He sort of appeared in my life around the time my brother was born. My shrink says it was because I was jealous and craved attention. Oh, yeah – I've been seeing a psychiatrist on and off for nine years. Are you ready to run yet?"

Morgan smiles. "Not at all. My sister and I both went to therapy after her disappearance. No judgement here."

I nod. "I invented this creepy character to keep me company because I felt lonely at my aunt's house. My parents dumped me there for two weeks when Tim was born so they could settle in at home without the added complication of me to look after. To eight-year-old me, it felt like they didn't want me around."

Morgan chuckles. "Why did you make this character so creepy? Why not a big cuddly teddy bear or something?"

"See, that's the thing – I don't remember deciding to create him at all. He just turned up in my bedroom one night wanting to play a game. He just *existed* all on his own. My psychiatrist reckons my subconscious made him gruesome to gain more comfort from my parents. Like, the worse I made him, the more concerned they'd be and the more they'd regret sending me away."

"Wow, you were quite the little schemer!" Morgan jokes.

"Apparently," I say, with a shrug. "Although Dr Ingrid put it in much nicer terms with a big side order of psychobabble."

Morgan shakes his head, smiling. "What did he look like? A messed-up clown or something?"

"Uh, no." It feels weird talking openly about Sparrow, yet there's still so much I'm withholding. "He looked like a person, I suppose. A sick one. Really skinny, with these deep hollows in his face right here." I place my hands underneath my cheekbones, pressing my cheeks into the void of my mouth. "He had these rotten teeth and his skin was really pale. His arms and face were covered in weeping sores."

"*Jesus*," Morgan says, with a mixture of amusement and horror. "He's like a bogeyman. No wonder you don't like getting trapped in a dark room with an image like that in the back of your mind."

It's not worth explaining the things Sparrow did; how it runs much deeper than being afraid of his appearance. What's the point? He was only imaginary.

"My mum sure grew tired of the nightmares about Sparrow for months afterwards. She and Dr Ingrid think that was part of my ongoing attention-seeking, but I was genuinely terrified he was going to come back. I'd sometimes imagine seeing him out of the corner of my eye."

I still do.

Morgan's eyes narrow and I feel my pulse stutter. For a split second it seems like he's assessing me, weighing things up. Before I can interpret it properly he's on his feet.

"Well," he says, stretching, "gotta say, you seem pretty well adjusted for someone with that grisly little nugget from your childhood. It's so weird the way kids' minds work. Thank god we grow out of these things, right?"

Returning his smile with a weak one of my own, I battle that ever-present voice inside my head.

Tell him. Tell him everything. Now.

Morgan slings his backpack over one shoulder and I fuss with the zipper on my bag, wondering if I can possibly explain how intrinsically Sparrow is woven into my psyche. Even inside my head the words seem complicated and disturbing, so I revert to my usual script: telling people what they want to hear.

"Yeah," I agree with Morgan. "Thank god we grow out of these things."

14

THEN

"Do you want to play a game?"

I look up from my colouring book at the sound of his voice, and one of my pencils rolls onto the floor. He's leaning around the doorway, his fingers gripping the doorframe like a scrawny bird claw. I haven't seen him for two days and he's never come to me in daytime. Maybe that's a good thing. If I'd met him in daylight I might've been too scared to talk to him at all.

Sometimes people look different, Mum would say. It's rude to stare.

I can't help it, though. I've never seen anyone that looks like him before.

He's not wearing his hood today and he has no hair. His eyes are pressed deep into his face making his forehead look all big and bony. There are red sores on his chin and bumpy scabs on his ears like he's been picking them instead of leaving them alone. And his skin is weird. Sort of dull. The colour is all faded, like that time I accidentally left my Wonder Woman comic in the sun.

Maybe he's sick. Except he doesn't move like somebody who isn't feeling well. He jerks and jitters like he's excited, like he's trying to wriggle out of his own body. He rushes into the room now, glancing over his shoulder at the staircase and the sound of Aunty Ally's shower upstairs.

"I've hidden something," he says. "You go down into the cellar and see if you can find it."

I place my blue pencil on the coffee table and uncross my legs. "Find what?"

"The door to my secret room."

"I don't like the cellar," I tell him. "I don't like the sound the water heater makes."

Even with the cellar door closed I can hear it – a thump and a shudder and a high-pitched wheeze like an animal in pain. It makes me think of the story Gran told me about this house, about some fancy doctor who built it for his family two hundred years ago. They had a Scottish convict working for them as a servant and the cellar was where he slept. They locked the cellar door every night. They trapped him down there in the dark.

"You'll have to hide it somewhere else," I say, "if you want me to play."

He glances at the stairs again and makes a growly noise in the back of his throat. "Just come now. It won't work if any grown-ups find out."

He moves in front of the window and I see he has dark

purple shadows under each eye. The sunlight shows up the lines across his forehead and creases around his mouth. I've tried to guess his age but it's impossible. He's like a pixie or a goblin from a fairytale book, one that looks old and young at the same time.

"Why are you here?" I ask him. "Are you allowed to be in the house?"

He picks at a scratch on his arm, his eyes looking towards the upstairs landing. "I'm here to play with you."

"Who invited you?"

"You did." He folds his arms. "You need to come now or we're going to run out of time."

Upstairs the shower stops and some floorboards creak. A door is opened and closed. I stand up and back away from the coffee table just as Sparrow lunges forwards. He grabs hold of my arm.

"I don't want to play down there!" I try to pull myself away. His grip is tight and his fingers are pinching. He might look small and sick, but he's also strong. "It's too dark. I don't want to. It's too dark!"

His face changes as though something has grabbed it and twisted, like that time Dad accidentally hit his thumb with the hammer. His eyebrows scrunch together and his jaw tightens like he's holding in a roar. I shrink away from him, my legs going weak. He drags me halfway across the living room, towards the hall.

"I don't want to!" I try to dig my heels in but my socks slide over the floorboards. "Please. Don't!"

"You have to, or else I'll sneak into your bedroom while

you're sleeping," he says, "and I'll lock you in a box. No one will find you and you'll starve to death. Is that what you want?"

The thought of something so horrible makes me quiet. Is visiting the cellar worse than that? I didn't ask him to come here, so why do I have to choose?

"I–I don't want to play."

Just as we reach the cellar door, there's a growling streak of golden fur on the upstairs landing. Benny bounds for the staircase, his collar tinkling like a tiny bell. Sparrow's hand opens and he shoves me so hard I fall onto my knees. When I look behind me, Sparrow is gone.

Benny leaps off the bottom step and skids sideways on the floorboards, his claws tippy-tapping as he flies past. His barking is like an explosion as he scratches and growls at the cellar door.

Aunty Ally dashes down the staircase in a faded green bathrobe.

"Tash?" She glances up and down the hallway. "Who are you talking to?"

"Sparrow." I rub the tender spot on my arm and hold it up as evidence. There aren't any red marks though. "He was here again. This time Benny saw him too."

"Sparrow ...?"

My cheeks get hot. "I just call him that. He hasn't told me his name so I made one up."

Aunty Ally doesn't say anything else. She stands on the bottom step watching me, her forehead all frowny.

"I swear," I tell her, pointing at the cellar door. "He was standing right there and Benny growled at him."

"Honey," Aunty Ally says gently. "Benny's just growling at the water heater again. Listen, you can hear it filling up now after my shower."

She brings a finger to her lips and nods her head at the cellar door. Behind it comes the hiss and squeal from the horrible dark room below. Benny growls and paces in front of the door.

"I hate that noise," I say, putting my hands over my ears. "Make it stop!"

Aunty Ally steps across the hallway and slips her arm around my shoulders. "Come on," she says. "Come away from there. Let's fix you some breakfast. I think you must be light-headed."

She leads me towards the kitchen and whistles for Benny to follow us. I glance up at her face. "You believe me, don't you? About Sparrow?"

Giving my shoulder a squeeze, she says, "I believe that you believe it. But your parents won't understand, honey. They might think something is wrong."

"What do you mean?"

"They might think something's a little glitchy inside your head." She steers me over to the kitchen table and slides a chair out for me. "They might think you're seeing things that aren't really there."

As I sit down, my aunty reaches for an old tin on the windowsill. I think she might be giving me a biscuit until she pulls out a cigarette packet and a plastic lighter.

"When I was growing up," she says, "I was convinced there were fairies at the bottom of the garden. See those ferns there? At the edge of the bush?" She lights her cigarette and waves it at the large window overlooking the backyard.

Straightening in my chair, I peer over the sink and through the grubby glass at the lawn full of bindies, past the washing line to the rusty back gate.

"I even built some little houses out of twigs and bark so my fairies would have somewhere to sleep at night," she says. "My brother – your dad – was cutting the grass one day and he mowed straight over the top of them."

"Oh no," I say. But what does any of this have to do with Sparrow? I wonder if he's listening to this story. He might have the cellar door cracked open so he can hear everything we say.

"I was so upset," Aunty Ally says, "because I thought my fairies were inside those little houses. I cried and cried. My mother told me I was overreacting. And my brother never had to apologise. No big surprise there."

She flicks cigarette ash into the sink, her lips pressed small and tight like she has something yucky-tasting in her mouth.

"My point is, I was different. I've always been different to them." She moves back to the table and stands over me, reaching out to place her hand on top of mine. "It's okay to be different. But sweetheart, take it from me – your parents just won't understand."

"If I–"

"Trust me," she says with a firm voice. "No more talk about this." She leans down and tucks a strand of hair behind my ear. "This will be our little secret, Tash."

15

NOW

The first week of March brings with it windy mornings and rain-soaked evenings, creating a much smaller window of opportunity for photography after school. I've taken far too many images of silos against storm clouds, none of them addressing the theme of *Dreamscapes* for our art project, and all of them too bland for my university submission folio.

Tim usually wants to tag along with me when I head out to take some shots, but Mum invariably keeps him occupied. There's always homework or chores or some other thing that prevents him from coming, all of them much less blatant than Mum telling me, "I don't trust you."

He looks at me now with a sad puppy dog expression as I load up my backpack with art books and photography magazines.

"Where are you going this time?" he whines. "You

promised to play Minecraft with me."

"I will, buddy. When I get home later." I slide my camera case out from underneath his hand. "I have to go to Morgan's house to work on our project. We're supposed to show our art teacher some work in progress next week."

Which is a problem since we've got a whole lot of nothing to show so far. Rachael refuses to spend any time on it, using class collaboration sessions bent over her journal, while Morgan and I toss around half-hearted ideas about futuristic worlds and desolate wastelands. We tend to get sidetracked talking about books we've read or what shows we're currently binging on Netflix. We spent most of yesterday's art period trying to guess each other's least favourite bands and foods, delighted in our joint dislike of Coldplay and coriander.

"Why are you doing school stuff on a Saturday?" Tim asks, shadowing me down the staircase and into the living room. "Are you going to be there all afternoon?"

I feel bad that Tim's dismayed at this prospect while I'm trying to keep a lid on my excitement. Morgan invited me a few days ago after telling me his parents were driving to a wedding in Coffs Harbour for the weekend. The idea of hanging out with him for a whole afternoon outside of school resulted in a new T-shirt purchase and twenty minutes of hair styling after this morning's shower.

It's not just seeing Morgan that has me full of nervous energy. Today will give me an opportunity to see Mallory again too.

"I'm not sure what time I'll be home," I tell Tim. "Maybe

Dad will play with you in the meantime."

Dad glances up from his newspaper and pats the couch for Tim to sit next to him. "Your mum will probably like to know if you'll be here for dinner," he says to me.

"Yes, she would," Mum says, appearing in the kitchen doorway. "Where are you off to?"

"She's going to Morgan's house," Tim sulks.

Mum arches an eyebrow just enough for me to know she has an opinion about this.

"You do realise I know Morgan is the Fisher boy," she says. "You conveniently left that part out of the introductions a couple of weeks ago."

"It didn't come up," I say, as I fiddle with my backpack's shoulder strap. "Anyway, what difference does it make?"

Mum folds her arms and lowers her voice. "You know why it makes a difference. You don't need things derailing your progress."

My eyes dart towards Tim, hoping this cryptic conversation is going over his head. Thankfully, he's reading the newspaper's comic strip over Dad's shoulder.

"*And*," Mum says, "the Fishers don't need to know about a certain embarrassing police interview from 2008."

"I'd never say anything about that," I mutter. "Morgan and I are in the same group for an art assignment, so it's not like I can avoid him."

Mum purses her lips like she knows avoiding Morgan is the furthest thing from my mind. She saw how he looked at the shops with his green eyes and boy-band hair.

"We should move your check-in session with Dr Ballantine

forward a couple of months," she says. "In light of all this with the Fishers moving back to town. Not to mention what happened at Watergardens with Tim."

"Elaine ..." Dad starts.

"Great!" I blurt, yanking the straps on my backpack way too tight. "I can talk to her about Willow Creek while I'm at it. Because, guess what? I'm going up there for a visit."

"Watch your tone, Tash," Dad warns.

"Willow Creek?" Mum says. "You didn't actually return Ally's call, did you?"

"She's invited me up there next weekend. I said yes."

"What?" Mum jerks her hands to her hips. "Were you actually going to ask permission, or were you just going to sneak off without telling us?"

Dad sets his newspaper down. "Tash mentioned something to me about it."

"Oh, well, terrific Richard," Mum says. "Were you ever going to let me know?"

Dad shrugs. "I don't think it's such a bad idea."

"You must be joking."

"You two could use a break from one another," Dad says. "A couple of days apart could be just what you need. Plus, we don't even know how much longer the old house will be in our hands. Tash may as well enjoy the place while she still can."

Mum gives Dad a look that could sour milk. "And everything that happened there—"

"Happened almost a decade ago," Dad says firmly. "She's not a child any more. She'll be perfectly fine." He slides me a meaningful look that implies, *I'm going out on a limb here, kid. Don't screw this up.*

"You think associating with your sister is in Tash's best interests?" Mum asks. They seem to have forgotten Tim's on the couch, listening with eyes as big as saucers. "She can barely sort out her own life."

I regard Mum curiously. I've never heard her let loose about Ally in front of me and Tim before. It's usually only snide comments to my dad under her breath when the two of us are around.

"Tash is almost eighteen," Dad says. "She won't be reliant on Ally and can look after herself."

I'll be doing exactly that since Ally won't even be there. I neglected to mention that part to Dad.

"*Well*," Mum says, snatching up a coffee cup Dad hasn't finished with, "I'm so glad the two of you are making decisions behind my back." She marches into the kitchen.

"She'll come around," Dad says to me. "Eventually."

I think of my university plans, my chance at an independent life. "I seriously hope you're right."

*

I'm not sure if it's eagerness to see Morgan or desperation to get away from home, but I pump the bike pedals so hard I'm sweating by the time I reach Banksia Avenue. I only realise, as I roll into the Fishers' driveway, this morning's blow-dry is now limp and stringy. When I take off my backpack, I discover two large damp circles in the armpits of my new T-shirt.

I yank my faded hoodie from my backpack and slip it on to hide my sweat marks even though I'm warm all over from my ride. Sucking in a deep breath, I press the doorbell.

This is still just a homework session, Tash. Don't get ahead of yourself.

The timber door swings open and my excitement takes a nosedive. Rachael Tan steps forwards and leans against the doorframe. A red sundress settles gracefully around her hips, her legs bare from her thighs all the way down to her matching red toenails.

"You look disappointed to see me," she says, smirking. She fiddles with one of her loose silky plaits. "I'm sure you'll get over it. Nice to see that ratty old hoodie's getting another run."

She disappears inside the house and I feel myself deflate like a punctured balloon. I don't know why I expected it would be just me and Morgan. We're working on a group project – it makes sense he'd invite Rachael too.

I follow music to the back of the house, to a rumpus room that was closed off during the Fishers' party. There's a foosball table, two plump couches and a huge flat screen TV.

"There you are!" Morgan says as I hesitate in the doorway. He's bent over a coffee table with books and papers spread out in front of him. Rachael drapes herself across a cane armchair beside the bi-fold doors leading out onto a bright patio. Christopher lounges across one of the couches nursing a packet of Doritos and surfing TV channels.

"Hey, Tash," he says, clearly bored. "Please tell me you three aren't really doing homework when there's a computer market on at the town hall."

"Afraid so," I say, trying to hide my own disappointment that this homework date is actually all about homework and nothing to do with the *date* part.

"He carries on like that swap meet's not on every month," Morgan says, standing to greet me.

"Not the point," Christopher replies, pitching a corn chip at Morgan's head. Morgan lunges and manages to catch it in his mouth to much whooping and laughter. I lower my backpack onto the floor with a thud and Morgan's attention swings back to me. His face is adorably flushed from his corn chip victory.

"You brought photography books?" he asks, raising hopeful eyebrows. "'Cause I'm seriously struggling to come up with anything here." He leans in close to lower his voice. "And the only thing Rachael's researched is which Kardashian has the most cellulite."

He winks at me and my pulse flickers. I want it to mean something more than Morgan's affable nature.

"Dunno how much inspiration these will be," I say, unloading books beside Morgan's sketches. He's agreed that if we stick to our strengths – his drawing and my photography – we might be able to merge the two somehow. I take a seat next to him on the couch and we pore over the books for a while, earmarking pages that catch our interest. The sun-drenched room is warm, almost stuffy, and I wish I could take off my hoodie. I wish I'd worn an eye catching red sundress and toenail polish. I wish a lot of things, none of which are going to happen.

Before long Rachael has persuaded Christopher to hook

up the PlayStation. The two of them embark on a noisy mission of butchering aliens, and it becomes harder to concentrate on the project.

"Sorry about this," Morgan murmurs. "It was Mum's idea to invite them over to keep me company. She organised it with Mrs Tan before I even knew about it."

"Isn't Mallory here?" I say, picking at a fingernail. I try to keep the sulkiness out of my voice. "It's not like you were going to be all alone."

"Mal's not exactly a big conversationalist," Morgan jokes with a subdued smile. "Mum thinks we both need more contact with the outside world."

Shifting in my seat, I place the book I'm holding onto the coffee table. "What was it like in Brisbane for the two of you after you left here? Was it hard?"

Morgan looks at his knees as he mulls over an answer. "Probably easier for me after I got over missing this place. No one in Brisbane knew about Mallory's disappearance. No one was pointing accusing fingers at me and I could make friends without worrying kids were trying to get close to me out of morbid curiosity." He slides me a sheepish look. "I got to start afresh where nobody knew me."

I nod earnestly, because this is exactly what I want for myself.

"For Mallory, though, it wouldn't have mattered if she was in Brisbane or on the moon," Morgan says. "There's no such thing as a fresh start when your past keeps haunting you on a continuous loop."

His words could be describing me too. I feel a melancholy

connection with Mallory, like we're both tethered to that one horrible summer.

"Does she have any friends?" I say. "Did she have anyone to hang out with in Brissy?"

"She mostly talks to people online," Morgan says. My face must give away my surprise because Morgan chuckles before he goes on. "When I said she doesn't talk, I just mean she's non-verbal. Mal texts and emails, and she's on Twitter and Instagram all the time. Although I think it's less about socialising and more about lurking."

"Sorry, of course. I just thought … I don't know what I thought."

"She's not good with face-to-face stuff," Morgan says. "She definitely prefers her own company. Not a big fan of *outside*."

"That's called agoraphobia, isn't it?"

"Yeah. Like the opposite of you and your fear of small spaces," Morgan says. "You and Mal should get together and swap phobia stories."

I smile. "In an uncrowded room that's neither too big nor too small."

Morgan snorts. "Exactly." His smile fades a little and he looks down at his hands. "I might just check on her, see if she needs anything. She won't come down if there are people here, even if she's starving."

"I'll do it if you like." I knock my knee against Morgan's. "Then you can tell your mum you both socialised today. I can take a plate of food up to her like I did at the party, if you think she'd be okay with it."

His head tilts as he considers my offer, perhaps assessing

me for ulterior motives. At this very second, I have none. All my burning questions for Mallory have been drowned out by a desire to show her she has a friend in me if she wants one.

"Promise I won't bore her with my phobia stories." I grin to reassure him. "Not until at least our second conversation."

Morgan gives a small laugh. "Okay. Let me text her first, give her a heads up." He reaches for his phone on the table and smiles sheepishly. "I know, it's kinda weird – this is how we communicate most of the time, even at home."

"Here, let me." I pull my phone from my pocket. "You grab her some snacks and I'll text her. What's her number?"

He recites it to me as we make our way out of the family room. I can feel Rachael's eyes burning a hole in my back as we go. When we reach the kitchen, Morgan rummages through the fridge as I compose my text message.

Hey Mallory. Morgan's making some food for you. I'll bring it up if you like? –Tash.

I glance up to find Morgan's laid out half the fridge's contents all over the benchtop. I grab some grapes, strawberries and a wedge of cheese. "Got any crackers?"

He searches the pantry and returns with a box of Jatz. I arrange everything on the plate while Morgan steals two crackers and stuffs them into his mouth.

"That looks pretty good," he says through bulging cheeks. "You should get a job with a catering company."

I flick a tea towel at him and he swerves to dodge it, cracking us both up. He grabs a can of lemonade from the fridge and places it on the benchtop beside the plate.

"Okay, run along," he teases, shooing me with his fingers. "Go and make friends."

Rolling my eyes and smiling, I balance the plate with one hand while Morgan places the soft drink in the other. He holds onto the can for a second longer than he needs to, compelling me to look up.

"Thanks, Tash," he says. "It means a lot that you want to reach out to her."

*

Morgan's words gnaw at my conscience as I climb the staircase. I'd be lying if I didn't admit I'm doing this for myself as much as for Mallory. I just don't know how many opportunities I'll get to be alone with her, so I can't squander this chance now that it's presented itself.

Her door is ajar when I reach the end of the landing, and there's no noise inside the bedroom when I tap lightly with my knuckle. Assuming she's in the bathroom, I nudge the door open to place the plate of food on her desk.

The blinds are pulled against the coppery afternoon sunshine, giving the bedroom a muted glow like a candlelit cave. It takes me a second to realise Mallory is curled up on the bed under a knitted blanket with her eyes closed. Her head is angled against the pillows, white earbuds nestled in her ears, her straw-coloured hair framing her face like a halo. Her skin is so pale it's almost translucent. I see shades of the six year old I followed around the carnival nine summers ago.

"Mallory?" I whisper, unsure if she's sleeping or zoning out to music. Her phone is on the floor beside the bed. I move a step closer. "Mallory?"

Her eyes don't open as she shifts on the mattress, her right leg stretching and knocking a small book onto the floor. A pen slips from its pages and skitters underneath the bed.

The notebook lands on its spine with its pages splayed open. As I bend for it, my jacket rides up, hood flopping over my head as I strain for the pen. It's a drawing journal filled with dozens of black ink illustrations. Even in the dim light, I can appreciate how exquisitely detailed they are.

Straightening to a stand, I flip through the pages. There are two recurring themes: a canopy of trees viewed from the ground looking up, tree trunks bowed in exaggerated perspective, and an ornate Victorian wardrobe like something from one of the fantasy novels on Mallory's bookshelves.

The images of the wardrobe far outnumber the pictures of trees, each one subtly altered as though Mallory is still tweaking the design. Carved flourishes in the wood, delicate floral borders, the size of the doors, the number of drawers. In some drawings the wardrobe is overlaid with a grid, as though viewed through a panelled window.

I close the book wistfully, wanting to see more, but also aware that what I've already seen is an invasion of Mallory's privacy. I smooth my hand across the book's cover, and lean over to place it beside Mallory on the bed.

Her eyelids flutter open.

The whites of her eyes grow wide as she struggles to sit up.

Oh shit.

"What?" I spin to look over one shoulder, then the other. Behind me, the room is empty. Mallory scrambles away from me across the bed, her legs kicking pillows and blankets onto the floor. She lunges for the bedside table, her hand closing around the base of a ceramic lamp.

She cocks her arm and pitches it at me like a baseball.

I flinch and duck, yelling something indecipherable. There's a loud crack as the lamp's power cord hinders its flight. It jerks backwards in midair, crashing to the floorboards and cracking apart. The lampshade pops off and skids into the wall.

"What the hell are you doing?" I gasp, backing away from the bed until I collide with the desk. I knock into it so hard the plate of food scatters all over the tabletop. The lemonade can barrels across the wooden surface before tumbling onto the floor.

Mallory jumps at the sound, groping wildly behind her. Her fingers latch onto a glass picture frame.

"Wait!" I hold up a defensive hand. *"Wait!"* I glance desperately towards the door, my view obscured by the side of my hood. I quickly yank it off, and that's when it occurs to me. My face was hidden. The room is dim and my face was in shadow.

I raise my hands in surrender. "Mallory, it's me. It's just me – Tash. *See?*"

She's frozen on the bed, gripping the picture frame, her chest heaving like she's run a marathon. Strands of blonde hair are stuck to the corner of her mouth as her ice-blue eyes map my features in confusion.

"I brought you some food," I say, gesturing behind me at the mess on her desk.

Her shoulders slump. She loosens her grip on the picture frame and it lands lightly on the mattress beside her. I sink to a slouch and prop both hands against my thighs, releasing a quivery breath. Down the hall comes the hammering of footsteps on the staircase.

I blink at Mallory, my pulse still jackhammering. She only breaks eye contact with me when her brother bursts into the room.

"What's going on?" he cries, flicking on the light switch. Rachael and Christopher cram into the doorway behind him as Morgan's eyes bounce from the broken lamp to me doubled over in front of the desk. "What the hell happened in here?"

"It was a misunderstanding," I manage. "Mallory was dozing and I think I startled her. It's completely my fault."

Morgan stares at his sister, stunned. "Jesus, Mal. You threw a *lamp*?"

"It's my fault," I repeat. "I'm sorry."

Rachael snorts and mutters something to Christopher under her breath but he frowns and shooshes her in response. Morgan throws Rachael an unimpressed look.

"Are you okay?" he says to me. "Are you hurt?"

"I'm fine." I reach for the lemonade can near the foot of the desk. "Let me just clean up this mess."

"Don't," Morgan says, clearly impatient. "You don't have to do that."

His gruff tone makes me recoil. Rachael clears her throat,

rearranging her features into a picture of concern.

"Look, Tash," she says. "It's probably best if you go home."

"No," Morgan snaps.

"All right," I mumble, moving towards the hall. Rachael steps aside.

"*No*," Morgan says again. "Can everyone just … *God!*" He whacks a hand against his thigh and glares at the three of us in the doorway. His eyes are wild and so uncharacteristic of the Morgan I know, I feel like I'm looking at a different person.

"Look," he says sharply. "Can you two please go back downstairs?"

"Sure, man," Christopher says. "Just take a deep breath, okay? No one's hurt. Everybody's fine." He nudges Rachael. "We'll give you some privacy." He retreats into the hallway and I slip past Rachael to follow close behind.

"No, Tash. Wait," Morgan says, his voice losing its edge. "I didn't mean you." He gives Rachael a pointed look, but she folds her arms and doesn't budge.

Morgan quickly turns to his sister, softening his tone. "What's going on, Mal?" He drops his voice lower still, shooting a quick look over his shoulder. "I thought we talked about this. Do you need me to call Mum?"

Mallory's eyes find me over her brother's shoulder as she shakes her head no. The heat off her stare sets my pulse racing.

She remembers something.

I back out onto the landing and rush downstairs to retrieve

my things. Christopher approaches me in the rumpus room, shaking his head. He releases a puff of air and widens his eyes, as though we're in on the same joke. "Seriously though, what the hell did you say to her?"

"*Nothing*," I tell him. "She was asleep. She woke up and got a shock I was in her room."

Christopher smirks. It's unintentionally reminiscent of his sister and I have to turn away.

"Crazy," he says, with a shaken kind of awe.

I ram the last book into my backpack and spin to face him. "She's *not* crazy. And it's really unkind to call people that."

Christopher's face drops. "No, wait. I didn't mean—"

"Yeah, whatever." I march down the hallway dragging my backpack beside me. Morgan appears at the bottom of the staircase with Rachael close on his heels.

"Wait," he says to me. "You're going?"

"Toodles," Rachael purrs, pushing past me to join her brother.

Wasting no time, I head for the door. Morgan glides in and scoops up my heavy backpack for me, his voice low and beseeching. "I really wish you'd stay longer."

I yank the door open and step out onto the deck. Murky storm clouds have slunk in from the ocean, erasing what was left of the afternoon sun. "It's definitely time I went home."

Morgan rakes a hand through his hair and makes a small frustrated growl. "*Damn* it."

I whirl around, wide-eyed. "I'm sorry. I really didn't mean

to startle her. I can go upstairs and apologise again if you think—"

"No." Morgan sighs heavily, his frown softening. "It's not that." He scuffs a toe against the doormat. "It's just … today really didn't go the way I'd hoped."

I'm not sure how to respond so I glance out at the road where a breeze is scattering leaves underneath the parked cars. There's a brown ute near the corner that reminds me of Ally's. It makes my stomach squirm.

Next weekend. Willow Creek. All alone.

"I really wanted to hang out with you today," Morgan says, drawing my attention back to his face. "*Only* you, without anyone else."

He moves a step closer and the backpack bumps between our knees. I bend to take it from him, almost headbutting his shoulder. As I glance up to say goodbye, Morgan ducks his face to mine and presses his lips against my mouth. He lingers just long enough to send a rush of heat from my face to my toes. There's barely time to react before he pulls away and straightens up.

I have no idea what I should do next. Was that a *real* kiss? Or a friendly kiss? Do friends kiss each other like that? I don't have enough of them to know.

I'm ridiculously confused now, not to mention embarrassed by how hot and dizzy I feel. "Thanks," I murmur. "I–I'd better go."

I scurry across the deck and climb onto my bike, throwing a quick wave over my shoulder as I pedal out onto Banksia Avenue. It's only when I'm halfway down the hill that I sneak a look behind me at the Fishers' house.

The deck is empty now.

But a pale face watches me from the porthole window.

16

THEN

15 APRIL 2008
TRANSCRIPT FROM THE OFFICE OF DR INGRID BALLANTINE, PHD
CHILD AND ADOLESCENT PSYCHIATRY,
NEWCASTLE CHILDREN'S CLINIC
PATIENT: NATASHA CARMODY, 9 YEARS OLD

IB: You seem a little frustrated today, Natasha. Would you like to come and sit down here on the couch?

NC: ...

IB: Do you want to talk about what's upsetting you today?

NC: Mum says coming here is supposed to help, but it isn't.

IB: Oh? Why do you say that?

NC: No one believes me about anything. I thought coming here to talk about all the stuff that happened at Aunty Ally's was so everyone would understand.

IB: Well, we're trying to understand.

NC: I have to keep going over and over everything!

IB: We're still trying to figure out why you saw some of the things you saw and said some of the things you said.

NC: Because they happened. Why else would I say so?

IB: Sometimes people *think* they hear and see things because they really want them to be real. Except those things might not have really happened in reality. Does that make sense?

NC: No ...

IB: We've talked before about how it feels to be lonely and how sometimes it helps us feel less lonely to daydream ourselves into different scenarios. A bit like writing movie scenes for ourselves inside our heads where we get to be the main character, the centre of everything.

NC: ...

IB: We've also discussed the difference between fact and fiction, and what's happening in real life compared with those movie scenes inside our heads.

NC: I know the difference between fact and fiction.

IB: Okay, good. Do you think we could now talk about one of the things that happened to you at your aunt's house?

NC: I s'pose.

IB: All right. Let's talk about the afternoon in the bush behind your aunt's house. The day you went looking for tadpoles in the creek.

NC: My dad used to do it when he was a kid. There's a place where the creek widens into a little waterhole. Dad says it's the best spot.

IB: And it's close to your aunt's house?

NC: Sort of. You have to walk for about ten minutes into the bush to get there.

IB: I see. So your aunt wouldn't have been able to see you from the backyard?

NC: No, there are trees and then you go down a little hill.

IB: So what happened that day you went to find tadpoles?

NC: Aunty Ally was working. She was arguing with someone on the phone in the upstairs study. The door was locked.

IB: Then what happened?

NC: I knocked on the door because I wanted to play with Benny. That's Aunty Ally's dog. But she told me to go outside and play.

IB: So you decided to go down to the creek?

NC: Yeah. It was fun. I had ten tadpoles in my bucket when he came along and ruined it.

IB: Who ruined it?

NC: Sparrow. He was hiding in the trees.

IB: Sparrow?

NC: That's what I call *him*.

IB: Did he speak to you?

NC: Yeah. He wanted me to follow him somewhere. I didn't feel like it. He said he knew how to make my dad come and get me since I wanted to go home so much.

IB: How was that?

NC: A game. I told you about it before.

IB: The one where you held your breath and put your face in the creek?

NC: Why do I have to talk about it again?

IB: I want to understand why you did it. Do you know breath-holding games can be dangerous?

NC: People hold their breath when they swim all the time.

IB: Yes, except you weren't swimming. You were kneeling on the bank, weren't you? Even in the pool people play breath-holding games where they hang on for so long they get dizzy and pass out under water. When they become unconscious their bodies automatically breathe for them again.

NC: Then they'd breathe in water instead of air.

IB: Yes, and they drown. It's very dangerous, especially if you're alone.

NC: I wasn't alone. Sparrow was there.

IB: Yes, of course.

NC: He did it first. He said if I could hold my breath longer than him he would call my dad to come and get me. It would be my prize for winning.

IB: So if your parents heard all about it they'd come and collect you?

NC: Sparrow promised.

IB: Did he keep his promise?

NC: No. It was a trick! He put his hand on the back of my neck – like this – and held my face under water. He wouldn't let me come up for air. He said I wasn't playing it right. He said, "Stop struggling".

IB: So what did you do?

NC: I kicked and scratched and punched as much as I could, and I must have hurt him because he let go. I ran back to Aunty Ally's house and told her what happened and she went down to the creek to look for Sparrow. But she didn't see him. She never saw him.

IB: Mmm. Why do you think Sparrow held your face under water?

NC: I think he wanted me to go unconscious, maybe? Like you said.

IB: Why would he want that?

NC: Because I wouldn't go to his secret room with him.

IB: Oh ...?

NC: If I went unconscious he could take me there while I was asleep and I wouldn't have any choice.

IB: You've never mentioned this secret room before.

NC: Sparrow said I'd like it because no one else knew about it. It would be our secret place.

IB: Why didn't you want to see it?

NC: Because if I went there he might never let me go again.

IB: Do you still see or hear Sparrow now?

NC: Sometimes I have bad dreams about him. Sometimes I think I see him here – just off to the side of where I'm looking.

IB: Out of the corner of your eye?

NC: Yeah. But when I turn around he's not there.

IB: Have you spoken to him since you've been home in Port Bellamy?

NC: No. He might be stuck there.

IB: Stuck where?

NC: In Willow Creek House. Maybe he can't leave.

IB: Have you been back to Willow Creek since the summer?

NC: No way.

IB: Why don't you want to go back?

NC: Because he might be there. Waiting.

17

NOW

The hour-and-a-half drive north to Willow Creek is a somewhat sombre affair. Dad and I abandoned small talk less than fifteen minutes from home. He and Mum shared a quiet and intense exchange as we left the house, and while Dad pretended to be unruffled as we wound our way out of Port Bellamy, I noticed a tic working away in his jaw. He seemed relieved when I suggested an audio book to pass the time, but I can tell his mind is elsewhere.

Between this weekend at Willow Creek and Morgan and I acting like his kiss never happened, I have my own preoccupations. It certainly doesn't help that Sadie warned me to slow things down with Morgan until I know him better, making me wonder what she senses about him that I don't.

The thing bothering me most is my last interaction with Mallory. It's not just that I startled her awake and she reacted violently; something about me being there was so disturbing that she was terrified enough to lash out.

Does she remember something about her disappearance?

More specifically, does she remember something about me?

As we pass the neat grounds of Greenwillow's golf course, I shift uncomfortably in my seat. It's ten minutes to Ally's house from here. A strange mix of familiarity and unease hums through me as we cruise up Greenwillow's main street, past the strip of brick shopfronts that have been here forever, the two-storey pub on the corner, the Palace Theatre with its blue-tiled frontage. I spot a wooden sign with arrows pointing towards the local caravan park – the Fishers' holiday house is nestled along the same stretch of river. It's enough to set off nervous flutters again, because if they're not here already, they will be soon enough.

"It's gone," Dad says, when he catches me peering up Old Meadow Lane, the back road police suspected Mallory was snatched from that fateful summer. "The carnival. Closed down about five years ago because of low attendance after that water park opened near Port Macquarie."

"Oh?" I'm surprised I hadn't heard about this. I crane in my seat for a glimpse of the carnival's entry gates, the peaked roof of the dodgem car pavilion. All I spot is the top of the buttercup-yellow Ferris wheel before my view is obstructed by a clump of trees.

"It was in the paper," Dad says, slowing at an intersection. We turn left and head west, the carnival site slipping away behind us. "The food trucks all left first, then one by one

153

they sold off the rides and moved them off-site. Not much left there now, I imagine. The end of an era."

I chew my thumbnail and slump against the door's armrest. I don't know why I feel disappointed by this news. Maybe I thought the carnival might still hold some answers. Now it's just another dead end.

As we leave Greenwillow township, the road meanders past grazing cattle and murky dams, hillsides scarred by rocky escarpments and towering gums. Willow Creek is a smattering of timeworn farmhouses and rusted iron sheds, large properties separated by nothing more than a few wooden posts strung together with fence wire.

We turn up Cowpasture Road and I get my first glimpse of Willow Creek House, its red corrugated roof flanked on both ends by crumbling stone chimneys. The symmetrical facade is at the same time proudly classic and completely banal. From a distance the house appears hunched against the looming mountains like a stubborn old creature, struggling to stay upright but flat out refusing to fall down.

As we draw closer, Dad takes in the sagging verandah eaves and cracked window panes. It's hard to tell if it's nostalgia washing over his features, or quiet defeat about the state of disrepair.

We hit a pothole in the dirt driveway and the car lurches to one side.

"Bloody hell," he murmurs, slowing to a stop in front of the house. A breeze whispers through the droopy boughs of surrounding willow trees as we get out. Dad inspects the wheel rim for damage.

"Didn't hurt your precious baby, did you?"

We both glance up at Ally's voice. She ambles barefoot down the verandah's stone steps, tugging a knitted cardigan around her sundress. Benny squeezes past her and bounds down the driveway directly for Dad.

"I'm touched by your concern," Dad says dryly, bending to scratch Benny behind the ears.

"That car's such a prissy little thing," Ally teases. "Guess it takes one to drive one, eh, big brother?" She makes a beeline for me, engulfing me in a brief, enthusiastic hug infused with a scent I'd forgotten about: gardenias and cigarettes. "I'd invite you in for a cuppa, Rich, except I know you'll want to be on your way."

It's true. Dad hasn't stopped looking over his shoulder like he can't wait to get back inside the car.

"Come on, Tash," Ally urges, holding her hand out for me like I might actually take it. I retrieve my backpack from the boot as Benny pants hot breaths around my ankles. Dad steps into my path as I move towards the house, his voice softening in a way that's reminiscent of the time he dropped me off here as a child.

"Listen," he says, "just call me if this isn't working out, and I'll come and get you. Whenever you're ready, okay?"

He kisses the top of my head and makes a quick exit. I stand beside Gran's old brown Ford as I watch him go. After the dust has settled, I run a hand along the curve of the truck's bonnet, following the line of orange pin-striping down the door panels.

"Barely use it any more," Ally says. "Only for long-haul

trips or bigger deliveries. I use Molly to get around town these days." She thumbs at an old silver moped propped up beside the shed. "She costs a hell of a lot less to run."

A thought pops into my head. "You could give the truck to Dad? I know he'd really love to have it."

Ally's eyes narrow, her gaze fixed on the horizon. "Richard got everything he wanted when our mother was alive. He doesn't get to have this as well."

*

"So, what are your plans for the weekend?" Ally asks as she retrieves the dented kettle from a burner on the stovetop. She's given me a tour of the house and gardens, and everything looks to be exactly the same. It seems I'm unchanged too, the way I keep checking corners and standing with my back to the wall. I thought I would have outgrown my fears of this big house simply because I'm now bigger in it. But my nervy stomach tells me that's not the case. When Ally offered me any room in the house to sleep in, I chose the one furthest from the downstairs guestroom I slept in all those years ago.

"Plans? Umm ... twenty-minute showers and sleeping in?" I answer, grinning. Ally nods as though her own mother got on her case about those things when she was the same age. "Other than that, I'm not entirely sure yet. I'm going to get together with a guy from school to work on our art project."

She looks at me with renewed interest as she pours two cups of tea, dolloping a spoonful of honey into each mug even though I asked for mine with milk and sugar. She arches an eyebrow. "Define 'get together'."

"Oh! No, nothing like that," I say. "We're just working on a group art project for school. He's staying at his holiday house in Greenwillow, so we thought it would be good to meet up and get some work done."

Ally smirks at my over-explanation. I swallow a large gulp of tea. It's way too hot and burns all the way down.

"You like him."

"Well … I mean …" I sigh. "Um, yes?"

She brings her mug to her mouth and smiles around the rim. I can't imagine ever having a conversation like this with my mother.

"You know," she says, "I met my soulmate in high school." I feel myself blush even though the story is about Ally. "Patrick Jonas. He was wiry and athletic, fastest runner on our school athletics team. The Pocket Rocket, they called him. Meanwhile, I spent all my time smoking behind the cricket sheds with the mopey drama kids. God knows how PJ and I even clicked, but it was so easy we didn't have to try."

I think about how Morgan and I have fallen back into our friendship after all these years. How right it felt when he kissed me, and how much I want him to do it again.

"Did your mum like him?"

"Pfft. My mother didn't like anything when it came to me," Ally says, waving a dismissive hand. "She always resented how close Dad and I were before he died. Imagine being jealous of your thirteen-year-old daughter." A bitter look washes over her face. "So of course she hated PJ because he filled the cold, loveless void she'd created at home. *He became my family.*" She places her chin in her hand and stares wistfully out the window. "We fought and broke up so many times, and always found our way back to each other. He's the only one who's ever really understood me."

Glancing around the drab kitchen with its yellowed curtains and washed-out floor tiles, I'm very aware Ally's currently flying solo. There's no PJ in her life now. She's still here alone in the cold, loveless void of her mother's home.

"Things get messed up sometimes," Ally says. Catchlights twinkle in her eyes. "I won't lie – I've made mistakes and I have regrets. But I truly believe that if things are meant to be, they have a way of working out." She draws her gaze away from the window and refocuses on my face. "People come back into our lives for a reason."

Like Morgan and Mallory, I think, though I'm still figuring out what that reason is.

Ally surprises me by leaning over and squeezing my hand. I flinch slightly, then feel guilty for doing so. "I'll leave you to settle in," she says. "Get reacquainted with the house. I'm going to pack a few things and put petrol in the truck for tomorrow's road trip. Might grab us some takeaway while I'm out."

My aunt slides her chair back and pushes herself up from the table. For a brief moment, she looks much older than her forty-five years. Weary and uncertain, almost vulnerable. The image disappears as quickly as it came, erased by a flick of her wavy hair as she strides purposefully from the kitchen.

*

When I come into my bedroom after my shower I find two new texts from Sadie. First:

Yo, kanga. How's things going at your aunt's place?

Then:

Btw, what did you say to Christopher Tan? He thinks you hate him.

I feel pretty bad about biting Christopher's head off at the Fishers' house last week; he didn't deserve it. The adrenaline was pumping and I was rattled. I need to message him this weekend to clear the air.

Hey, kiwi, I type to Sadie. *All good here so far. How's it going at the party?*

She sends me a response straightaway and we text back and forth for several minutes until it's time for her to go and wash up some cocktail glasses.

Ally's in the living room pouring red wine when I come downstairs. She's lit a small fire in the hearth as the last remnants of sunset drain from the sky. Silhouettes of scribbly gums stretch across the horizon, their disjointed arms flailing like an army of the undead advancing on the house. I shiver at the chill leaching through the window panes and quickly draw the curtains against the darkness. I don't like the feeling of being a window display. Anybody could be out there watching us.

On the coffee table are takeaway boxes of Indian food. Ally's already started on the samosas and found some trippy sitar music to accompany our meal.

"Had to drive over to Ellenbrook for this," she says. "So dig in while it's still hot." She tosses me a large embroidered floor cushion to sit on while she plonks herself on a Moroccan pouf by the fire. Benny trots in from the kitchen to join us, pausing in the hallway long enough to growl at the cellar door.

"Stop that, Benny. C'mere." Ally tosses him a piece of roti, which he catches in midair. He settles on the rug at her feet in the hopes more food scraps might come his way.

"He still does that?" I say, nodding towards the wooden door tucked underneath the stairs. I shudder without meaning to. I can still feel the clutch of Sparrow's bony fingers digging into my arm, and I find myself frantically trying to rub the sensation away.

Behind the door comes the rumble of the water heater filling up after my shower. The hiss and squeal of the pipes from below still hits a nerve.

This house won't let me forget.

"Not for a long time," Ally says, stroking her foot along Benny's rump. "I suppose old habits die hard." She frowns into her food for a second like she might say something else, then seems to change her mind.

She nudges a tumbler of wine across the table towards me.

"Um," I say, "are you sure this is okay? I mean, I'm underage and everything ..."

She snorts. "God, you're your father's daughter, aren't you? You don't wanna know what *I* got up to when I was seventeen." She takes a generous slug from her own wineglass. "Don't worry. Promise I won't report it to your prison guards."

I tentatively sip my wine between mouthfuls of lentil

curry, and it's not long before I'm feeling loose and relaxed, maybe even a little woozy. I've tried wine before and not enjoyed it very much. It goes down much easier with food.

"So, what other stuff did you get up to when you were younger?" I ask her, the wine making me bold.

She pours herself another glass and side-eyes me. "I don't want to talk about all of that. I don't need any more grief from my self-righteous brother about how I've lived my life."

"Oh, I wouldn't say anything to Dad. And he's really not—"

"Let me tell you a little something about Richard 'Golden Boy' Carmody," Ally says, throwing up air quotes. "He wouldn't know the first thing about actually living. He thinks he's so worldly when all he's done with his life is marry his first-and-only girlfriend and move an hour-and-a-half away from where he grew up. He's jealous he doesn't have the freedom I do, and I'll be damned if I'll let him sell this place to fund his pathetic mid-life crisis. I won't lose my home so a sad little man can buy himself a sad little Volvo to park in his sad little garage."

Ally looks at me like she's just remembered she's talking about my father, and that his sad little life thus far has resulted in producing sad little me. She mumbles something I don't catch and reaches for her cigarette packet. I concentrate on shovelling food into my mouth as I try to process her outburst.

It occurs to me my aunt is a walking contradiction. She rabbits on about the benefits of her organic diet, yet she smokes like a chimney. She extols the virtues of cleansing yoga and meditation, but carries around a shit-tonne of resentment about my dad. When I was a little girl, Ally said she and I were alike, and she assured me it was okay to be different. Yet she didn't want a relationship with me after I left here, changed.

She glances at me now, blowing smoke out of the corner of her mouth. "He'll find some other way to pay for your university fees."

I'm not sure how I'm supposed to respond.

"He'll never get his grubby little hands on my half of the house," she continues. "I'm leaving it to somebody else."

It's hard to know if she's serious. "Why?"

Ally swallows another mouthful of wine, her lips glistening. "Why not? It's not like I'm the beneficiary of *his* estate, am I? So why should I leave my half to him just because I don't have kids?" She chuckles conspiratorially, as though we're two girlfriends in a wine bar. "Had a legal will drawn up years ago. Can you imagine the look on Rich's face when he finds out?" She snorts into her glass and takes another swig.

There's something really jarring about Ally's nature, inconsistencies between what she says and what she does. Maybe it's the wine, or the way she's insulting my dad, or some long-held suspicion about what really happened in this house that stirs up a challenge brewing in my belly.

"Can I ask you something?"

She blows a thin stream of smoke towards the fireplace and settles into an armchair. "Of course, honey."

"That day at Greenwillow Carnival, when I was eight. You know, when Mallory Fisher disappeared?"

She narrows her eyes. "Yeah ...?"

"Why did you think it must've been me?"

"What do you mean?"

"When you came to pick me up, you'd heard in the car park that a little girl had gone missing. When we met up you grabbed me by the shoulders and said, 'I thought it must've been you'."

Ally frowns, shrugging her shoulders. "Why would I say that?"

"Exactly. Why *would* you say that?"

She sits back and assesses me like she's seeing me for the first time. She waits a few beats before speaking and I have to resist the urge to babble on to dilute the growing tension.

"I'm not sure what you're getting at, Tash," she says, folding one arm across her body. She takes a long drag from her cigarette.

"You seemed certain that it must have been me who disappeared."

"I don't know how you could possibly remember a conversation from when you were eight."

"I remember everything about that day."

Her eyes flash. "Even the fictional parts?"

There's a hardness in her voice that makes me want to back down. This isn't the empathetic aunt murmuring assurances about her niece's healthy imagination. This feels like her throwing it back in my face.

"Did you feel guilty?" I fire back.

"Of course not. Why would—"

"Because you left an eight year old alone at a carnival for five hours."

Ally scoffs, sitting up straight in her armchair. "You were perfectly fine!"

"If I'd disappeared instead of Mallory Fisher, I wouldn't have been fine."

She gives me a bitter look. "I had so many errands to run that afternoon, Tash. I knew you'd have more fun at the carnival. I was doing something nice for you."

"By leaving me alone to fend for myself?"

"You were eight years old, not a bloody toddler. When I was eight my mother made me walk all over town delivering pamphlets for her antiques business. Everyone knows everyone here. It's perfectly safe."

"Except for when it's not."

Ally leans forwards and stubs out her cigarette in the ashtray on the table. I find myself shrinking away from her.

"Why are you picking a fight with me, Tash?"

"I'm not. I'm just trying to understand why you looked so terrified that day, why you were so convinced it was me who'd gone missing."

She sighs, pushing herself up out of the armchair. She wanders over to the stone fireplace and stares at the flames through the grate.

"You'd been saying and doing some weird shit that summer," she says, resting a hand against the mantel. "It's like you were living in your own little world. Seeing things, inventing people. I was worried you'd run off from the carnival in one of your made-up fantasies."

Wrapping her cardigan around herself, Ally wanders back to the coffee table to retrieve her wineglass.

"I wasn't going to tell your parents about any of it, you know," she says, standing over me. I feel like a small child again sitting here on my cushion, looking up at her. "I knew how they'd overreact and make a big drama out of nothing. It was going to be our little secret, remember?" I open my mouth to speak and she talks over me. "I knew you were doing it for attention. I also knew the less attention I gave it the sooner you'd grow bored of it. Then you made up that story about seeing that Fisher girl getting snatched. You left me no choice – after that I had to tell them about everything else you'd made up."

Her last sentence makes me bristle. She says it like I told those stories on purpose, like there was intent or malice on my part. Yet, as riled as I feel, I can't find the words to speak up for myself. I drop my gaze to the table, shamed. Whichever way you slice it, I still told those stories. In everyone's eyes I was a liar.

"I'm not hungry any more," Ally says in a way that's reminiscent of Tim when he's sulking. She won't look at me as she tops off her wineglass and carries it with her towards the hallway. "I'm going upstairs to finish packing."

Her battered brown suitcase is already sitting by the front door.

"See you at breakfast," she mutters, creaking her way up the staircase. Benny lopes along behind her, throwing one more longing glance at the takeaway containers.

I pick at the remainder of my food before clearing off the coffee table and cleaning up the kitchen. I return to curl up on Gran's old patchwork couch as the dwindling flames lick around the charred wood in the fireplace.

Trying to empty my mind and let go of old frustrations, there's one question I can't seem to silence, one I wish I'd asked Ally while I had the chance.

If I was acting so weird and spacey in that week leading up to the carnival, why on earth would she leave me there alone?

18

THE CARNIVAL

Two balloons.

One pink and one yellow, tethered to each other like sisters holding hands. Fighting and pulling, kissing and twisting, the updraft yanking them to and fro in a wrestling waltz.

Away they go, drawn to the ocean sky dusted with fairy floss, away from the clatter and whirr of the carnival rides, the discordant clang of the sideshow. Away from the stink of muddy grass and deep fryers, high above the fairgoers slick with sunscreen and sweat.

Away they go, their ribbon strings flickering a fond farewell.

To the girl on the ground.

As he lures her away.

19

NOW

I wake up with a start, the carousel's melody still pealing in my ears, the metallic tang of panic coated on the back of my tongue. My heart thumps as I blink into the darkness of the bedroom where moments ago there was blazing blue sky. I grab for the sheets and blanket I've kicked off in my sleep, then hug them to me as I curl into a ball against my pillow. It's the third time I've woken since going to bed, each restless dream a variation of that dreadful moment at the carnival.

It's this house. It won't give me peace. It won't leave me alone.

Shaking my sleep-deprived paranoia away, I remind myself I chose to come here this time. I am *not* powerless. I am *not* a child.

I doze on the very knife-edge of sleep, the pulsing trill of cicadas seeping through the window cracks, preventing me from fully slipping under. The old house ticks and groans as the cool night pulls it closer, and my initial jitters give way to numb, exhausted indifference. When the floorboards creak on the landing outside my bedroom door, I give it a half-hearted glance with barely one eye open.

The door is ajar. A shadow hovers outside in the hallway.

"Ally?" I rub my eye with the ball of my hand. "What is it?"

I lean up on one elbow, straining to make her out in the dark. When I squint, the outline of her shoulder becomes more defined.

"Ally ...? Are you okay?"

The shadow doesn't move. My heartbeat thumps a warning while my bleary mind sifts through questions.

Can't she hear me?

Does she sleepwalk?

Is that even Ally?

I shrink against the mattress, tugging the blanket to my chin. "I–Is someone there?"

The shadow shifts in the doorway. I blink rapidly, trying to distinguish shapes, refusing to let my mind wander where it shouldn't–

this house, this place, where he first appeared

–and concentrate on logical explanations.

Ally's just checking on me, or she's got up to let Benny outside. Maybe she's leaving now for her road trip to Byron Bay.

So why won't she answer me?

I fumble for the frilly lamp on the bedside table behind me. The small room floods with golden light, spilling through the doorway and out into the hall. Apart from a few wispy cobwebs and peeling wallpaper, there's nothing to see.

I kick off my sheets and march over to the bedroom door, throwing it wide open. The dim hallway is empty in both directions, and when I move to the top of the stairs, I hear only the ticking clock in the living room below. I pad down the landing to Ally's bedroom door and press my ear up against the cool wood. The door swings inwards and I almost topple over.

I'm not sure what I was expecting on the other side, but it wasn't Ally passed out across her bed, limbs splayed and fully clothed, Benny nestled at her hip. She makes a low groaning noise in her sleep and one of Benny's paws twitches. An empty wineglass is upended on the rug beside the bed.

Standing in the middle of Ally's bedroom, I watch them sleep for much longer than I need to. I'm almost afraid of going back to my own room, frightened to be alone with my thoughts. I eventually close Ally's door softly behind me, then do a full circuit of the house, flipping on every light switch as I go. I check door bolts and window locks, inside cupboards and behind the shower curtain, until I'm satisfied no one could've possibly broken in.

But it's no comfort at all.

If there's nobody here, the only other place they can be hiding is inside my head.

*

On Saturday morning, I wake to the sound of Benny scratching. I think it's at my bedroom door until I shake off the remnants of sleep and realise it's somewhere downstairs instead. I feel completely wrung out, like I haven't rested at all, though in actuality I must have snatched a few hours. I nudge a curtain aside to find powdery mist lingering over the surrounding hills, the violet-grey light hinting that the sun is on its way. And so, it seems, is Ally – her brown truck is gone from the driveway.

Benny's scratching becomes insistent and it occurs to me he probably needs to be let outside. I shrug my hoodie on over my pyjamas and slide out of bed. The floorboards are chilly underfoot, and I glance around for my sneakers. Benny barks so urgently that I hurry downstairs to find him in the hallway. He's not standing in the front entry, though. He's pacing outside the cellar door.

"Come on, Benny-boy," I croak, rubbing the sleep from my eyes. "You wanna go outside?"

I open the front door and Benny scrambles for the verandah, launching himself onto the gravel driveway and disappearing around the side of the house. I trail into the kitchen, and everything's exactly how I left it after cleaning up last night. No used coffee cups or dirty ashtrays, no cereal bowl in the sink. I guess Ally decided to leave early and get breakfast on the road, and really, can I blame her? Things got tense between us last night, and I feel sort of guilty about how we left it.

By the time I've put the kettle on and filled a bowl with dog kibble, Benny still hasn't come inside. I find him growling at his reflection in the ground-level windows around the side of the house.

"Come here, you old coot." I pat my thigh and hold up the dog bowl. "Time for breakfast. C'mon." He gallops over and follows me inside. Once he's eaten, he trails behind me upstairs and waits outside the bathroom door while I shower. I'm grateful for it. The house is too quiet and I can't wait to get outside.

I grab my camera and barely touch Benny's dog lead on the entry table before he comes bounding towards me with a look of goofy expectation on his face. The sun has burned off the dawn mist, leaving the morning bright and crisp – my favourite kind of light to photograph in. We hit the dusty backroads of Willow Creek, steering clear of the bushland behind the house, well away from the creek I'd be happy to never visit again.

Benny runs ahead of me chasing butterflies and things that whisper through the tall grasses on both sides of the road. I call Sadie, and she fills me in about last night's cocktail party. Her neighbour Lilly dropped a tray of spring rolls into a pot plant, and Alice, her crush from the Seaspray, was a guest at the party. She and Sadie have now added each other on Snapchat.

"What about you?" she asks. "How was it hanging out with your aunt?"

"All right."

"By that you mean weird. I can hear it in your voice."

"Yeah. Things got a bit tense. Seems she's got a few million hang-ups about my family."

Sadie snorts. "Lucky she didn't smother you in your sleep then. You sure she doesn't have an ulterior motive for inviting you?"

Sadie chuckles to herself, but her words unsettle me. What *did* prompt Ally to invite me here? Why did she get so hostile when I brought up *that* summer? And why did she leave this morning without saying goodbye?

"Funny you should say that," I tell Sadie, trying to keep my voice light. "I thought she was standing in my doorway last night watching me sleep."

"Ding, ding, ding! Creeper alert!" Sadie laughs. "Please tell me you pegged a pillow at her."

I force a laugh as well. "It wasn't her. I mean, it wasn't anyone. It was just my sleepy head playing tricks."

"Or," Sadie says, lowering her voice and adding a quiver, "it was the ghost of Convict McPants coming to check out your frilly little nightie."

"McTavish," I say, sniggering. "I wish I'd never told you that story. Stop trying to spook me."

"Didn't he die in the pantry or something?"

"The cellar, supposedly. He was the Blackwell family's servant, and the cellar was his living quarters. There's no record of him actually dying at Willow Creek House, though. He probably finished his sentence and happily trotted off to Sydney."

"Yeah, you hope."

We continue chatting about everything and nothing while Benny bounds ahead of me up the side of a hill. It's not until I reach the top that I realise we've made it all the way to

Greenwillow. We're standing in the middle of Old Meadow Lane. I cross the road on autopilot and follow the gravel shoulder towards the open field that served as Greenwillow Carnival's car park.

"Uh-oh," Sadie says in my ear. "You've started responding in Vague-a-nese."

"Huh?"

"You keep doing this lately. You flake out halfway through a conversation like your brain's gone AWOL."

"I'm just distracted by Benny," I say, long grass whipping at my legs. "I'm trying to keep an eye on him."

"Sure, chief. Don't worry, I'm going anyway. Gotta see a girl about some ice cream."

I'm hungrily rummaging for my camera by the time Sadie hangs up, my attention fixed on the scene ahead of me.

The carnival site is a graveyard of grungy amusement rides, dead mechanical arms bent at the elbows as though struggling to keep upright. The dry grass is littered with hollowed-out rocket carriages, sun-bleached and brittle, like a minefield of oversized cicada shells. Broken sideshow games slump into one another, lightbulbs missing from their signage and leering clown faces riddled with graffiti. One or two grubby stuffed animals hang here and there, too high to bother with. Benny barks at one before trotting off to mark his territory on everything possible.

Even in its heyday this place would have been eerie without people around. Now, abandoned and dying, it's so surreal it feels like a dream. I dig out my phone and dial Morgan's number without thinking.

"Hey!" he answers. "Are you here? We arrived last night."

"Morgan, you have to see this," I say, poking my head inside a red-and-white striped ticket booth. Somebody's scraped the words *No ticket, no ride!* on the dirt-covered countertop with their finger. A roll of green paper tickets is unravelled all over the floor. "I've found us our dreamscape. It's seriously perfect. You need to get over here with your sketchbook."

"What, here? In Greenwillow?" He sounds excited, his voice muffled like he's pulling on a jacket. "My parents said we can use their car today. Mal and I can leave now. Whereabouts are you?"

It suddenly hits me – where I'm standing, what I'm suggesting. I glance towards the rear of the grounds where the concrete toilet block is perched on the edge of the hill overlooking the car park. "Mallory wants to come?"

What the hell was I thinking? I can't invite them here! *Either* of them. It would seem like some kind of sick joke at their expense.

"Yeah. She suggested it, actually." Morgan lowers his voice. "I think she feels bad about what happened last weekend. She wants to show Mum she's making an effort to socialise."

I keep my voice low too, although Mallory can't possibly hear me. "Listen, it's a bad idea. Forget I mentioned it. We can find something else."

"Are you kidding?" Morgan says. "We're the only group in class with nothing to show so far. If you're that excited about it I will be too. Let's go for it. Just tell me where you are."

My shoulders slump. "I ... I'm at Greenwillow Carnival."

There's a pause so long on the other end of the phone I think Morgan must have hung up on me. Common sense tells me I need to suggest somewhere else right away, but a defiant internal voice urges me to stay. Recording this decay might help me think of this place differently. It might help me move forward. I selfishly need to do this for me.

I'm about to end the call when Morgan exhales. "So, are we going for the nightmare angle or what?"

"I'm sorry. I just stumbled across it while I was out walking. You really don't have to come here. I can meet you somewhere else later on."

"You know what?" His voice is a little more upbeat. It's hard to tell whether or not it's put on. "Didn't Mrs Liotta say our best work will stem from something that actually holds meaning for us? Maybe it's time to go back there, face this particular demon head-on."

"You sure?" I say. "But Mallory ..."

"I'll tell her where I'm meeting you. It's her choice whether she comes or not."

"And your parents ...?"

Another pause. "They don't have to know."

*

I've taken close to fifty photos by the time I see a black SUV pull into the field below the carnival. I think Morgan might be alone until the passenger door opens too. I press a firm hand against my stomach to quell the nerves before moving to the edge of the hill to raise it in greeting.

Morgan follows the dirt track up from the field, sketchbook in hand, Mallory trailing a couple of metres behind. I catch only glimpses of her head or her shoulder behind her brother, as though she's using his frame as a shield.

"What happened to this place?" Morgan calls, his eyes drawn to what remains of the carousel. It's been hollowed out and stripped of ornamental horses, the elegant fretwork and mirrors shot through with holes. "Why isn't this all fenced off?"

"My dad said they closed it down a few years ago," I tell him, as Benny trundles over to meet them. "Maybe they want people to come and steal stuff so they don't have to cart it all away."

Morgan leans over and sinks both hands into Benny's fur, murmuring, "Who's a good boy?" and, "You are. Yes, you are." It's Mallory my aunt's dog is most interested in, though. He sniffs around her legs, panting up at her, his tail wagging hopefully.

"Hi, Mallory," I say. She nods in response, avoiding eye contact. She places her earbuds in and turns away from us, wandering towards what's left of sideshow alley.

Morgan's barely looked at me, distracted by the deterioration of this once flamboyant place. He seems in awe of its decline, but also wary, as though this fallen beast might still have some teeth.

"This is not what I expected," he murmurs, more to himself than anything. The faint smile on his lips tells me he recognises the artistic possibilities. Without saying another word he slips off his jacket, finds a place to sit and opens his sketchbook. I leave him to draw while I seek a path through the overgrown grass to the Ferris wheel on the other side of the park.

After an hour, we reconvene in the picnic area where the food trucks used to sit. Morgan spreads his drawings out across a wooden table so we can decide which ones might work best overlaid with my photos. I scroll through the images on my camera, offering him a look at the LCD panel. He slides closer on the bench seat until our shoulders touch. There's a brief lull in conversation as I enlarge an image on-screen to see if it's in focus.

"Are we okay?" Morgan says quietly.

I half-turn towards him. "Yeah, of course. What do you mean?"

He drops his gaze to the papers spread out in front of him. "You just haven't said anything about ... you know." He taps the pad of his finger against a splinter on the edge of the table. "I think I may have misread the situation."

His sentence ends with an inflection, as though it's really a question. My pulse races. Is he talking about our kiss? Or does he mean what happened in Mallory's bedroom? I place the camera down and rub my palms across the thighs of my jeans.

"I have a habit of jumping into things too quickly," he says. "I guess I panic that anything good in my life is going to get wrenched away." He glances in the general direction of his sister, but he could just as easily be talking about his hometown, his happy childhood. "When Mallory disappeared, I was swallowed up by this overwhelming bleakness, like I'd never feel happy again. I'd always complained about my little sister tagging along with me everywhere until suddenly she wasn't there any more. I hated myself for every time I wished she was out of my hair."

Nodding, I wait for him to go on.

"When they found her, it was like I'd been given this second chance. I made a pact with my eight-year-old self then and there: don't ever take good things for granted, and hold onto them tight so they can't be snatched away."

I stare down at the table, my chest aching for everything eight-year-old Morgan went through.

"Only problem is," he says, strumming his fingers against the table, "sometimes I get a bit full on. I completely understand if you just want to be friends."

"Morgan?"

He slides me a sheepish look, as though he knows what I'm going to say next. He looks as surprised as I feel when I slip my hand onto his knee and lean my face up to his. For the briefest of moments, I'm breathing in the same delicious air he's breathing out.

He holds eye contact as he brushes his mouth against mine, as though needing visual confirmation this is really what I want. I open my mouth slightly and catch his bottom lip between mine, tugging softly. It's all the invitation Morgan needs for his eyelids to flutter closed, for his hand to slide to my jaw as he tentatively explores my mouth.

A nagging voice questions whether I actually deserve this. Would he still want me if he knew things are more than a little messed up inside my head? But as the kissing intensifies,

I can't think straight. I close my eyes and surrender to it, every nerve ending in my body on fire. All that exists is the taste of Morgan Fisher, the heat of him through his T-shirt, the tremble in his breath in the brief moments our mouths break apart.

I don't know how long the kiss consumes us before there's a loud thump on our picnic table. Morgan pulls away from me and we both jerk around to find Mallory glaring at us from across the table. She's gripping an empty water bottle, her chin jutting towards Benny sniffing around some old bins.

I shake my head. "I don't know what you …?"

Mallory rolls her eyes and pushes herself away from the table. She strides towards the rear of the park with the bottle in her hand. Morgan chuckles as we watch her go.

"What's her problem?" he says, shaking his head.

The penny drops. "Water," I say, jumping up. "She wants me to get water for Benny."

"Well, *she's* doing it now," Morgan says, standing too. "So you don't have to go anywhere." He threads a hand through mine and tugs me towards him, his shy smile sending a tingle through me. As he moves to kiss me again, something occurs to me.

There's only one place with running water around here.

Mallory's headed towards the carnival's toilet block.

"I, um–" I slide my hand out of Morgan's and stumble over the bench seat. "Sorry. I'll be right back."

His raised eyebrows tells me he's more amused than offended. "Okay. But this trend of you running away every time I kiss you is a bit worrying." He smiles to himself as he starts gathering up drawings to slip inside his sketchbook.

I force myself to walk casually even though I'm dying to sprint after Mallory. I'm not sure why I need to stop her going inside that toilet block. Do I even *want* to? Maybe I'm following her because I want to witness what will happen if she does.

Once the carousel hides me from Morgan's line of sight, my pace quickens. I shiver as a breeze kicks up. It coaxes creaks and groans from the rust-eaten rides, whispering along the deserted walkways like the ghosts of carnival patrons. I spot the graffitied toilet block ahead, silent and ominous like a slumbering creature not to be disturbed.

As though sensing this, Mallory has stopped a few metres from the entrance. I slow to a creep and pull up alongside a wooden stand that used to sell popcorn and fairy floss. It's exactly where I was standing the day I watched Sparrow tug balloons from the wrist of a trusting six year old and release them to the sky.

I glance above me now like I might actually see them there, one pink and one yellow. Irretrievable pieces of our childhood drifting away.

I scrape my shoe in the gravel to make my presence known. Mallory's shoulders twitch, yet she doesn't turn around, as though she knew I was here all along. I consider backing off and leaving her alone, but if there's a more fitting time to question her about this I sure as hell don't know what it is.

"Mallory?" I say to her back.

She turns slowly at her name, body as tense as a coiled

spring. Her nostrils quiver as she struggles to contain tears, glancing above her at the sky as though she, too, might spot her balloons floating away.

"What is it?" I ask, moving a step closer. "Is something coming back to you?"

I'm not sure I'm even prepared for her answer. She remains motionless like she hasn't heard me.

"Mallory, do you remember something about this place?" I urge. "About the moment you were taken?"

She finally looks my way and nods confidently. Aggressively. Her piercing eyes drill into me as she raises her hand and points a finger at my chest.

Her mouth forms a single word.

You.

20

THEN

13 MAY 2008
TRANSCRIPT FROM THE OFFICE OF DR INGRID BALLANTINE, PHD
CHILD AND ADOLESCENT PSYCHIATRY,
NEWCASTLE CHILDREN'S CLINIC
PATIENT: NATASHA CARMODY, 9 YEARS OLD

IB: Let's talk about Mallory. She's the little girl who went missing for a few days, isn't she? For about a week?

NC: ...

IB: Her face was on the news a lot, wasn't it? Pictures of her were on power poles and noticeboards. Did you see some of those?

NC: Mm-hmm.

IB: Everyone was very worried about her. She got a lot of attention, didn't she?

NC: Mm.

IB: You were all alone that day at the carnival, weren't you? You weren't really getting any attention from anyone.

NC: ...

IB: It feels good to get attention, doesn't it? To feel like someone is listening to us?

NC: Umm ... yes?

IB: And you told the grown-ups at the carnival that you think you saw Mallory just before she went missing?

NC: I *did* see her. With Morgan. Mallory was holding balloons.

IB: Was she?

NC: They were tied around her wrist so they wouldn't fly away.

IB: So you were quite close to them to see all of this. Did you say hello?

NC: No.

IB: So Morgan and Mallory didn't see you following them?

NC: I don't think so.

IB: Why did you follow them?

NC: I was scared. I wanted to go home.

IB: Did you?

NC: I didn't know anyone else there. Aunty Ally wasn't coming back for me until later so I thought Morgan's mum might take me home. I wanted to ask Morgan if I could go home to Port Bellamy in their car.

IB: You wanted to go home because you'd got trapped in the wooden box?

NC: Yeah.

IB: I understand. It must have been a bit of a fright.

NC: I wanted to tell Mum and Dad.

IB: But they were busy with Tim, weren't they?

NC: Yeah.

IB: Telling them you'd got trapped in a box and saw the little girl being taken – that's a lot of news to tell your mum and dad, isn't it? You'd have all their attention with some news like that.

NC: ...

IB: Sometimes when we tell people our news we like to include lots of details to make the story sound exciting, don't we?

NC: It wasn't a *story*. I didn't make it up.

IB: Okay.

NC: I saw him do it. He took her.

IB: Did anyone else see this happen?

NC: I don't think so.

IB: Why is that?

NC: I don't think anybody else can see him.

21

NOW

I jog Benny home, my mind in freefall, unable to shake the image of Mallory's accusing finger, like she was picking a criminal in a line-up. I try to analyse what Mallory communicated from every possible angle: she remembers I was at the carnival. Did she see me at the moment Sparrow took her?

Was I involved?

Did I follow her into those toilets?

I shake the last thought from my mind. It's impossible – I'd remember if that were the case. It was definitely Sparrow who took her.

Yeah, exactly – your imaginary friend who doesn't exist.

I'm shaking by the time I reach Ally's driveway, my head pounding wildly. It takes much longer than it should for me to catch my breath.

On the back verandah, I spend fifteen minutes composing text messages to Mallory that I end up deleting without sending, ignoring a bunch of texts from Sadie that pop up when I'm trying to think. I recall how Morgan interrupted our little stand-off at the carnival's toilet block, excited about his sketches and keen to catch up again tonight. When he invited me for dinner I fell over myself with reasons why we should do it here instead. There's no way I can sit across the dinner table from Mallory, her parents flanking her on both sides.

Leaving Benny in the backyard to doze underneath a tree, I unlock the garden shed to find the bicycle Ally mentioned during yesterday's tour of the house. The shed is poky and cluttered, and I have to shift an old dog cage and three bags of mulch to get to it – an exercise in clumsy panic in my efforts to get quickly in and out.

The bike is a rusty old thing with white wall tyres and a large wire basket, hopefully sturdy enough to get me to Greenwillow's supermarket and back without falling apart. I return the shed key to the kitchen and lock up the house behind me, grateful for the distraction of organising dinner, even if I'm just replacing nervous thoughts about Mallory with a whole other set about being alone with her brother.

It takes me thirty minutes of wandering the supermarket before I finally choose ingredients for a pasta dish, my earlier headache intensifying as I dither over my decision. The searing pain in my head makes it difficult to steer the handlebars on my ride home, and I can barely see straight by the time I reach Ally's front door. I dump the groceries in the kitchen and take two Panadols before collapsing on the couch for a minute to close my eyes.

When I open them again, it's dusk. The living room is cloaked in shadows.

No, no, no. It's done it again. This house is always shifting and changing on me.

I lunge from my seat and swipe at the light switch on the wall, then move around the room to switch on every single lamp I can find. In the kitchen, I yank open the back door and whistle for Benny to come inside. There's barely fifteen minutes until Morgan's due to arrive and I haven't prepped dinner yet or even showered.

After filling Benny's dog bowl, I tap my fingers against the stainless steel as I carry it out onto the verandah. I feel horrible that I've left him out here for hours – some dog-sitter I am. It's only after I've placed the bowl on the steps and done a full circuit of the garden that panic sets in.

Benny's not in the backyard.

The gate is securely latched, there are no gaps in the fence, no holes dug signalling an escape. He can't get under the house and I seriously doubt he could scale the wall up and over the garden shed.

"Benny?" I attempt to whistle but my lips are quivering. If he got out he could be miles away by now. How am I supposed to find him in the dark with nothing except Ally's ancient bicycle to get around on? *"Benny?* Here, boy. Come on!"

There's a faint whine behind me and I turn to find the yard empty. Something in the bush? I call Benny's name again and hear another weak cry in response. I spin and run towards it, not even sure what I'm looking for. Only when I've reached the garden shed do I notice the door is slightly ajar.

I closed it after I got the bike out. I mean, I locked it, right?

Nudging the door open, I fumble for a light switch, dreading the idea of stepping inside. I hear Benny panting, weak and shallow, a moment before the fluorescent bulb hums to life. White light bleaches out the cupboards and work benches, illuminating the cardboard boxes and piles of junk. And there, crammed between an old fridge and the wall, I spot a mound of golden fur.

Not just golden.

Patches of crimson glisten all over his coat.

I launch myself towards him. "Benny? Oh, god. What have you *done*?"

He's somehow ensnared himself in a coil of fencing wire. It's looped around his neck several times, the sharp barbs snagged deep in his fur. The more he's struggled, the deeper the barbs have dug, piercing his skin to create gaping wounds. As I attempt to loosen the wire, Benny releases a low growl.

"I'm sorry. Am I hurting you, boy?" My hands are shaking so much I'm probably doing more damage than good. I scour the workbench for something to cut the wire, trying not to think about Benny struggling out here for hours while I dozed on the couch. It's cramped here in the corner, and sweat breaks out across my top lip. The shed feels even smaller this far away from the door.

My hands find a pair of rusty pruning shears and I set to work on the tightest loop of wire. Benny must have really panicked to get it so dangerously constricted. The wire bends and buckles under the blunt blades. It's not even close to severing. Benny growls again and nips at my hands, his limited mobility the only thing stopping him from taking a bite.

"I know, I know," I coo. "I'm so sorry." I drop the shears and lean over to hug him in a bid to calm us both down. "Sshh. Ssshhhh." The shed walls press in on all sides and the metallic tang of Benny's blood is making me woozy. He whines, his breath laboured. He struggles to sit up and it pulls the wire tighter.

"I'm going to get my phone, boy." I give him a reassuring rub behind the ears and my hand comes away sticky. "I'm going to call someone, get some help."

I practically crawl out of the shed on hands and knees, dry-retching on the weed-riddled pavestones.

The kitchen glows with golden light, though there's no warmth inside the house. A roaring fire might stave off the cloudless night but wouldn't touch the chill in my bones. I glance towards the hook by the back door where the shed key is kept. It's not there. It wasn't in the shed door, either. None of this makes any sense.

I scour the kitchen benchtop for my phone, then riffle through my backpack, leaving smears of Benny on everything I touch.

Where the hell is it?

I dash into the living room in case my phone fell out of my pocket while I napped, careful to wipe my bloody hands across my jeans before upending the couch cushions. Nothing. I dart in and out of every room searching for a landline.

Frustrated, I whimper at the pointlessness of my time-wasting. I need to get on Ally's bike, ride to the closest neighbour and raise the alarm. Grabbing the house keys from the kitchen, I turn and run flat out for the front door. As soon as I reach the hallway, a figure lurches into my path. I hit it hard, ricocheting clumsily into the wall.

For a moment everything's black – a high-pitched wail in my ears, skull aching at the point it connected with the wall – and I hear a groan and think it must've come from me. I glance down, surprised to see I'm still on my feet, the tangle of house keys firmly clutched in my hand.

Weapon, my brain thumps. *Intruder.*

I blink away the white dots encroaching on my vision, threading two keys between my knuckles. I turn to face my attacker, swinging my hand up to strike.

"Whoa!" he says, raising his forearm to block my blow. "What are you *doing*? It's me. It's just *me*." Morgan backs into the wall, dropping his shopping bag in surprise. A carton of ice cream rolls across the floor.

Lowering my hand with the keys, I raise the other to the growing lump on my forehead. "How did you get in?" My voice is raspy, on edge.

"I knocked a few times. You didn't answer," Morgan says. "The front door was unlocked ..." His words trail off as he takes in the rusty smears on my arms, the patches of crimson on my T-shirt and jeans. He moves towards me, his hands hovering near my waist. "What is–? Are you–?"

I shake my head quickly, pulling away from him. "It's not my blood. Benny's got himself tangled up in barbed wire in the shed. He's really hurt and I need to get help. I can't find my bloody phone."

"Show me," Morgan says.

I lead him outside and wait by the shed door while he crouches to examine Benny. I want to comfort Benny while he does it, but I can't bring myself to set even one foot inside the doorway.

"We need to get him to a vet," Morgan says over his shoulder. "Like, right now. Do you know where one is?"

"In Ellenbrook – I saw a magnet on the fridge," I tell him. "There's a cage thing, a dog crate we can use. I saw it when I got the bike out earlier." I lean around the doorway and point underneath the workbench, finding nothing but a patch of dusty concrete floor. *What the hell?* "It was here. I swear it was right here."

"It doesn't matter," Morgan says. "We can't stuff him inside a cage when he's hurt like this. Better to lie him down in the back of my dad's car." He crouches in front of Benny, strokes him gently around the neck while assessing how to move him. "Better yet, let's see if the vet can make a house call. I don't know how to get this wire off without making things worse."

"Okay." I rake shaky fingers through my hair, my heart thumping fast as I throw another doubtful glance at the empty space under the workbench. "Okay. I'll go and call."

I'm about to run back towards the house just as Morgan stands and catches hold of my hand. He squeezes it gently before pressing his phone into it.

"Take a deep breath," he assures me. "Everything's going to be fine."

It's after eight and pitch black by the time the vet – a matronly fifty-something named Margaret – has administered Benny a sedative and disentangled him from the barbed wire's chokehold. She and her assistant load Benny into the back of their white van while Morgan and I light the way with torches. Margaret explains she needs to stitch Benny up back at the surgery once they've properly cleaned his wounds.

"It's all right, sweetheart," she assures me. "He'll be okay. Stop beating yourself up."

"I left the shed door open." Even as I say the words I don't really believe them. "I'm supposed to be looking after him and I let him get in there and into all that stuff."

Margaret removes her latex gloves with a snap of authority. "I've seen a few things in my time," she says. "Animals in all sorts of scrapes and mishaps. They do get up to mischief, no doubt. But my gut feeling is this was a deliberate act."

"I'm sorry?"

Morgan steps forwards. "Someone *did* this to him?"

"That wire was wound pretty tight," Margaret continues. "Even if he got his head through the looped roll, I can't see how he managed to pull it tighter and tighter around his own neck until he became incapacitated."

I gasp. "Who would do something like that?"

"Bored kids?" Margaret shrugs. "Some kind of prank gone wrong? I know Sergeant Blake dealt with a case in Jamison recently where a cat was tortured by a guy trying to punish his ex-girlfriend. Can you think of anyone who might be trying to get your attention?"

The dead bird on my doorstep. Sparrow at the shops.

"No," I say, shaking the ridiculous thoughts away.

"Have you been home all afternoon?" Margaret asks.

"I left Benny here when I went to the supermarket around one o'clock. I was gone for maybe an hour."

"Was he in the backyard when you got home?" Morgan says. "Did you notice the shed door open?"

"I–I don't know. I had a headache and fell asleep on the couch."

"What? For three hours?" Morgan's tone is dubious. "You didn't notice anything unusual?"

"No!" I snap. Why are they grilling me like this? "I was *asleep.*"

His face softens. "Sorry, Tash. It's not your fault. I just don't like the idea of you falling asleep in a strange house with the doors unlocked. Especially if some sicko is prowling around the backyard."

"The house *was* locked," I say, but my voice has lost any conviction. I can't seem to recall anything from this afternoon beyond that debilitating headache.

Morgan squints. "Okay. But the front door was unlocked when I got here …"

Glancing towards the house, I suddenly feel exhausted, suddenly unsure if anything I'm saying is reliable. Margaret closes the door of her van and turns to me, notepad in hand.

"Benny's not one of my regular patients," she says. "So I'm going to grab your aunt's details. Do you have a number I can contact her on?"

194

"I've misplaced my phone," I mumble, realising how much of a space cadet I must seem to her. "And I don't know Ally's number off the top of my head. She's in Byron Bay for the weekend and will be back on Monday. I'll call you in the morning to check how Benny's doing. I'm sure I'll have found my phone by then."

Margaret reaches out and pats my arm. "You go ahead and get cleaned up now. Benny's in good hands." She glances at Morgan. "You keeping her company tonight? I think she's a bit shaken up."

"Yeah," he says. "That's a good idea." He slides me a reassuring look. "I'll call my parents and let them know. I don't think you should be alone."

*

Morgan gets a fire going in the living room and makes us pasta while I shower. I leave my rinsed clothing draped over the shower rail, the faint blood stains a permanent reminder of my negligence. Before we eat, we do a final check of the house together, making sure all doors and windows are locked, eventually ending up side by side on the patchwork couch. Morgan kicks off his shoes, nestling cross-legged on the seat cushions, and I relax into my own seat, relieved he's settling in for the night and I won't be alone.

I'm so wiped out I can barely keep my eyes open, but my mind keeps replaying uncomfortable images as though I don't deserve to rest: Mallory upset with me at the carnival; Benny growling at me as I tried to free him; Morgan's flicker of disbelief when I mentioned three hours of my time unaccounted for. I rest my head against the back of the couch as drowsiness overcomes me, vaguely aware of my pasta bowl being removed from my hand, a blanket spread over my knees and tucked around my shoulders. I swim in and out of consciousness, the crackling fire and the TV's canned laughter lulling me deeper. At some point I'm roused by Morgan's gentle snoring to find myself curled in the foetal position, using his lap as a pillow.

When I next open my eyes, morning sunshine is streaming through a gap in the curtains. It hits me square in the face like I'm under an interrogation lamp. I find myself horizontal on the couch with cushions bunched underneath my head, and I panic that Morgan has snuck out in the middle of the night.

Then I sense the solid warmth of his body against my back, his arm folded across my waist and warm breath tickling my hair. I snuggle into him and he mumbles something soft and dreamy, flexing his arm around me before relaxing it again and pulling me close.

We're suspended in a deliciously dozy state, our bodies spooning, Morgan's weight pressed against me in a way that is both familiar and a promise of the unknown. I feel myself resubmerging into our warm, safe slumber when I hear two shrill beeps from somewhere down the hall.

I jerk upright.

My phone.

I extract myself from the couch as gingerly as I can, but Morgan's disturbed by my repositioning. He yawns and throws his arms above his head in a feline stretch. I pad my way to the kitchen, and I'm staggered to find my phone sitting in the middle of the round breakfast table, plain as day. Apart from a couple of missed calls and some texts from Sadie, there's one other new message. From Mallory, of all people.

It reads, *What do you want?*

I frown at the speech bubble. Above it is my message from last Saturday about bringing food up to Mallory's bedroom. I don't understand the context of this new message. What do I want? In relation to what?

Doubt burrows in my gut like a poisonous seed. *Mallory knows.* She knows my questions about her disappearance are more than polite curiosity. She wants to know what my motives are, why I'm trying to get close to her.

Hey Mallory, I text back. *Not sure what you mean?*

I'm aware of Morgan moving around in the living room down the hall. I catch a glimpse of him scratching his stomach and mussing up his hair.

I'm still gripping my phone when it chimes with Mallory's response.

My phone's showing three missed calls from you in the middle of the night. Why didn't you leave me a message?

I make a small scoffing noise and scroll to my call history. There are calls to Mallory's phone at 2.41 am, 3.36 am and 5.02 am. *What the hell?* I haven't even seen my phone since one o'clock yesterday afternoon. If Morgan found it, why would he place three calls to his sister from my phone in the early hours of the morning?

And why would anyone call Mallory anyway? They must know she's unable to talk back.

As I'm grappling with how to reply, Morgan shuffles into the kitchen. "Found it last night," he says, pointing at the phone. "On my way to the loo."

"What? Where?"

"On the floor in the hallway." He moves towards the kitchen cupboards. "You must've dropped it yesterday when you ran into me."

"No," I say, shaking my head. "That's not right. I'd already misplaced it by then."

He grabs two coffee mugs from the cupboard above the stove and glances over his shoulder. "You sure?"

"Yes, I couldn't find it. That's why I was rushing out to the neighbour's house. To use their phone."

Morgan shrugs. "Okay."

"And how many times did we walk up and down that hallway yesterday evening? Why didn't we spot it earlier?"

He raises defensive hands. "Hey, I'm just sayin' – that's where I found it."

Just sayin'.

There's a hint of impatience in his words and I think of his doubtful look yesterday when I insisted I'd locked the house. Does he think I'm lying? Or is he the one not telling the truth?

"What time did you go to the toilet?" I ask, thinking of the calls to Mallory's phone.

He moves towards the pantry, shrugging. "Dunno. Maybe around one? Why?"

"What did you do with the phone after you found it?"

His hand pauses over the coffee jar. "Umm, I placed it here on the kitchen table? What's with the interrogation?"

"I'm just a bit baffled, that's all."

"Huh. You and me both."

His frown clears and he wiggles the coffee jar at me, as though a shot of caffeine will rewire my muddled brain. I return my attention to Mallory's message and respond the only way I can that stops me from looking like a weirdo.

Sorry, I must have butt-dialled you. Promise it won't happen again.

I slide my phone away from me across the table like it's untrustworthy. Yet history tells me *I'm* the unreliable one.

"Where's the kettle?" Morgan asks.

Moving to the stovetop, I grab the old copper kettle from the burner. As I stand at the sink filling it, my gaze drifts out the window overlooking the backyard. The garden shed sits banal and unremarkable by the edge of the bush, no hint of the horror that took place there fifteen hours ago.

On impulse I glance towards the wall hook by the back door where the shed key is kept. The kettle slips from my grip and clatters into the sink, the stream of water hitting the handle and flicking out in all directions.

"Whoa, there," Morgan says, jumping forwards to turn off the tap. "Somebody's not quite awake yet." He chuckles and gently nudges me aside to mop up the splashed water with a dishcloth. I back away from the sink in a daze, and it barely registers when Morgan passes me a tea towel to dry myself off.

"Everything okay?" he says, touching a hand to the small of my back.

No, it's not! I want to yell. *Because the shed key is now hanging exactly where it was missing yesterday.*

I press my lips together and a dull pain surfaces behind my eyes. I want to ask Morgan if he just happened to find the shed key in some random place too. I want to ask him what he did after we left the carnival, where he was when I went to the supermarket and Benny was here all alone. I want to ask him how he let himself into my aunt's house yesterday evening when I'm certain – *certain* – I locked the front door.

But really, how can I be certain about anything?

"Why don't we get out of here?" Morgan suggests, turning me to face him. "Come and spend the day with my family down at the river." He tucks a strand of my hair behind my ear and smiles at me hopefully. "You could meet my parents properly."

I shake my head, unable to meet his eyes. "I–I've got to get things in order here. Phone calls to make. I need to clean up the shed."

"Let me help you," Morgan says. I decline his offer. I send him on his way much sooner than either one of us expected even though the last thing I want is to be here all alone. I then straighten up the living room, clean the dishes in the kitchen and take a bucket of sudsy water out to the backyard. It takes me two hours of stops and starts, tears and panic, to finally scrub every last trace of Benny's blood from the shed floor.

I call the vet clinic to check up on Benny and provide

Margaret with Ally's details, then leave a detailed message on Ally's voicemail.

And finally, I do what I wished I could have when I was eight years old.

I call my dad to come and take me home.

22

THEN

The Mid Coast Times | Archives
Section: News
Date: 15 March 2008

PORT BELLAMY, NSW – Fisher family leaves Port Bellamy and bad memories behind.

The family of Mallory Fisher, the six-year-old girl who went missing for a week in January, has now relocated to an undisclosed interstate address "to put the past behind them", according to a source close to the family. It ends speculation about the family's possible move after Mallory's father, Daniel Fisher, closed his orthodontic practice in Newcastle indefinitely last month.

After two months of investigation, police are no closer to uncovering the mystery of how Mallory disappeared from the Greenwillow Carnival and came to be discovered in Barrington Tops National Park.

Daniel and Annabel Fisher, who were cleared as suspects early on in the case, released a statement earlier this month confirming the investigation continues. "We believe we are drawing ever closer to finding out exactly what happened to our daughter," the statement reads. "And we are cooperating with police in every way we can to make sure the perpetrator is apprehended. We urge members of the public with any information to please come forward."

A source close to the family explains Mallory has been traumatised by events and is still not speaking, slowing progress in the investigation.

Inspector Owen Morris confirmed, "While Mallory was able to indicate she remembers waking up and wandering alone in the national park, she seems unable to recollect how she actually got there in the first place."

Inspector Morris went on to clarify Mallory's responses were still non-verbal at this stage. However, questions had been carefully constructed by a child psychologist to ensure answers were clear and unambiguous.

"With an investigation as delicate as this one," Inspector Morris explained, "it's important we give the child time to recover. Emotional trauma can often affect the victim's recollection of events, but we are willing to be patient. In the meantime we intend to keep all lines of inquiry open."

Family friends say the Fisher children are suffering under the intense media spotlight and have not returned to school.

"They need a fresh start," the source said. "Maybe one day, when this has all died down, they'll come home to Port Bellamy."

23

NOW

I must have read every old newspaper story ever written about Mallory's disappearance. In the last few days, I've used my editing time before school to scour for clues about possible abductors, no matter how small or seemingly insignificant. Every article is the same: there were no named suspects, not even a bad facial composite photo. There were no suspicious vehicles ever mentioned in the media reports, no dodgy hikers in Barrington Tops at the time.

Not a single indication Mallory was abducted by *anyone*.

It's like whoever it was disappeared off the face of the earth.

Or got very good at hiding.

Our *Dreamscapes* deadline is looming and I should be editing my carnival photos, but every time I start I'm drawn into memories of Willow Creek, and the shock of what happened to Benny hits me anew. I've left so many messages for Ally I think I've filled up her voicemail. I can't seem to get many words in before a beep cuts me off mid-sentence every time.

Why won't she return my calls? Then again, there's a lot I don't understand about Ally. What does she do for work? Who are her friends? At what point did she and my dad stop getting along?

I feel helpless sitting here at school while Benny recovers in some sterile vet clinic a hundred kilometres away. So I just keep trawling old articles on news sites, looking for–

What? Evidence Sparrow is real?

"Hey, stranger."

Behind me, Sadie's peering around the doorway of the computer room. Apart from a few casual texts here and there, we haven't spoken much since Sunday night when I filled her in about the weekend. I played down the kiss with Morgan because I knew she'd have an opinion about it, especially considering all the weirdness that came next.

"Lucky he was there *yet again*," she'd said, with a hint of what seemed like jealousy. It only occurred to me afterwards that it might have been suspicion.

Even though I've questioned some of Morgan's behaviour myself, I feel strangely defensive when Sadie makes a comment about his motives, the same way I feel protective about his whole family. It's what compels me now to minimise the computer's web browser, leaving a very obvious blank desktop on display.

Sadie frowns briefly at the screen before her attention moves to my face. "Thought I'd find you here. This where you live now? Wanna add a few pot plants?"

"I've just got a lot of editing to do," I say. She's complained three times this week because I've chosen to spend my lunchtimes up here too. It's all right for her – she doesn't have a major assignment due after Easter. And, for the same reason I've been avoiding Morgan since the weekend, I need time alone to think.

"Okay," Sadie says, holding up both hands like she's backing off. "Just confirming you're still good for Francine Tan's fundraiser on the weekend?"

"I said I'd be there, didn't I?"

Carting around hors d'oeuvres and smiling politely at the Tans is the last thing I feel like doing. But I don't want to leave Sadie's mum short-handed, and I need the money for Benny's vet bill if Ally ever calls me back to let me know the amount.

Sadie slumps against the doorframe. "Is there anything you want to talk about? Not that I'm not delighted by these short responses where you bite my head off."

I swivel in my chair to face her, leaning my elbows on my knees. "It's just this stuff with my aunt's dog. Ally won't reply to my messages. I think she's pissed off at me for what happened." That's not the full extent of my worries, but it will do for now.

Sadie considers this, chewing the inside of her cheek. "I wouldn't read too much into it; she's probably still a bit shocked. It's been less than a week since it happened. And if she does blame you, that's out of line and you don't want to talk to her anyway."

"It was my job to care for Benny." I try not to think about those hours unaccounted for, the missing key and my disappearing phone. "Who else's fault is it?"

She shrugs, glancing over her shoulder at someone passing by in the corridor. "How could you know the dog would even go in that garden shed, let alone get all tangled up in Ally's junk? Sometimes shit just happens, you know?"

She's being blasé and it makes my blood simmer. She has no idea how responsible I feel, how much I need a better explanation for what happened.

"Look," I say, "I'm kind of busy here …"

Sadie raises unimpressed eyebrows at my brush-off. "You wanna talk about what's really bothering you?"

"Not particularly."

"And that, my friend, is the problem. You're being cagey and secretive."

"No, I'm not."

She juts her chin at the computer screen. "So, tell me what you're reading about."

"Nothing."

"Didn't look like nothing. You said you were up here editing photos."

I roll my eyes. "Oh. I'm sorry, Detective. Please arrest me for taking a little break."

"Umm, okay," Sadie says. "This is getting weird. Call me when my best friend is back because I'm not really up for whatever the hell this is."

"Agreed. Do you need anything else?"

"Guess not," she says blandly. "Oh, except–" She rummages

in her schoolbag for a second before producing a small wrapped package tied with a yellow bow. She tosses it towards me and I react just fast enough to catch it.

She's already walking away when I hear her mutter, "Happy birthday."

*

The remainder of my birthday is equally subdued. I don't mention it to Morgan when I see him in the art room, even when Rachael stares at me like she's remembered what day it is and refuses to let on. At home, I ask Mum if we can postpone my celebration dinner until the weekend because I'm not feeling up to it. Since I've been pale and listless after returning from Willow Creek, Mum insists it's a virus and bundles me off to bed for the next two days. I haven't told her or Dad about what happened to Benny.

On Saturday afternoon, Sadie's gift still sits unopened on my desk. She hasn't texted me while I've been absent from school, and I feel a knot of resentment tightening between us that I'm not sure how to loosen. Things are no better when I turn up at Port Bellamy Sailing Club for Francine Tan's fundraiser. Sadie screws her face up as soon as I walk into the staff kitchen.

"I said the *white* shirts for today," she says, plucking at the collar of her *So Delish* polo shirt. She turns to Kiri. "I'm sorry, Mum. I did tell her."

Glancing down at my black shirt, I try to recall that conversation.

"It's fine, it's fine," Kiri says, her own white polo shirt stark and crisp against the stainless-steel fridges. "It's not a problem, Tash." She pats Sadie's arm on her way past, murmuring that it's no big deal, before diverting the conversation to today's order of events.

Upstairs in the function room I move silently between guests, offering tall-stemmed glasses of sparkling wine and orange juice, squirrelling discarded empties back down to the kitchen to load the dishwasher before doing it all over again. When Sadie falls behind with the hors d'oeuvres, I assist Kiri in plating up risotto balls and smoked salmon blinis, then circulate the room to help catch us up.

Guests mill in front of a small stage where Rachael is assisting her mother. She works a PowerPoint presentation on the laptop while Francine gushes about a bunch of auction items flashing up on a large projector screen. There's a flurry of bidding, the knock of a gavel, then more eating and drinking before the process is repeated for the next item.

"Thanks for picking up my slack," Sadie says on one of our trips down to the kitchen. "These cashed-up yachties sure know how to put it away."

She gives me a wry smile and I feel a flutter of relief – some of the animosity between us seems to be melting. I still need to clear the air about what's going on with me.

"Hey, Dee? At the end of our shift, can I talk to you?"

"Sure," she says without hesitation. "Is everything okay? You're not going to quit on my mum, are you?"

"No, nothing like that," I assure her. "It's about Mallory and Morgan Fisher."

Sadie's face is impassive but her eyebrow flickers, as though she knows exactly what I want to talk about. "Let me guess," she says dryly. "You and Morgan are getting married and you don't know how to break it to me that Mallory's maid of honour."

"Hardy har," I say. "Anyway, you've always said you won't 'do' bridesmaid. Best man or bust, remember?"

"True," she says, her mood lifting. "You know I can't deal with taffeta."

She gives me a careful smile as we move to our different stations in the kitchen, and I can tell she's feeling uneasy. But true to her word, she meets me upstairs after all the guests have gone home.

We leave Kiri to load the last few boxes into her van while we sweep the function room, making small talk until we reach the doors that lead out to the foyer.

"So, you gonna spill?" Sadie says.

Sighing, I slouch against the end of my broom. "Okay. About the Fishers. You know I've been spending some time with them lately …"

"I had noticed."

"Well, I knew them when they lived in Port Bellamy, before."

"Yeah, I know," she says. "You've mentioned that."

"What I didn't tell you is that I was there when Mallory Fisher was abducted."

"What? From that carnival? Didn't she wander off or something?"

Sadie's not as familiar with the story as the rest of us

locals since she and her mum moved to Port Bellamy a year after it happened.

"I was staying at my aunt's place at the time," I say. "I was at the same carnival on the day Mallory disappeared."

I swallow, second-guessing my decision to say the next part aloud. I've never told Sadie about it for fear of driving her away. I feel like I'm losing my grip, though, and she's the one person I trust more than anyone.

"Police think Mallory wandered off from the carnival and got snatched by someone on Greenwillow's back roads," I tell her. "Except that's not what happened. I watched her being taken."

Sadie frowns. "What do you mean?"

"My aunt left me at the carnival by myself and I spotted Mallory and Morgan with their parents. I was desperate to go home, and I thought the Fishers might take me with them back to Port Bellamy."

"Okay," Sadie says, coaxing me with her hand. "Get to the abduction part."

"I followed Mallory and Morgan to the toilets," I say. "But *he* was following *me*. I led him right to her unintentionally."

"Wait. Who? Morgan?"

"*Sparrow*." His name catches in my throat and I hear the wobble in my voice. I've never admitted to myself, let alone anyone else, the only reason Sparrow chose Mallory out of all the kids at the carnival is because I led him right to her.

"Whoa, back up." Sadie straightens. "Your imaginary friend, Sparrow? That's who you think is responsible for abducting Mallory?"

212

I wince at Sadie's incredulous tone, sense her subtle withdrawal. It sounds as ridiculous as ever when I say it out loud, somehow worse because I'm nine years older and I should know better.

"I know how it sounds," I say. "That's how I remember it. He looked right at me as he waited for Mallory to come out of that toilet block, as if daring me to stop him. It was either me or her, and I didn't want to play with him any more. I thought it was a game."

"Tash." Sadie's solemn face makes my pulse quicken. "You're talking about Sparrow as though he's real."

"Yeah."

"You made him up, though. That's what your shrink says, right? You made him up because you were lonely?"

"He seemed real."

"Okay but, dude, there's a big difference between what *seems* real and what *is* real. I still remember the aerodynamic rocket cake my nan made for my sixth birthday. In reality it was this sad-looking Swiss roll with an upturned ice cream cone for the nose. I've seen the photos. Nothing at all like I remember it."

I lean my broom against the wall and fold my arms. "Well, sorry, but Sparrow was a little more disturbing than your sad-looking Swiss roll."

Sadie gives me a long look, and for a moment I think I've offended her. Then she clicks her fingers. "You know what? That's actually a good point."

"What is?"

"What if you're remembering the aerodynamic rocket

cake instead of the Swiss roll?"

"Huh?"

"Your mind could be remembering things differently to how they really were."

"Um, yeah?" I say. "That's kind of the general consensus, hence the therapy and all."

She huffs impatiently. "What I mean is, is it possible your mind created this Sparrow persona to block out the identity of someone you know? To prevent you from being traumatised or something?"

I laugh self-consciously. "God, that sounds a bit far-fetched."

Sadie widens her eyes. "Are you friggin' kidding me? This from a girl who just told me her imaginary friend stole a kid from a carnival."

"Ssshhh!" I say, glancing around the large function room. It's still empty but the sliding doors beside us are open a crack. "Keep your voice down. And don't you reckon Dr Ingrid would have covered off that scenario in the last *decade* of head-shrinking?"

Sadie points her broom handle at me. "Okay then, riddle me this: did you ever see your aunt and Sparrow in the same room at the same time?"

I throw my head back and shake it at the ceiling. "Jesus. Now you're getting all Scooby Doo on me."

"Well, what do you want me to say, Tash? You come to me with this wild idea your make-believe buddy abducted a living, breathing child from a public toilet. Sorry if I'm trying to find a more plausible reason that doesn't sound so batshit crazy!"

Her final word hangs in the air like a dirty stain. She closes her eyes as though willing it back inside her head where it's obviously been residing for a while.

"Okay. Good talk." I raise trembling fingers to the door. "Appreciate your honesty."

"Tash …" Sadie reaches for my arm and I shrug her away.

"Don't. Please tell your mum I'll walk home."

I yank the door open and find myself nose to nose with Rachael Tan.

For a moment we both stand there as Rachael's silky hair resettles around her shoulders, her lips parted in quiet surprise. Not about me almost slamming into her, or even because I've caught her eavesdropping. She's wide-eyed about what she's just learned.

In the blink of an eye she composes herself. "Forgot my laptop," she says, shoving past me. The rap of her heels across the function room floor might as well be nails hammering into my coffin.

My eyes meet Sadie's and they reflect what I already know.

It's only a matter of time before Rachael uses her new information against me.

24

THEN

It's too hot tonight.

There's no air inside my bedroom and I'm lying on top of the sheets waiting for Aunty Ally to go upstairs. The bed feels like a warm driveway underneath me, and my hair is sticking to my neck like seaweed. I think I hear a breeze blowing down the side of the house but I won't open the window to find out. It's stayed locked since the night Sparrow flew in and landed on the window seat.

I keep the curtains closed and the lamp on all night now, and I've pushed the bedside table behind the door. It's so hot in here and I'm so thirsty. Aunty Ally doesn't give me a glass of water to take to bed like Mum and Dad do at home.

She was in the kitchen tonight banging things around, so I stayed out of her way. When I came inside from playing this afternoon, the coffee table was flipped over and one of

Grandma's vases was smashed against the fireplace. When I asked her what happened, she got cross and told me to go upstairs and take a bath. But at dinnertime she made spaghetti and said she'll take me to Greenwillow Carnival tomorrow as a treat. She smiled at me a lot. There was nothing smiley around her eyes, though.

And now I'm so thirsty.

What's worse? Going to the kitchen while Aunty Ally's still in there? Or having to go later in the dark, alone?

I hear her in the hallway mumbling something to Benny, and his collar tinkles as he follows her upstairs. I hold still until the floorboards stop creaking and the water stops running, until there's no sound from upstairs at all. I slide off the bed and move to the door, shoving the bedside table to one side. Aunty Ally hasn't left a light on for me in the hallway, and the switch is all the way down near the front door. It's as black as space, and from here to the kitchen seems three times longer than normal.

If I hold my breath and tiptoe, no one will hear me. If I keep close to the wall, nobody can sneak up from behind. I wait in my bedroom doorway for another minute, making sure the shadows aren't moving, looking for places he might hide.

When Dad called after dinner, I wanted to tell him about what Sparrow did at the creek on Tuesday. It was mean and scary, and Dad would definitely want to know. When I started explaining it, he told me to put Aunty Ally back on the phone. She looked cross when she tugged it from my hand, frowning while she listened to Dad talking on the other end.

"*You put me in a very awkward position there,*" she said afterwards. "*I thought we agreed we weren't going to bother your parents with this Sparrow business. They already have their hands full with that new baby, you know.*"

But now there's only a few days left until Dad drives up here to take me home – I'll tell him all about it then. I'll make sure Mum and Dad know every single tiny little thing that's happened here. It's important. They need to know not to send me away again.

I run quickly for the kitchen, forgetting to tiptoe and hold my breath. When I make it to the sink I don't worry about anything except how thirsty I am. As water gushes into my glass, I glance at my reflection in the window.

Something moves near my left shoulder.

I spin around to look behind me but the kitchen is empty. When I glance at the window again I see that the shape isn't a reflection at all – it's on the other side of the glass. I stand on tippy-toes for a closer look at the figure lying across the end of the verandah, one arm and leg dangling off the edge like a ragdoll.

I move to the back door and pull aside the chequered curtains to peek through the small window. Even in moonlight I can recognise his bony arms, his sharp shoulders, the outline of his shaved head.

I know why he's here. He's come to ruin my day tomorrow. He won't let me have any fun unless he's there as well.

I flip on the outdoor light and tap my knuckle on the door's window. Sparrow doesn't move an inch. I keep tapping until his head rolls towards me. His eyelids are droopy as though he's been dozing.

218

"Don't come here any more," I say. "I don't want to play with you. Just go away!"

He mumbles something I can't hear. I've never seen him so limp and floppy. I drag a chair over from the table and reach for the lock at the top of the door, sliding it free so I can open the door a crack.

"Did you hear me?" I say. "Don't come here any more. I don't like how you play."

He chuckles to himself, rubbing a hand down his face. "Game's not finished yet. We haven't got to the good part."

"I don't care. I'm not playing with you. Why would I want to be your friend?"

He pats a heavy hand against his chest. "Because I have magic powers."

I pull the door open wider and lean my hip against the doorframe. "No, you don't." But sometimes I wonder if he does since no one else can see him. He always seems to appear out of nowhere.

"I know how to turn a fistful of hair into a pot of gold," he tells me, wiggling his fingers.

"That doesn't even make sense."

Sparrow rolls onto his side and props himself on one elbow. "I can read your mind." He taps a finger against his head. "I'm already in there right now, crawling and scratching around."

"No, you're not."

"I'll tell you something," he says. "Something you're thinking right at this moment."

"I'm not thinking anythi—"

"My name. You've made one up for me."

I wasn't thinking about that at all. Now I am. I try to empty my mind and think about nothing. There's no way he knows this — I've never said it to his face.

"You call me Sparrow." He taps his head again. "You can't hide from me."

"That's not magic," I say, my chest tightening. "It's just a lucky guess."

He gives me a sleepy smile before his eyes roll back in his head like he can't stay awake any longer.

"Game's not over," he murmurs, cracking one eye open to watch me as I back into the house. I try not to look at him as I swing the door closed and slide the lock in place. If I just ignore him, maybe he'll disappear.

As I reach for the light switch I can't help peering outside one last time. Sparrow raises a heavy arm and points at me, his voice a silly singsong.

"Coming to get you. Ready or not."

25

NOW

A week into April, I'm suspended in a perpetual state of unease. It's been over two weeks since the sailing club fundraiser, and I know Rachael's just biding time with her new information. Whenever Morgan approaches me at school I wonder if it's because Rachael's spilled my secret, or whether he's going to interrogate me about why I've gone cold since the weekend at Willow Creek.

As much as I want to explore this thing with Morgan and keep getting to know him better, I also can't shake the feeling that, any minute now, Mallory's going to remember something concrete about her disappearance. Whatever that something is will involve me. I feel in constant risk of being exposed.

I try to keep distracted by working on my photography folio every chance I get. But even now, sifting through photos of the derelict carnival, my thoughts are hijacked by childhood memories of Sparrow stalking me around sideshow alley. I think of Sadie's suggestion about my child's mind creating Sparrow to mask somebody's true identity, trying to recall whether this actually *was* territory we covered in my sessions with Dr Ingrid. I keep coming back to my other behavioural problems at the time, the fact that nobody else saw Sparrow, Dr Ingrid's questions about whether I heard other voices.

Gathering up a handful of photos to hand over to Morgan to use as reference for his final *Dreamscapes* sketches, I have to wonder if any of my photos stand alone well enough to be included in my submission folio. I hunch over Mum's laptop, scrolling through images in the hopes something will jump out at me, going back as far as those I took at the pier in February. I skip past a couple of artless wide-angle images of the beach, when something snags my attention. Only not for the reason I'd hoped.

I double-click a thumbnail picture and it enlarges in my browser. It's a landscape view of Port Bellamy Beach looking east. Beyond the sand dunes and scrubby grasses, a snatch of Marine Drive curls away from the camera along the coastline. Maybe a kilometre down, a lone car is parked facing the pier. I zoom in as much as I can before the image becomes pixelated. Despite the graininess, there's no denying what it looks like.

A metallic-brown ute with orange pin-striping.

Thinking back to that morning, I remember it was the day I called Ally about coming to visit. I'm certain she was just waking up, Benny curled beside her on the bed. Is it possible she was sitting in her car here in Port Bellamy? And if so, why?

I consider how many old utes there must be around the port, not to mention those that roll in for daytrips at the beach. I recall at least one other occasion recently when I spotted a similar car parked on Banksia Avenue near the Fishers' house. It's probably paranoia brought about by everything else that's happened, but I grab my phone and text Ally anyway. It's been almost three weeks since Benny was injured and she still hasn't got back to me. She's avoiding me and it doesn't sit well.

Hey Ally. Have you been getting my messages? I really need to talk to you when you get this.

The doorbell rings as I hit *Send*, followed by a bright and breezy voice. Francine Tan. I'd forgotten Mum invited her over this afternoon to organise school committee stuff. It's not long before I hear footsteps on the staircase, no doubt Tim looking to hide from Mum in hectic-hostess mode.

Instead, Rachael Tan appears in my doorway.

"What are *you* doing here?"

"Mum says I have to invite you to this." She thrusts a postcard at me. It's an invitation to the twins' eighteenth birthday party at their uncle's restaurant. "I know you won't come, so can you just tell your mum you got the invitation? Because mine will check."

I hand it back to her. "Why bother giving it to me then?"

She tosses it into the bin underneath my desk. "Because I don't want to lie to my mother."

"Right. Like that's never happened before."

Rachael scoffs. "Really? You're going to lecture me about lying? Should we start with your imaginary friend abducting Mallory? Or the part about you keeping this whole twisted side of your personality from Morgan?"

"Look," I say, rising warily from the bed, "I don't know what you think you heard at the sailing club—"

"We both know what I heard. To be honest, I'm not even surprised."

"What do you mean?"

Rachael folds her arms and narrows her eyes. "There's always been something off about you, Tash. I knew it from the moment I moved here, even before I heard all the rumours."

"You *started* the rumours," I say, folding my arms too.

"Please. Kids were calling you Weirdo and Whackjob long before I ever arrived. I heard all about you freaking out at school for attention, always playing helpless so everyone would feel sorry for you."

"You think I actually wanted that attention?" I hate the way my voice sounds, shrill and emotional. "I had genuine anxiety attacks. Not that I need to explain myself to you."

"When are you going to explain yourself to Morgan?"

A shard of panic stabs my insides. I wait too long to respond and there's a glint of victory in Rachael's eyes.

"What do you want, Rachael?" I intend it to sound disgusted but it comes out like I'm pleading for a deal.

"Leave that poor family alone," she says, like she actually cares about anything beyond snagging Morgan for herself. "Don't call. Don't go to their house. Just don't go near them."

"Why the hell would I listen to you?"

"Because I'm doing you a favour! I'm giving you a chance to drop it before you completely humiliate yourself."

"And if I don't?"

Rachael rolls her eyes at the ceiling. "What do you think, genius? I'll tell the Fishers what I overheard and they'll think you're a psycho."

I fume silently at the floor. Rachael's motives are so transparent. "So, either way, I'm supposed to have nothing else to do with Morgan?"

Her features settle into a smug half-smile. "Well, I didn't say I wasn't doing myself a favour as well."

*

An hour later, when the Tans' car is pulling out of our driveway, I'm still fuming about my conversation with Rachael. I grab my phone and dial Sadie's number, despite how awkward things have become between us since our talk at the sailing club. We've been keeping things lightweight and civil, but they don't feel like real conversations. Neither of us have broached the topic of the Fishers or Sparrow.

"Hey," she says, answering after two rings. "What's up?" Her voice lacks that warm familiarity that I've come to depend on.

"I've just had another run-in with Rachael."

"Ugh. What did she want?"

There's music in the background. Sadie sounds distracted. "Are you able to talk, or ..."

"Yeah. It's cool. I'm at the cinema with Alice."

"What, like a *date*?" I don't mean it to come out as sulky as it does.

"Umm, yeah. That okay with you?" Sadie says, laughing. My mood takes an even bigger nosedive.

"Sorry. I'll let you get back to it."

"Hold up," she says. "Are you okay? What do you need?"

Need? Why does it always become about me being needy? I swallow my growing frustration. "Rachael's threatening to tell Morgan about what she overheard at the sailing club."

"Hm," Sadie says. "Not good. I suppose you'll just have to get to him first."

"What?"

"Beat her to the punch."

"I can't tell Morgan about that stuff," I say. "He'll hate me!"

Sadie's phone goes muffled, like she's covering it with her hand. When she comes back on the line, I hear her last few words to somebody else.

"Dee?"

"Look," she says. "I know you have this thing for Morgan Fisher—"

"A *thing*? Could you make it sound any more tragic? I seem to recall you encouraging this *thing* from the very start."

"Yeah," Sadie says. "That was before."

"Before what?"

"The laundry incident and Tim going missing at the shops. And don't you think it's weird how Morgan turned up inside your aunt's house?"

"Like letting himself in is a huge crime," I say dryly.

"Morgan really helped me with my aunt's dog that weekend, you know."

"I know. I'm just saying."

"Didn't realise you were keeping a tally of things to be suss about."

Sadie sighs. "I'm not. I know you like him, but ... something about all of this is worrying me."

"Okay. Let's pretend I never brought it up."

"That's the thing, though – all you ever talk about these days is the Fishers," Sadie says. "I mean, what is it with you and that family?"

I'm about to respond when my phone dings with a text. I'm dying to read it. It could be Morgan. It could be *Mallory*.

"Look, I've gotta go."

"Tash," Sadie says quickly, "when's your next appointment with Dr Ingrid?"

"Huh?" My stomach drops. "Why are you asking me that?"

Another sigh. "I just think it might be good to–"

"I've gotta go," I say again, cutting her off before she implies things I don't want to hear. *Batshit crazy. Batshit crazy.* Now that Sadie's words are out there I can't unhear them.

I hang up and scroll to my new text message, almost dropping the phone when I see Ally's name onscreen.

Don't worry my dog's fine when are you coming here again

In my flustered state, I have to read it a second time.

Not only is Ally assuring me everything's okay, she's inviting me back to Willow Creek? Why did it take her so long to put me at ease about Benny? My hands tremble as

I type a vague reply. I'm almost tempted to call Sadie back and ask her what she makes of Ally's message, except I know she'll accuse me of overthinking like I always do.

Slumping onto my bed, I feel the acute sting of isolation.

I *am* overthinking because I have nobody to talk to about this stuff, no one who understands. The only person I can think of who could relate to what I'm going through is the one person who can't actually talk back.

I pick up my phone and scroll to Mallory's name in my list of recent messages. My thumbs fly over the keys.

Hey, Mallory. I hope you don't think this is rude – I'm just really curious. When we were at the carnival a few weeks ago, I asked you if you remembered something and you pointed at me. What did you mean?

I hit *Send*, then push the phone away from me like it's infected. Did I really just initiate this conversation? Do I really want to know?

Within minutes, she responds.

I recognised you when you waitressed at my parents' party. Couldn't remember where from. When I saw you next to that popcorn stand at the carnival, it felt like deja vu. Like we'd both been there before. Am I right?

I chew the inside of my cheek as I type my reply.

Yes. Do you remember anything else?

There's no response for a couple of minutes, and I think Mallory mustn't be interested in divulging more details. Then: *A sharp pain in my wrist, like the snap of an elastic band. Mum says she'd tied balloons there. Guess they were hurting so I pulled them off.*

No, I want to tell her. *It was Sparrow. He yanked them off your arm before he led you away.*

I take a deep breath to steady my hands as I type the next question. This is the moment I find out the truth – either Sparrow really did exist, or he was a fabrication.

Was somebody with you when you left that toilet block?

The message sends and I place my phone down delicately on the bed. When it buzzes again, I'm almost scared to pick it up.

Like I've been saying for years, Mallory's message reads, *I just can't remember.*

I release a defeated sigh. I was pinning my hopes on Mallory having the answers, but we're no closer to uncovering the truth. And my instincts tell me she's not being entirely truthful. She was upset about something when I found her at that toilet block three weeks ago. There's something she's not telling me.

Another message appears from Mallory.

Tbh, I'm not comfortable talking to you about this. I barely know you. It's not really any of your business.

It's absolutely my business, I want to say. *More than you know.* I tap my fingernails against the edge of the phone trying to come up with the right words to keep her on side.

I want to help you remember, I tell her. The honest truth.

Mallory takes a while to respond this time.

Why? How do I even know I can trust you?

Because, I type feverishly, *I know what it's like to feel confused and alone, for your brain to betray you by screwing up your memory. That day at the carnival holds answers for both of us. I need this as much as you do.*

I read over what I've written, then reluctantly tap the backspace key, swallowing up the characters. In their place I type three words that mean the same thing.

You just can.

*

My conversation with Mallory is still weighing on my mind when Morgan corners me at school the day before the Tans' birthday party. I've played a good game of dodging him since Rachael delivered her ultimatum. For the most part it's been easy since Morgan and I don't share many classes, and for those we do share I slip in the door at the last second and make sure I'm the first to leave.

Art class is the one place I can't distance myself from him, though, sitting side by side under Rachael's watchful eye. For the last few lessons I've managed to steer his attention back onto our *Dreamscapes* project whenever his voice drops into that low, familiar tone that's just for me.

It's temporary, I remind myself. *To keep Rachael's mouth shut until I figure things out.*

But Morgan's onto my ploy of arriving last minute for class. He's waiting outside the art room door even though it's closed and everyone's already inside. His face is sombre as he steers me into an alcove of lockers off the main corridor.

"What's wrong?" I say. I'm dreading the answer. Has Mallory talked? Has Rachael followed through with her threats?

"Why didn't you tell me it was your birthday three weeks ago?" Morgan says. "Rachael mentioned it earlier. I feel like a jerk."

"Because it's not important. I'd had a rough week – it didn't come up."

This isn't what's really bothering him though, I can tell.

"I thought we were–" Morgan glances around even though the corridor is deserted, "–I thought we were *together*. I mean, at Greenwillow, the way you kissed me was ... I thought you were into me. Since then you've been avoiding me and I don't know what I did to screw things up."

I want to reach up and smooth the crease between his eyebrows. Instead, I shove my hand into my pocket and avoid his worried eyes. Is withholding a secret the same thing as lying? Because it certainly feels just as wretched.

"Are you ... I mean, are we–" Morgan stares at a point over my shoulder, as though his question is for the row of lockers behind me. "Is this over already? Are you dumping me?"

I shouldn't be surprised Morgan's arrived at this conclusion and it rattles me to hear him suggest it. I wish I could beg him to be patient, explain it's just for now. Even if Rachael wasn't threatening to divulge embarrassing secrets that make me look unstable, I ought to cool things with Morgan while I sort myself out to prevent him getting hurt.

But the wounded look in his eyes tells me he's hurting already, and I feel myself longing to fix him, soothe him, fill up his hollow parts. I don't want to detach myself from Morgan at all. I want to give *more* of myself to him.

Morgan thinks he's found an answer in my silence and he makes a move towards the corridor. I step into his path and place my hands against his chest. I slide my arms inside his jacket, pressing myself into him, inhaling his soapy, slightly salty scent. He stiffens, probably unsure if this is pity or maybe my way of saying goodbye.

"I don't know what's going on," he murmurs into my hair.

I lift my face and kiss him because I don't trust my words, confessions that will confuse him and drive him away. My lips feel as deceitful as if they were whispering lies, silencing Morgan's questions and keeping my mouth too busy for explanations.

While my body surrenders to the heat and taste of him, my mind crackles with anxious static: the longer this kiss goes on, the more complicated things become. Because thirty metres away, inside that art room, Rachael is glowering at those two vacant seats beside her.

Retaliation is inevitable.

26

THEN

27 MARCH 2012
TRANSCRIPT FROM THE OFFICE OF DR INGRID BALLANTINE, PHD
CHILD AND ADOLESCENT PSYCHIATRY,
NEWCASTLE CHILDREN'S CLINIC
PATIENT: NATASHA CARMODY, 13 YEARS OLD

IB: Welcome back, Natasha. It's lovely to see you again. I feel like we should be having a little celebration.

NC: Why?

IB: Last month marked our fourth anniversary of talking together. With six months between visits now, you always look so much more grown up every time I see you.

NC: I always feel like I'm exactly the same.

IB: Well, that's not true, is it? Your behaviour is certainly very different to the nine-year-old girl who first came to visit me.

NC: I was eight when I first came here.

IB: Ah, yes. So you were–

NC: I remember everything about that year.

IB: It was a difficult one for you. You faced a lot of challenges.

NC: ...

IB: How have the last six months been for you? It's your first year of high school, isn't it?

NC: Mm.

IB: Are you still good friends with Sally?

NC: Sadie.

IB: Sadie. Of course.

NC: She's my best friend. We make each other laugh.

IB: It's wonderful that you've found each other. I know in the past it was a bit challenging for you in regards to making friends.

NC: *Keeping* friends.

IB: You could put it like that too. Have you and Sadie expanded your circle a little more or do you still like keeping things just the two of you?

NC: We met a new girl at the beginning of the term. Her name's Rachael Tan.

IB: Well, that's good news.

NC: We had a slumber party at Rachael's house a few weeks ago. I didn't really like it.

IB: Why's that?

NC: It was really hot in my sleeping bag and I accidentally rolled underneath Rachael's desk in my sleep. I think I had a bad dream.

IB: That can sometimes happen if you get too hot in bed.

NC: Rachael said I woke her up because I was talking in my sleep. She said I was saying Sparrow's name. I tried to sit up and hit my

234

head on the desk. I thought I was back in the box.

IB: That must have been upsetting.

NC: It was dark and I didn't know where I was. I panicked a bit.

IB: Did you?

NC: I had an accident.

IB: You injured yourself?

NC: No, I mean I wet myself. Like I used to do when I was younger.

IB: I see.

NC: Ever since then Rachael's been asking me over and over who Sparrow is. But I don't want to talk about him. I don't want to talk about any of that stuff any more.

IB: That's understandable.

NC: I think Sadie blabbed to her about it. She told Rachael I used to have an imaginary friend or something.

IB: Why do you think that?

NC: Because Rachael's stopped asking and now she keeps looking at me funny.

IB: Do you think it's worth sitting down with Rachael and explaining it all properly? It might help you feel better.

NC: It won't. It makes me feel afraid.

IB: Afraid of what?

NC: That dark place.

IB: Sparrow's secret room?

NC: No, I don't mean that. I know Sparrow wasn't real. His secret room was never real.

IB: What do you mean, then?

NC: I don't want to go back to that dark place where my mind sees things that aren't really there.

IB: Does that still happen sometimes?

NC: Not really. Every now and then I feel like Sparrow could be watching me. Like he's come back to finish his game.

IB: What game is that?

NC: I don't know. There is no game, is there? It was all in my head.

IB: Remember how we discussed your anxiety and how it often comes on when you're feeling a bit stressed or lonely? Have you been feeling that way lately?

NC: Maybe a bit. It's just ... ever since Rachael came to our school and started hanging out with us, I feel like sometimes Sadie likes her better than me.

IB: What makes you think that?

NC: Because she doesn't have to look after Rachael or make excuses for any strange stuff she does. Rachael's confident and I'm a weirdo. People still call me that at school.

IB: Does it matter to you what other people think?

NC: It matters what Sadie thinks. I don't want to lose her.

IB: Perhaps Rachael's not trying to take her away from you. Do you think she might simply be looking for close friendships of her own?

NC: Not with me. I'm worried she's going to tell everyone at school I wet the bed at her sleepover.

IB: You were having a panic attack. Perhaps Rachael understands it was out of your control.

NC: I doubt she cares about that.

IB: What do you think she cares about?

NC: Having Sadie all to herself.

IB: If Sadie and Rachael *do* become good friends, you'd have to think about how you'd react. Do you feel comfortable sharing Sadie's friendship with someone else?

NC: Not really.

IB: Why's that?

NC: I'd be lonely.

IB: You might feel lonely some of the time—

NC: No! That can't happen. Things don't go well for me when I'm lonely.

27

NOW

I spend most of Saturday at Watergardens with Morgan while he shops for Rachael's and Christopher's birthday gifts. He and his father are going to the party tonight while his mum and Mallory are opting to skip it. When Morgan drops me home afterwards, I make him park his dad's car near the boatsheds at the end of my street. I kiss him until the windows fog up and my mouth aches, and it still doesn't feel like enough.

"Please tell me you'll be at Willow Creek for Easter," he says, peppering light kisses all the way down to my collarbone.

"You'll be at Greenwillow?"

"Mm." He lifts his face up to mine and I wonder if my lips look as punished as his. "So I can visit you at your aunt's house. Please say you'll be there." He arches a flirty eyebrow.

"Uh ... I might," I tell him, suddenly drunk on the idea

of me and Morgan pressed together on that patchwork couch. Spending time alone with him is Willow Creek's only drawcard. "My aunt's invited me to stay. I haven't given her an answer yet."

Morgan grins, pretending to frantically pat down my pockets. "Why are we still talking? Where the hell is your phone?"

When I eventually climb out of the car, my body is humming and I feel deliciously light-headed. I duck home for my camera and head over to the old mill, wanting to capitalise on this high. I shoot frame after frame in the cool wind, warmed by the promise of a future with Morgan, as if reinventing myself is entirely possible after all.

I'm still smiling when I make it home as the sun is slipping behind storm clouds. Mum picks up on my positive mood as soon as I walk into the kitchen.

"Looks like you've had a good day," she says, glancing up from slicing carrots. I think there might be affection in her eyes as her gaze follows me across the room. If my hormones hadn't already surged enough today, I feel an unexpected rush of emotion.

"I have." I'm almost tempted to tell her all about it, but my stolen moments with Morgan are something I want to keep just for me.

"Well," Mum says, grabbing a tea towel to wipe her hands, "maybe this will make it even better." She moves to the alcove beside the fridge and returns with a shoebox-sized package wrapped in brown paper. "This was on the doorstep when I came home."

She holds it out to me. It has no postage mark and my name is scribbled across the top in black marker. The letter "O" in my surname has a diagonal line through it the way some people write zeroes.

"A late birthday present, perhaps?" Mum says.

I think of Morgan finding out about my birthday and how he hasn't said a peep about it since. I smile coyly as I take the package from Mum, wondering how he managed to swing this when we've been together for most of the day.

It's very light, and when I give it a shake something rustles inside. I can tell Mum's fighting the urge to ask what it is, but she resumes chopping vegetables and tells me dinner's at seven when Dad and Tim get home from the footy. She's granting me some privacy and it feels like a breakthrough ... which is exactly why I shouldn't push it. I just can't stop thinking about the possibility of more time alone with Morgan.

"Mum?" I say, pausing in the doorway. "Aunty Ally's invited me to stay with her at Easter. I'm thinking about saying yes."

Mum places her knife down. "Oh, Tash, I don't know ..."

"Just a couple of days," I add. "It will help me finish my art project for school."

"But Easter is family time."

"Ally is family too."

Mum huffs at the technicality. "I'll have to talk to your father about it."

Which means it's not a no.

"Okay. Thanks, Mum." I smile at her and she returns a faint one of her own.

I rush up to my room and slip the door closed before she changes her mind, nestling in the middle of my bed to tear my package open like a kid on Christmas morning. Inside is a black shoebox. I fumble with the tape holding the lid in place, my eager fingers suddenly all thumbs. Holding my breath as I pop the lid off, I know there's every chance I'll adore whatever this gift is simply because Morgan chose it.

I peel back two layers of crumpled white tissue paper.

In the bottom of the box are five dead sparrows.

*

I eat dinner in silence, barely able to swallow, pretending to listen to Tim's account of the close-scoring footy match. Mum throws me confused glances, wondering what could cause such a turnaround in mood. Those dead birds circle my thoughts like they've become reanimated, dipping and swooping, teasing and taunting.

Sparrow's sending me a message.

No. There's an actual box of dead birds underneath my bed right now. Not imaginary. Not make believe.

What if he's come back?

How? From where, exactly? Mum handed me that package herself – whoever left it is a hundred per cent real.

What if he's real too?

How is that even possible? What evidence is there that Sparrow *ever* existed anywhere other than my flawed memories?

No, those birds came from someone who wants to rattle

me. Someone who stands to gain if I start spiralling.

It has to be Rachael. It's the only possibility that's close to making sense.

Why didn't I confront her months ago when I suspected she was behind the first sparrow on my doorstep? It might have nipped things in the bud, might have taken the fun out of trolling me if I'd called her out publicly. Now there's the added complication of Morgan. Rachael told me to back off from him and I haven't. She won't take that lying down.

I push food around my plate as my stomach churns. Rachael and Morgan are together at her party right now and she could tell him anything she wants without me there to defend myself. If he's going to hear about what I told the police all those years ago, Sadie's right – it has to come from me. I need to be able to explain myself.

Excusing myself from dinner without finishing, I race upstairs to phone Morgan. My call goes straight through to voicemail, so I slip on sneakers and a hoodie. As an afterthought, I tug the shoebox out from underneath my bed and slip it into a plastic bag. I may need it as evidence of what Rachael's done.

When I come downstairs, Mum and Dad are clearing the dinner plates.

"Need to drop something at Sadie's house," I tell them. "She's invited me to hang out and watch a movie."

Mum frowns. "I thought Sadie was going to the Tans' party tonight."

I pause. "What?" I shake my head. "Not possible. No way."

"That's what Kiri said when I ran into her at the

supermarket." Mum shrugs. "Must have had her wires crossed. Don't be late."

There's no chance Sadie would be caught dead at Rachael's party; she must be using it as a cover story for something else. Maybe something to do with Alice. It shouldn't even matter anyway since I'm not really going to her house, but it still stings that I'm not privy to whatever Sadie's up to tonight. If anyone's going to be her alibi, it should be me.

"I'll drive you over there," Dad offers.

"I'll take my bike," I say, grabbing my helmet from the hall table. "It's only five minutes away."

The Korean restaurant owned by the twins' uncle is actually more like two kilometres from my house, in a strip of shopfronts on Marine Drive near the pier. Christopher has been waiting tables there for almost a year and has just scored Morgan a job interview for a kitchen hand role on Friday and Saturday nights. Tonight, instead of the usual hustle and bustle along this strip of eateries, the whole block is deserted thanks to light rain falling and thunder rumbling out at sea. I catch snippets of music and laughter from Kimchi before I spot the glow of its neon sign reflected on the wet footpath ahead.

As I roll up to the plate glass window, it's like watching the party on a movie screen. Guests buzz around white-clothed tables as waiters dart between them with lavish trays of food. A large banner has been strung across the wall above the restaurant's bar – *Happy 18th Rachael and Christopher!* – and clusters of silver helium balloons are tethered to the centre of each table.

An antique sideboard by the window is buried under a stockpile of presents beside an elaborate three-tiered chocolate cake. I watch as a red-haired girl covertly dips her finger in the cake's glossy icing, then sticks it into her mouth and giggles. Her friend takes a much larger swipe, and the two of them double over with laughter.

It takes me a second to realise the redhead is Alice and her friend is *my* friend. Sadie's inside at Rachael Tan's party.

Blood rushes to my head and I back away from the window, digging for excuses about why Sadie is a guest here tonight. No matter which way I slice it, her presence feels like betrayal. Why would she come? Why wouldn't she tell me?

And why do I feel like the punchline of some inside joke?

Yanking the plastic bag from my handlebars, I dump my bike against the bus shelter, shoving the restaurant door open before I lose my nerve.

Kimchi's cramped foyer is lined with black vinyl chairs and potted ficus trees. The leafy plants form a privacy barrier to the dining room, which does well to hide me, while also making the space feel too cramped and cluttered. I grope for the assurance of the door at my back, knowing I can be through it and outside any time I need to be.

A young maître d' in a three-piece suit materialises, explaining the restaurant is closed for a private function.

"Thank you, yes," I say. "I'm not staying. I just need to speak to someone." I catch a glimpse of Morgan by the bar, relaying something amusing to his father judging by the way Mr Fisher is chuckling. Morgan's dressed in a black collared shirt with the sleeves rolled to his elbows, his hair scooped into his trademark quiff. He looks handsome. Happy. And just like three months ago at school when he stepped out of his dad's SUV, the world around me stills as I drink him in.

Do I really want to have this conversation with him right now? He may never speak to me again.

Before I can say anything else, the maître d' scurries away from me into the dining room. I lurk awkwardly for a moment until I see him returning with Christopher.

"Hey, Tash!" he says as he approaches. "Glad you could make it." He smiles warmly and I feel another pang of guilt about how I snapped at him at the Fishers' house last month. He made it so easy for me in the weeks that followed by acting like it never happened, insisting there was nothing to apologise for. He's a stand-up guy and I won't let my thoughts about his sister prevent us from becoming friends, especially for Morgan's sake.

"Hi, Chris," I say, taking in his dark knit jumper and pinstriped pants. "You're looking sharp. Happy birthday."

"Thanks." He grins. "Can you tell my mum I'm officially an adult now? Because she laid these clothes out on my bed earlier – I think she missed the memo."

I force a laugh in spite of my nerves. "Your mum's very well organised."

"If that's a polite way of saying she has control issues, then yes."

Smiling, I feel my resolve softening. I'm getting too relaxed. I'm here for a purpose and need to stick to the plan.

"Listen," I tell Christopher. "I'm sorry, I can't actually stay."

"Oh, okay. You want Rachael?"

"No, no. I was—"

"Hang on," he says, glancing around the restaurant. "I think she's over with the DJ."

Before I have a chance to stop him, he jogs back into the restaurant. I hear him calling out Rachael's name. It amazes me how sometimes guys can be oblivious to friction and fallings-out. He still thinks his sister and I are the same girls who used to see movies together and paint each other's fingernails. Or maybe he just wants us to be those girls again.

Rachael skips over to the foyer in a black cocktail dress, her face lit up and flushed. When she spots me, her shoulders drop and her smile flatlines. To say the feeling is mutual is an understatement.

"You have *got* to be kidding me," she says, looking me up and down. "Why did you even bother turning up?"

"I couldn't care less about your bloody party," I say. "I'm not here to see you."

Glancing past her into the crowded dining room, my eyes fall on Morgan. Rachael sidesteps to block my view. "What happened to staying away from him?"

"Like I take orders from you."

"You need to leave," she says, folding her arms. "There is no way I'm letting you cause a scene and ruin my party."

"As if I'd *want* to cause a scene."

"Hello, attention-seeker?" she says. "It's what you do."

Maybe it's the cutting look she gives me that helps her words find their mark. I'm suddenly hyper-aware of the restaurant's cheerfulness, the stream of carefree conversation,

Morgan and his father cracking jokes by the bar. And here I am in my torn jeans and faded hoodie, my hair wild from my bike ride and the look in my eyes even wilder.

It was a mistake coming here. This isn't the time or place to talk to Morgan about my problems. I don't even care about humiliating myself – I don't want to embarrass *him*.

The plastic bag crinkles in my hand. I feel powerless. Desperate.

She sent you a box of dead birds, for Christ's sake. Do something about it!

"I need to talk to you." I hold up the bag. "Now."

"God, spit it out then. I'd like to return to my guests."

"Not here," I say, my eyes finding Morgan again. I nod towards the opposite side of the street, the row of lamps dotted along Port Bellamy Pier. "Meet me at the Seaspray, and don't bring your rubber-necking entourage."

"You can*not* be serious."

"Unless you want me to announce to everybody here what you've been doing?"

Rachael scoffs in disbelief, but there's a flash of uncertainty in her eyes. Even before the dead sparrows, her nastiness goes back years and she knows it. Not exactly the kind of speech she was anticipating for her eighteenth.

I glance past her and realise Sadie has spotted me through a gap in the plants. She's weaving her way towards us looking baffled. I slip outside and hurry across the street just as Sadie reaches Rachael near the doorway. I pick up the pace knowing Sadie will try to follow me, call out for me at any moment. But that moment never comes.

*

Out on the pier the ocean surrounds me like an inky mass, slopping and sloshing against boat hulls in the marina. Every now and then, a flash of lightning illuminates the horizon, sending a rumbling wave across the sky. When I reach the small weather-beaten shed of the Seaspray, I rest a hand against the wall to steady myself. The wind buffets me back and forth, lashing at my hair, blasting through my skin to seize my bones.

No sooner have I had doubts about whether Rachael will actually turn up, the wind carries the sound of her clicking heels on the boardwalk behind me. She appears and disappears as she passes under lampposts, illuminated one second, swallowed up by darkness the next. As she draws close she shivers, tugging her leather jacket across her chest.

"You've got two minutes," she says. "What do you want?"

I tug the black box out of the plastic bag and Rachael's face remains infuriatingly deadpan. My prepared accusation flies out of my head. I rip the lid off the box and thrust it towards her.

"You wanna explain this?"

She glances down in surprise. "What–?" She squints at the contents in the low light, then flinches and jumps backwards. "Eww!" Her arm jerks up, knocking the box out of my hand. The dead sparrows plop onto the pier around us like hacky sacks.

"Are you insane?" she says. "What the hell is wrong with you?"

"What the hell is wrong with *you*?"

The wind catches the empty shoebox, toppling it end over end until it sails over the edge of the pier.

Rachael hugs herself tighter, slipping her hands inside her leather jacket. "God, you really are deranged."

I scowl at her in the darkness. "Why won't you just leave me alone?"

"Seriously? Has it ever occurred to you that not everything's about you?"

"I know that."

"Do you? Because we're all pretty sick of The Natasha Carmody Soap Opera."

"What?"

"Everything always has to revolve around you. 'Tash's anxiety attacks' and 'Tash's claustrophobia' and 'Tash doesn't want us to be friends any more because she's so fragile and needy.'"

"That's supposed to be Sadie, is it? Nice try. I know she wouldn't say those things."

She wouldn't, would she? Sadie doesn't think of me like that. She's got my back; she always says so.

"Did it ever occur to you that I just wanted to make friends when I first moved here?" Rachael says. "You and Sadie invited me to hang out, but you were always so possessive of her. You still are. Why couldn't she be my friend too?"

My skull aches as the wind blasts against it, jangling and scrambling my thoughts. "I don't know what ..."

"You probably can't remember it. You probably couldn't care less. But *I* remember all your private jokes and how you gradually excluded me. I remember how you turned Sadie against me, and I won't let you do it again with Morgan."

She bunches her arms up further inside her jacket, her black cocktail dress flapping across her thighs. I try to make sense of what she's claiming. Is that really how it was? It's not how I remember it. Then again, neither are a lot of things.

"I'm not turning Morgan against you," I tell her. "He can see you for what you really are."

"Me? What about *you*? He's dating a total head case and doesn't even know it."

"You can say what you want about me; Morgan won't believe you."

Rachael's face hardens and her gaze flits around as though she's grasping for her next insult. Suddenly, she yanks her phone out of her jacket and waggles it in front of me. Her cutesy Hello Kitty phone case is like a red flag in her hand. "It's just as well I recorded your confession to Sadie at the sailing club, then. Morgan can hear it in your own words."

My gaze darts to her phone. She's bluffing. She didn't have her phone in her hand when I caught her eavesdropping.

Did she?

Movement catches my eye at the opposite end of the Seaspray. A shadow slips behind the corner of the shed.

"I told you to come alone," I snap.

"I did." Rachael makes no attempt to turn around, as though she knows someone's been there all along. A witness. *Her* witness. "Letting your imagination run away with you again, Tash? Gee, what a shocker."

250

She shakes her head so disdainfully, I feel exposed and humiliated, as though there's an audience of dozens instead of one little spy. All it takes is one to get the story around school, to reignite the taunts and relentless name-calling. Year Twelve was supposed to be different. *I* was supposed to be different.

Nothing ever changes.

"You can take your phone recording and shove it," I mutter, my head fuzzy with anger. "And for the record, I didn't want Sadie to be friends with you because I needed her more. I had no one before she came along. Do you even know what that's like? To feel completely and utterly alone? You had everyone in the palm of your hand within two weeks of starting school. You didn't need us. You didn't need Sadie." I thump a fist against my chest. "*I* needed Sadie. I need her right now and she's at *your* birthday party."

Frustrated tears smudge my vision as I turn away, leaving her standing in a ring of dead sparrows. I head back towards Marine Drive, throwing a venomous glare over my shoulder at Rachael's accomplice. A figure is crouched low behind the Seaspray, clad in black and cloaked in shadows.

Yes, hello! I see you there, I almost jeer out loud.

They turn their head to follow me as I pass, watching me watching them. I blink back tears, unable to make out any features. The figure's face is shrouded from lamplight by a gaping hood.

Just like Sparrow.

No.

On the window seat. In the shopping centre.

Stop it.

Just like Sparrow in every single one of my nightmares.

My shoe finds a gap in the pier and I pitch forwards, knee cracking into the boards, followed by my hip and elbow. Rachael calls out a begrudging, "You all right?" and I'm aware of how feeble I must look, sprawled across the boardwalk like a foal struggling to find its legs.

Scrambling to my feet, I hiss at the tender parts of my skin that hint at multicoloured bruising tomorrow. My eyes scour the dark void behind the Seaspray. There's no hooded figure in the shadows. There's no one waiting to pounce, no one scurrying away down the pier. There's no one here except Rachael Tan gripping her phone, probably forwarding that voice recording to Morgan right now.

Resentment rolls over me like the black water beneath my feet. The sensible thing to do is walk away now before I say or do something I'll regret.

But if Sparrow's reappearance is proof of anything, it's that I'm no longer in the business of making sense.

*

I circle my bike around Port Bellamy's deserted streets, riding up past the high school to the top of Old Bluff Road. I ignore Sadie's constant stream of phone calls and texts, her frustration evident in the final one she sends before going dark: *WHAT'S GOING ON?*

Only when the rain has soaked through to my skin do I decide it's probably time to head home. Mum's dozing in the armchair when I get in – it's much later than I thought – and once again I feel like I somehow lost time. I rouse her gently to let her know I'm home, then retreat upstairs before she's alert enough to ask questions.

It feels like I've only just surrendered to the mattress when I'm woken by a ringing phone. Daylight seeps through cracks in the venetian blinds, striping up and down my bed. I half-heartedly pat down my jeans for my phone until I remember it's in the pocket of my damp hoodie crumpled on the floor.

My elbow shrieks in pain, and last night's events come flooding back to me: my fall on the pier, and the argument with Rachael. My secret about Mallory's abduction is most likely all over town by now.

I'm just about to pull the quilt over my head and hide for the rest of the day when my bedroom door is thrown open. Mum's holding the cordless phone in her hand, her cheekbones high in colour.

"That was Francine on the phone," she says. "Rachael's in hospital."

"What? Why?"

"Somebody attacked her last night on Port Bellamy Pier."

"You *serious*?"

"Natasha." Mum's face is grave. "The police want to speak to you as soon as possible."

28

THEN

The Mid Coast Times | Archives
Section: News & Views
Date: 8 February 2017
Story: Jennifer Nguyen. Photos: Jack Allen.

PORT BELLAMY, NSW – Fishers swim home to the port.

Over the weekend, a quiet suburban street in Port Bellamy hosted the return of a local family that made headlines almost a decade ago. Once again, speculation is rife about the events of that sunny afternoon in January, 2008, when six-year-old Mallory Fisher disappeared from a carnival in Greenwillow.

At the time, authorities stated Mallory was most likely wandering in Barrington Tops National Park for forty-eight hours maximum, with no account for the other five days she was missing. Her white sandshoes and pink cardigan have never been recovered in extensive searches to help pinpoint an area of the national park where she was freed. With no CCTV cameras installed around Greenwillow in 2008, there is no way of knowing whether Mallory was abducted from the carnival itself or whether she did indeed wander off.

For years conspiracy theories have revolved around Daniel and Annabel Fisher fabricating their daughter's abduction for media attention, to cash in on tell-all interviews. Others speculate that Mallory's older brother, Morgan, was somehow involved and that his parents withheld information from police to cover it up.

Adding weight to such theories is a statement from a press conference given by Inspector Owen Morris in the days following Mallory's abduction:

"We cannot discount the possibility that Mallory's abductor may be known to her, and we will certainly be pursuing this line of enquiry along with all others."

But after nine years, it seems we are no closer to answers in the abduction of Mallory Fisher. Did she know and trust the person who took her? Did she really wander off or was she willingly led away?

One thing is certain: Mallory Fisher is the only person who can tell us what happened to her that week she was missing. And she's not talking.

29

NOW

First thing Monday morning Mum drives me to Port Bellamy police station so I can be questioned about Rachael's attack. A thirty-something detective with cropped black curls and starched pants invites me into a small room with some couches and a window. It's nothing like those stark interview rooms you see on TV, and she invites Mum in to join us even though I'm no longer a minor. She pauses to grab us Cokes from the vending machine in the hall. I take all of this as a good sign I'm not under suspicion.

"So, by now you've heard your friend Rachael was assaulted on Saturday night at Port Bellamy Pier," says Detective Gordon. She has flawless dark brown skin and pristine white teeth. I feel like I should point out that Rachael and I haven't been friends for a long time, but I suspect such a slick-looking detective has done her homework. "Someone approached her from behind and hit her over the head so hard she lost consciousness."

Mum gasps at this even though Francine already gave us these details yesterday. Rachael doesn't know how long she blacked out for. When she came to she was alone on the pier and her phone was gone. She staggered back to Kimchi with a cracking headache and a vague recollection of talking to me shortly before everything went dark.

I nod politely. "She was mugged."

Detective Gordon neither confirms nor denies. "We just need to hear about your movements on Saturday evening before and after interacting with Rachael. I understand you were the last person to speak to her before her assault."

Mum gives me a worried frown. The detective simply sips her Coke. I can't tell if she's being genuinely laidback, or if it's a ploy to lull me into a false sense of security before she pounces. I slip my hands behind my knees, gripping the front of the chair as I give my version of Saturday night. I gloss over any distracting details. There's no point bringing up things that will confuse the issue at hand.

"You argued with Rachael then?" asks Detective Gordon pleasantly, scribbling something loose and brief in her notebook. She already knows the answer. Did Rachael also tell her what it was about?

"She'd played a prank on me," I say. "I wasn't happy about it. I asked her to leave me alone."

Detective Gordon nods. "Then you left?"

"Yes," I say, wondering why she's not asking me about the dead birds. Maybe Rachael didn't mention them. After all, it makes her look pretty sick and twisted, regardless of what happened to her next.

"Can anyone account for your movements when you rode your bike up to the bluff?"

"Um … no."

"You didn't run into anyone? Someone that could verify where you were after eight-thirty pm?"

"No."

"What about before you left the pier? Did you see anyone else?"

I dig my fingernails into the seat and swallow my rising panic. I know who I *think* I saw, but there's no way I can admit it out loud. Mum glances at me expectantly and suddenly I'm eight years old again, fumbling through explanations about Sparrow and the carnival, only to be met with confusion and impatience.

No one will make allowances this time. No one will write it off as childish whimsy. At best, I'll be accused of lying for attention. At worst, my mental health will come into question all over again and it's bye-bye university.

"No," I croak, quickly clearing my throat. "It was just us."

Detective Gordon's pen scratches across her notepad. She glances up – a slow blink, a mild smile – and I feel my cheeks redden. She asks a few more questions that don't seem to interest her much before standing and holding her hand out to shake mine.

"We're all finished?" Mum asks, sliding her handbag onto her shoulder.

"I'll call you if I need anything else," says Detective

Gordon, moving to the door. She points her finger at me. "Just don't go skipping town now, you hear?"

My stomach drops. "I–I'm going to my aunt's house for Easter," I blurt. "It's here on the coast, though. It's less than two hours away."

Detective Gordon chuckles, glancing from me to my mother. She winks. "I'm kidding. I've said it to all the kids I've interviewed from the party. *Relax.*"

I'm not the only one she's interviewed? Oh, thank god. I'm just a routine inquiry, a loose end to follow up. I smile as though I knew she was kidding all along.

Detective Gordon holds the door open for us. She leans into me as I walk past.

"If you think of anything else," she says, "don't hesitate to contact me."

I shrug on my jacket, leaving my untouched Coke on the table. "I told you everything I know."

She smiles like she doesn't believe me.

*

My mother doesn't say much in the short trip from the police station to school, but her fingers drum the steering wheel like she's preparing to broach an awkward topic.

"You didn't tell me you were going to see Rachael on Saturday evening," she says. "You told me you were going to Sadie's house."

"Sadie wasn't home so I went for a ride."

"At eight o'clock at night?" She arches an eyebrow. "Then

you just happened to swing by the Tans' party and an opportunity popped up to speak to Rachael?"

"Yep."

She turns the car into the high school car park. "I don't believe you."

"Well, hey, at least you're consistent."

She swings into a parking space and yanks on the handbrake, turning to glare at me. "What did you say to Rachael? Did you upset her?"

I jerk in my seat to face her. "What if she upset *me*? What about all the shit Rachael's put *me* through?"

"Mind your language."

I stare at a point on the dashboard and shake my head. "You haven't even asked me about Rachael's prank and why I was so bothered by it. Do you even care?"

The car continues its low humming idle. Mum's expression is weary, and her eyes lose focus. "Of course I care, Natasha. All I've ever done is care. Quite frankly, I'm exhausted after years of dealing with this stuff with no end in sight. The panic attacks and nightmares and dramas at school – and now you're being questioned about an assault?"

"Everyone's being questioned!" I say breathlessly. "I didn't do it. I didn't do *anything*."

Mum sighs and stares out the windscreen. "I know you've had your challenges–"

"Gee, thanks, Dr Ingrid."

"I'm just trying to help you," she says. "We all are. But sometimes I think you don't want to be helped. It's like you've convinced yourself the lies are all true."

"I didn't lie. I didn't mean to."

She glances at me, despondent, like she's somehow failed in her duty of care. "You've always struggled with the truth."

I pull my bag into my lap and busy myself with the straps. I know she's looking at me that way she so often does, like I'm a puzzle with missing pieces, a brain-bender she doesn't have the energy to figure out.

She switches off the ignition and leans for her handbag at my feet. Bringing it to her lap, she rummages inside.

"This came on Friday," she says, smoothing something against her thigh. She passes me a white envelope bearing the RMIT logo on the front. It must be the information I sent for about their Bachelor of Photography course.

"This," Mum says quietly, tapping her finger against the envelope. "You know this can't happen."

"What do you mean?"

"Living away from home is not a good idea for you right now."

"I'm eighteen, Mum …"

"Your anxiety's spiking again. You're acting irresponsibly—"

"I told you, I didn't have anything to do with Rachael's assault!"

"I'm talking about *Tim*. I couldn't trust you to watch him for one measly hour. How are you supposed to look after yourself at uni? How will you cope?"

My throat closes in and I pick at a loose thread on my backpack.

"I'm saying this because I'm worried about you," she continues. "You go through patches where you're doing really

261

well, then something trips you up and you start to unravel."

"Nothing's tripped me up."

"The Fishers," she says. It's not a question. "Now that they're back on your radar, everything about that summer is coming up again. It's like you're slipping into bad habits with the paranoia and attention-seeking." She sighs and shakes her head at the steering wheel. "I think we should hold off on any university plans until after your next appointment with Dr Ballantine. I'm sure there are campuses you can commute to from here. I think that's what she'll recommend."

"But I need this," I say, gesturing at the envelope. "A fresh start."

Mum looks at me so sadly it's how I know it's not going to happen. I think she actually wants it for me too. I'm the one sabotaging myself.

"Let me go to Ally's for Easter," I beg. "Let me show you how I can cope away from home. You don't have to worry."

Her expression is unconvinced. "Natasha, all I do is worry."

I open the car door and climb out. I'm just about to close it after me when I lean down and peer inside. "Please don't make any decisions about uni just yet."

"You're already late," Mum says, sliding her sunglasses on and starting the ignition. "We'll talk about this later."

Later never comes. That night at dinner, Mum and Dad are strategically silent about anything to do with my university brochures, and they don't mention Easter either. I text Ally to confirm I'm coming anyway She sends me a simple *Great* in return, which has me stewing about how she's going to act around me. Maybe enough time has passed since Benny's accident and all will be forgiven.

Or maybe this will be the last time I visit Willow Creek for good.

*

Rachael's attack is all anyone wants to talk about, and the remainder of my week is a study in the art of avoidance: ducking the suspicious stares of Rachael's friends, and dodging awkward questions from my own. I skip a number of classes and spend my lunchtimes hunkered down in the computer room, only catching up with Morgan in Art and English. Sadie's completely given up on trying to pin me down in the corridor.

On Good Friday there's a swift knock at the front door, and when I hear Tim's excited chatter, I know it must be Sadie. My spirits lift out of habit even though our friendship is in a thorny place right now.

"Hey," she says, as she enters the living room. "You got a sec?"

I lead her to the back patio where we'd normally squeeze onto the swing seat side by side. Today, Sadie takes the wooden chair opposite, perching on the edge like she's ready to jump up and sprint away.

"So, about Rachael," she says.

"Yeah?"

"Did you speak to Detective Gordon?"

"Yes."

"And …?"

"And what?"

"What did you tell her?" There's a guardedness to Sadie's words like she's holding back. It's not in her nature and probably why she looks so strained.

"Exactly what happened," I say. "Rachael and I spoke on the pier. Things got heated, so I left. I found out the next morning what had happened just like everybody else."

"You were the last one to talk to her before the assault."

"Yeah, I *know* that, Dee. What are you saying?"

Sadie pushes herself out of the chair and paces along the edge of the patio. "You looked upset when you turned up at Kimchi."

"So what if I was? And speaking of, why were you even at her party? Are you and Rachael besties now?"

Sadie's face darkens at the bitterness stitched into the fabric of my words. I hate how it sounds but I just can't seem to unpick it.

"I knew you'd overreact," she mutters. "Alice does taekwondo with Christopher every Thursday. He invited her to his party and *she* invited *me* as her date."

"So, you and Alice are officially a thing then?"

"Oh, good," Sadie says. "So you *are* aware of the outside world."

"What's that supposed to mean?"

"Something's going on with you, Tash. You're being sketchy. I've seen those online articles about the Fishers you're always reading. Now all this stuff is coming up again about Sparrow. You've been acting really …"

264

"What?"

"*Obsessed*. You're not yourself. Ever since the Fishers returned to town you've been paranoid and spaced out."

I turn away from her, gnawing the skin around my thumbnail.

"Did you tell the police you gave Rachael a box of dead birds?" Sadie asks. "Because *she* did. You need to make sure you're upfront about everything or else it will look like you've got something to hide."

"Are you accusing me of something?"

"Not gonna lie, Tash – none of this is making you look good."

"Rachael left those birds on *my* doorstep, you know. *Sparrows*." I fold my arms. "She heard everything I told you at the sailing club. She's screwing with me, trying to get inside my head."

Sadie scrunches her face, sceptical. "Why would she bother?"

"Because of Morgan."

Annoyance flutters across her features. "Seriously? I really don't think Rachael's gonna get all possessive over some pale dude in skinny jeans."

I lean back and look at her. It's suddenly so obvious why we've been drifting apart these past months. "You haven't given Morgan a chance since my panic attack in his laundry."

Sadie's expression is impassive.

"Is it because I trust him and you don't like it?" I ask her. "Are you jealous or something?"

"Whoa. Hold up."

I'm overstepping, but the words keep spilling out. A terrible mean-spirited part of me wants Sadie to take some of this weight from my heart, relieve me of some of this hurt. "Is it because you can't stand me relying on someone that isn't you?"

Sadie blinks. "Excuse me?"

"Serious question: what do you get out of all of this?"

"All of what?"

"Our friendship. Hanging out with me. Is it because I'm so needy? Does it make you feel important because I depend on you so much?"

"Tash, you'd better check yourself—"

"I don't need you to look after me all the time!" I tell her, standing too. "I need a best friend, not a babysitter."

"Well, clearly that's not the case," Sadie snaps. "You lose your brother in a shopping centre, your aunt's dog is injured while you're caring for it and now you're a suspect in Rachael's attack."

I gasp. "I'm not a suspect!" *Jesus, am I?*

"What's the common denominator here, Tash? That's all I'm saying." Sadie can barely look me in the eye.

"You think I'm responsible for hurting Rachael?"

She folds her arms, looks out over the backyard at the T-shirts flapping on the washing line. "I don't know what to think. You barely talk to me any more."

Something inside me fractures. How has it come to this? Everything seems to be slipping through my fingers.

Sadie sighs. "Look, I know you wouldn't hurt Rachael intentionally. But sometimes when people are really upset they can do things they don't mean and block it from memory. Alice says—"

"You talked to Alice about me?"

Sadie blushes, a rare event. Then I realise she's actually embarrassed for *me*. "You need to figure some stuff out."

"I'm trying."

"The *truth*," she says, holding my gaze.

I look down at my shoes. "I know."

"You're all knotted up, Tashie." Sadie's voice softens. "You're somehow tied to that summer when you were eight and it's messing with your head." I nod as she moves a step closer. "It's just going to keep pulling you further under unless you figure out what the hell is real and what isn't."

She places her hand on my shoulder and gives it a squeeze as she passes. I watch her trudge across the patio and into the house.

And I know she's right: I feel like I'm losing myself. I've forgotten how to trust my own mind, ensnared in a net of unreliable memories. I need the cold, sharp blade of truth, no matter how brutal.

It's the only way I'll cut myself free.

30

THEN

15 SEPTEMBER 2014
TRANSCRIPT FROM THE OFFICE OF DR INGRID BALLANTINE, PHD
CHILD AND ADOLESCENT PSYCHIATRY,
NEWCASTLE CHILDREN'S CLINIC
PATIENT: NATASHA CARMODY, 15 YEARS OLD

IB: Tell me about your aunt, Ally.

NC: Why?

IB: You haven't mentioned her for a long time.

NC: I haven't even seen her since Christmas a few years ago.

IB: Her name used to come up a lot in our sessions.

NC: Did it?

IB: That summer at her house certainly did.

NC: It was a long time ago.

IB: Do you think about her much?

NC: Not really. I don't have much to do with her.

IB: Is that because there's something unresolved between the two of you?

NC: What do you mean?

IB: Well, thinking back to that summer, you were upset when she told your parents you'd been making things up and misbehaving.

NC: Yeah. But I suppose she had to, didn't she? She thought my parents needed to know.

IB: Have you wanted any kind of a relationship with her since then?

NC: Not really.

IB: Why's that?

NC: I suppose it felt like I couldn't trust her any more.

IB: I see.

NC: She told me she was on my side and then she threw me under the bus.

IB: Is that how you see it?

NC: It's how it felt at the time.

IB: Do you still feel that way now?

NC: I think there'll always be a part of me that thinks it's unfair.

IB: Unfair?

NC: Yeah. Because at the end of the day, it was her word against mine.

31

NOW

Willow Creek has a completely different air about it this visit compared to last month. The light is muted, and everything has indistinct edges. Tall willow trees along the driveway droop listlessly, as though holding their breath. The bushy mountains behind the house seem murky and impenetrable, a few shrill bird calls the only indication something is living in there.

Ally's truck is not at the house when we arrive on Saturday morning. Dad glances at his watch a few times, needing to get away soon. He, Mum and Tim are attending a barbecue at the Tans' house at lunchtime.

"Typical," Dad says, peering through the front windows. He's already knocked three times and dialled Ally's phone twice. "How hard is it to stay put until your house guest arrives?"

"I have keys," I tell him, holding up his set. "Don't worry. She's probably just gone to buy hot cross buns or something."

Dad looks at me like that's wishful thinking and he's probably right. I don't care about Easter anyway. I'm here to talk to Ally. I'm here for answers.

Dad gives me an extra-long hug as he's leaving. "That's from Mum too," he says, kissing the top of my head. I really want to believe him.

As he drives off in a cloud of dust, I let myself into the house and notice straightaway that it's in need of airing out. I listen for the tippy-tap of Benny's claws on the floorboards, but he's most likely riding shotgun with Ally on her errands. I take my backpack upstairs to the room I stayed in last time, the bedding still crumpled from my previous visit.

An hour of channel-surfing later, Ally still hasn't returned. I pull out my phone and dial her number; it goes straight through to voicemail again. I think about my family on their way to the Tans' house without me, and I'm struck with aching loneliness. I find myself texting Mum.

Hope you have a nice time today.

The eerie quiet of Ally's house makes me pause for reflection, prompting me to add:

Please tell Rachael I hope she's feeling better.

Next, I call Morgan.

"Hey," he answers. "I feel like I haven't spoken to you for ages. Did you skip classes this week?"

"Just had some appointments and stuff," I lie. "So, are you here? At Greenwillow?"

"Not yet. We're coming up tonight."

271

"What are your plans for Easter Sunday?"

"I'm glad you asked!" he says, the smile obvious in his voice. "My dad's cousins are coming up for dinner at our holiday house. I'd love it if you'd come too."

My pulse flutters as I accept the invitation, and it's not just nerves about dining with Morgan's family. I feel responsible for my part in Mallory's disappearance, even if I'm not sure how big that role was. For better or worse, one thing's certain: my pull towards the Fisher family has never been stronger.

*

By dinnertime, I'm not sure whether to be baffled or livid at Ally's no-show. With her track record, I'm beginning to suspect she's making some kind of point. Is she trying to scare me? Punish me? Or has she simply forgotten about me after a boozy afternoon at the pub?

I yank open cupboards in search of ingredients to make some kind of dinner, but there doesn't seem to be anything new in the pantry since I was last here. I flip open the breadbin on the counter, pleased to find half a loaf in a plastic bag. When I pull out a slice, I see it's covered in patchy green fuzz.

Shuddering, I bundle the bread bag into the bin beside the back door, my shoe knocking into Benny's water bowl as I pass. It's bone dry. Not only that, a small spider has made itself a home, fine webs zigzagging across the bowl's rim.

I march over to the pantry and drag out the bag of dog kibble I fed Benny from weeks ago. It appears to be sitting at exactly the same level from when I last used it.

My pulse thrums.

Is Benny being cared for somewhere else? Did Ally lie about him recovering from his injuries?

God. Is it possible Benny didn't make it home at all?

On impulse, I pick up my phone to call Ally before realising I'll only get her voicemail again. Instead, I scour the fridge for the magnet from Margaret's vet clinic in Ellenbrook. A female receptionist picks up after two rings.

"Hello," I say. "I hope you can help me. I'm just enquiring after a dog that was treated at your clinic about four weeks ago."

"Name?" she asks pleasantly.

"Tash Carmody."

She giggles. "Sorry, I mean the name of your pet. It's how we put them in the system."

"Oh. Benny. Um … surname Carmody, I guess?"

I hear her fingernails tapping against a keyboard. Then, "Yes, I've found it. A ten-year-old yellow lab?"

"Uh-huh."

"It says here … oh. Umm …"

"Is something wrong?"

"Just a moment, please."

She places me on hold. I gnaw my thumbnail while I listen to crackly classical music, suddenly panicked that Benny didn't survive his injuries. Why would Ally lie about that? To spare my feelings? Surely she wouldn't keep that news to herself.

The music cuts out and a deeper voice comes on the line.

"Tash?"

"Hello? Margaret?"

"Yes!" She sounds relieved. "I must say, I'm glad someone's finally got in touch."

"What do you mean?"

"We're still chasing your aunt in regards to payment. In all the excitement of getting Benny into my van that night, I never got *your* phone number. So we really didn't know who else to call."

I drag a chair out from the kitchen table and lower myself into it. "Didn't you talk with my aunt when she came to pick up Benny?"

"Sweetheart," Margaret says. "No one ever came to pick up Benny."

"What?"

"We had to put him in foster care because we didn't have the space to home him here."

"I don't understand."

"We thought something must have happened to your aunt."

"No," I say, rubbing fingers across my forehead. "No, she's fine. We've been texting each other since Benny's accident."

"I can give you the details of the foster carer if you'd like to arrange for Benny to come home?"

"Yes," I say. "Yes, please. That would be great. He can come home with me to Port Bellamy if need be."

Margaret provides me the phone number of the foster home, and I arrange to have Benny's vet bill forwarded to my email.

"I'm so sorry about the mix-up, Margaret. I had no idea Ally no longer wanted him. Did she give you a reason?"

"Honey," Margaret says, "we never heard a peep from your aunt at all."

*

It's a restless night's sleep on an empty stomach, the old house's creaks and groans my only company. My body flounders on the mattress as though struggling to keep afloat, the mouldy walls and ceiling pressing into me from all sides. At one stage I wake with a start, convinced I heard Benny bumping around downstairs. Impossible of course, yet it didn't stop me from lying rod-straight in bed, heart jackhammering in my chest. I knew I wouldn't get a wink of sleep unless I went downstairs and double-checked every locked door and window.

On Easter Sunday I emerge from bed feeling dull and headachy. I make breakfast out of dry Weet-Bix, and it only now occurs to me I can't buy groceries today because the supermarket will be closed. Ally still hasn't returned any of my messages, and when I scroll through her scant responses from recent weeks, I become increasingly irritated. It appears she's been playing some kind of game with me, lying and luring me here under false pretences in a way that feels chillingly familiar.

Trying to use photography as a distraction, I ride out to an old hay shed on Greenwillow's outskirts. It's not long before I'm snapping anything at random, my mind turning over recent arguments and conversations. Some of Sadie's comments keep bubbling to the surface.

Your mind could be remembering things differently to how they really were.

Did you ever see your aunt and Sparrow in the same room at the same time?

Why didn't Ally want me talking about Sparrow to my parents? Is it possible she was harming me, and my frightened eight-year-old mind masked her identity? Or maybe *she* planted the idea of Sparrow in my head to cover her own tracks. It's no secret Ally resents my dad, and the easiest way to hurt him is by hurting his child. But what would Ally stand to gain? The sadistic pleasure at screwing up one of his kids? If that was her intention, it's fair to say she succeeded.

Unless, of course, she's not quite done.

Shivering despite the autumn sunshine, I tear up and down Willow Creek's dirt roads on Ally's bike. By the time I reach the house, I'm wired and dehydrated, a familiar headache flaring up around my temples.

My phone chimes with a text from Morgan.

We're here! Kitchen's a madhouse. Pick you up at 6?

I reply with something upbeat before downing two glasses of water and hunting for a Panadol.

Upstairs, I peel off my jeans and sweaty T-shirt, crawl into the claw-foot bath, and sit balled up at one end with the shower streaming over me. My skin prickles under the hot water, my chest tightening in a way that tells me a panic attack is sharpening its claws. I towel myself dry and upend my backpack on the bed, focusing my energies into finding something to wear to dinner. As I pick through my clothing, my fingers knock against something hard. I shake out a

T-shirt, and a red mobile phone case topples onto the floor.

The dead black eyes of Hello Kitty stare up at me.

Oh, god.

I have Rachael's phone.

32

THEN

The Ferris wheel is slowing down when I spot Sparrow hiding behind the ticket booth. He's staring up at the yellow carriage that I was lucky enough to get all to myself. Now I wish I'd squeezed in with that nice family in front of me, or maybe those teenagers two carriages behind. If I was with other people, then maybe he'd leave me alone.

"Go away," I tell him when I get out of my carriage onto the wooden platform. He follows me from the ride's exit, down the steps and onto the muddy grass. He hangs just far enough behind that people are looking at me weird for talking to myself. "You need to leave me alone."

He tugs his hood over his forehead but I can still see the purple smudges under his eyes. There's a long red scratch along his cheek as well. What's he been doing? Where does he go when he's not pestering me to play?

"Come with me," he says. "I've got something to show you. You're going to like this, I promise."

"I don't want to." I turn down a gap between two circus tents. It only leads to a bunch of dumpsters.

"You should really come and see," he says, a few steps behind me; he always walks too close. I reach the dumpsters and realise it's a dead end – Sparrow's blocking the path back to the rides.

I wrap my arms around myself. "I already told you I don't want to play with you."

"Even if I show you a magic trick?"

I roll my eyes and try to look like I don't care. But something wriggles inside me like a tummy full of worms. What if he is magic? He doesn't look like a wizard or a superhero. What does magic even look like anyway?

"I know how to make you disappear," Sparrow says.

The side of the tent flaps in the breeze and it's hard to hear the carnival noises. The rides and people seem really far away.

"I don't want to disappear."

"You don't want to stay here, do you? You're lonely and bored."

"I want to go home."

"Well, this is perfect then. You won't really disappear. It's a magic trick. You'll end up back at your house."

I fold my arms. He might do another mean thing, like when he forced my face into the water at the creek. I don't think I should listen to him. I don't think he tells the truth.

But I'm so thirsty and tired, and my legs are kind of achy. My skin feels hot and sore. Plus, I really don't want to go back to Aunty Ally's house. I don't like it there. I don't like the sounds and the shadows and the smell. *What if Mum and Dad get so busy with the new baby they decide to leave me there for even longer? Another two weeks? Maybe even a month. This could be my only chance to get home before they forget all about me.*

"What would I have to do?"

"I've found a special box," Sparrow says. "You just need to climb inside and I'll say the magic words."

"I don't know …"

Sparrow's smile goes away like it always does when I don't say yes. "Come on," he says. "Just come and see."

I'm worried and tired and hungry, and I miss Mum and Dad so much I might cry. I wish I was at home on my bed with my books and teddies, my green blanket and a huge glass of lemon cordial.

"So, I only have to climb inside the box for a minute?"

Sparrow grins at me with his black and yellow teeth.

"Hardly any time at all," he replies.

33

NOW

I don't know what I choose to wear. It doesn't even matter. Somehow I'm fully dressed and sitting in Ally's kitchen with Rachael's phone on the table in front of me. My wet hair is soaking through the back of my T-shirt, dripping onto the wooden chair at my backside.

How do I have this?

A shiver ripples through me. Next minute I can't stop shaking.

What should I do? Who should I tell?

I stand and pace around the kitchen. Morgan will be here in twenty minutes. I just need to calm down and think this through.

Moving to the pantry, I hunt for herbal tea or something that might help calm my nerves. I spot three bottles of red wine similar to the one I shared with Ally last visit. There's no doubt it made me feel warm and relaxed. It could be just the thing to take the edge off.

I twist off the bottle's lid and grab a coffee mug from the draining board, swallowing the first three mouthfuls in large greedy gulps. I refill the mug and wait for the wine's effect, impatiently swallowing two more mouthfuls before pushing the mug aside.

Did I do something to Rachael? Have I done other things I can't remember?

I've been fixating on Ally, but what if the problem *was* me all those years ago? What if there was a reason Ally kept those locked doors between us? Those tense phone calls late at night – was she talking about me to my dad?

Dark thoughts volley back and forth inside my skull until I'm woozy. It's probably the wine kicking in, only it's not dulling my anxiety fast enough. I top up my mug as I hear Morgan's car pull up outside.

Grabbing Rachael's phone, I dump it inside the breadbin, catching my hip on the side of the table as I pass. My mug of wine sloshes around conspicuously, so I grab it and move it to the sink. As Morgan knocks at the door, I gulp down most of the cup before tipping the rest down the drain.

"Hi," Morgan says, when I open the front door. He's in a fitted V-neck jumper and the tan pants he wore to his family's welcome-back party. His eyes scan me up and down and I feel like guilt must be radiating off me. "Um, am I early?"

"Nope. No, you aren't," I say too loudly. I bend over to pull on my Chucks, using the wall to steady myself. "Just let me grab my bag."

He waits by the door while I weave my way to the kitchen and back again. I can't tell if my grin looks forced, but he can't know anything's wrong.

"Err, Tash," he says. "It's kinda cool outside. Maybe a jacket?"

I glance down at my white tank top and ripped jeans. Huh. So *that's* what I ended up throwing on.

Despite my churning stomach, the car ride to the river feels warm and floaty. I rest my head against the window while Morgan talks, but I have trouble grasping hold of his words. I can't remember how much wine I had to drink – I'm pretty sure I'm only tipsy. I'm still being coherent. At least I think I am.

My gaze drifts along the shopfronts on Greenwillow's main street as their lights blink off, their door signs flipped to CLOSED. Up a cross street, a rotating neon OPEN LATE sign catches my eye. I sit bolt upright in my seat.

"Wait," I tell Morgan. "Stop!"

He flinches at my voice, eyes darting to the rear-view mirror, before braking and pulling over.

"Back up." I jerk in my seat to look behind us. "Reverse. Reverse!"

"Why?" he asks, doing it anyway. There's no traffic and he's able to roll all the way back into the intersection. "What is it? What's wrong?"

My face is so close to the window, hot breath fogs up the glass. I press the button to open it and crane my neck out as far as I'm able. "I thought I saw my aunt's truck. Up there in front of the chemist."

"Um ... so?"

I squint into the dusk. A couple of hatchbacks are hunched against the kerb, but the parking spaces in front of the chemist are empty. "I could have sworn ..."

Morgan touches my shoulder and it makes me jump. "Tash, are you okay? You seem a bit—"

"No, I'm good. It's all good." I slouch in my seat and sheepishly close the window. "My mistake. Forget I said anything."

Morgan's puzzled glances for the remainder of the car ride tell me that's easier said than done. I try to be subtle about glancing at the passenger side mirror, watching a set of headlights just far enough behind us that I can't tell if we're being followed.

When we pull up alongside a blue weatherboard bungalow overlooking the riverbank, Morgan jumps out of the car and dashes around to my door.

"Are you sure you're up for this?" he says, as I struggle to unbuckle my seatbelt.

"Of course! Looking forward to it." I spill out of the car and he catches me before I topple onto the gravel shoulder. I peer up the dark road behind us, relieved there are no other headlights around. "I'm just a lil' bit tired. I'll perk up once we're inside."

We're barely through the door of the small holiday house when Mrs Fisher greets me with a warm smile and a tray of bruschetta. She's wearing another elegant floral dress, her dark brown hair cascading in chunky curls around her shoulders.

"I know Daniel used to be your orthodontist," she says, leaning in to kiss my cheek. "It's so lovely to meet you again all grown up. Morgan talks about you nonstop, of course."

"Mum ..." he says, rolling his eyes.

I try to coax my lips into a smile; they feel numb and uncooperative. "Thank you for the invitation," I say slowly, taking care to form each syllable clearly. I reach for a circle of toast from her tray but it doesn't make it to my mouth. The diced tomato-and-basil topping dribbles down the front of my white tank top.

"Oops," says Mrs Fisher. She holds out a serviette. "Sorry, it's the messiest food ever. Should've stuck with a cheese platter." She watches as I smear the red splotch deeper into the fabric. "Morgan, show Tash where the bathroom is. A little water on that should help prevent a permanent stain."

As I follow Morgan to a small hallway off the main living area, I notice his relatives are throwing me curious glances. I only now realise how dressed up everyone is – smart shirts and pressed pants, shiny leather shoes. I glance down at my ripped jeans and ratty Chucks and wonder what the hell I was thinking.

My shoulder catches the doorframe as I stumble into the bathroom. I turn to face Morgan. "Your mum's really nice—"

"Are you smashed?" he hisses, throwing a quick look over his shoulder.

"Huh?"

"How much did you have to drink before I picked you up?" He glances towards his family taking their places around the dining table, a handful of men and women the same age as his dad.

"I didn't—"

"You're not exactly holding it together," he says, brows knitting. "Are you okay? Is something wrong?"

Everything's wrong, Morgan! I feel like I'm losing my mind.

"Just tired," I assure him. "Didn't sleep well last night. I'll be out in a minute."

I close the door as gently as I can, managing to lock it on the second try. I sway in front of the mirror, grabbing hold of the porcelain sink to stop the room tilting. I splash water on my face and comb fingers through my hair, assessing my bleary eyes in the mirror.

You look like a girl with something to hide.

In the dining room I try to keep up with the polite dinner conversation, thankful Morgan is sitting beside me so I can't see his face when I stumble over words. I can see Mallory's face though – watchful blue eyes, wispy blonde hair framing her elfin features. She's seated opposite me, sneaking glances when she thinks I'm not looking. At one point our eyes connect and she musters the tiniest hint of a smile. I try to return it, but inside I feel like crying.

"There was a bit of an incident at a party we attended recently," says Mr Fisher conversationally. "A friend of Morgan's was assaulted and left unconscious on Port Bellamy Pier."

One of his cousins clucks. "Awful," she says. "Did they catch who did it?"

"Still investigating," Morgan replies. "Somebody mugged her for her phone."

My mouthful of mashed potatoes turns to glue and I can't seem to get it down my throat. I sink further in my seat as another cousin speaks up.

"Incredible!" he booms, his moustache twitching. "Who in their right mind would risk an assault charge for something as trivial as a second-hand phone?"

Yeah, I almost say, *but what if they weren't in their right mind?*

"Is Rachael a friend of yours too, Tash?" Mrs Fisher asks, popping a dainty green bean into her mouth. She and her husband smile at me expectantly.

"Uhh—" I try to sit up, "—we used to be. We're not very close any more. It's terrible what happened, though." I reach for my water and gulp it down. I can see Mallory watching me through the bottom of my glass.

I think I did something bad, Mallory. And maybe more than once.

I place my empty glass on the table and attempt to refill it. The water jug is much heavier than anticipated. My elbow goes slack mid-pour, the base of the jug crashing onto the rim of my dinner plate, sending my cutlery flying. A large crescent-shaped piece of bone china snaps clean off.

"Oh," I say, jumping up, every set of eyes on me. "I'm so sorry!"

"It's fine, honey," coos Mrs Fisher. She leans across the table to take the plate from me. "Just a little accident. No harm done."

"*Okaay*," Morgan says, pushing his chair back and standing. "I think Tash and I might step outside for some fresh air before dessert." He throws his cloth napkin onto the seat of his chair like he's whipping a horse.

Glancing at everyone apologetically, my eyes fall on Mallory. Her face is pained, lips pressed together like she's connected to my distress. I wish I could talk to her but Morgan's already heading for the door. It takes me a moment to disentangle myself from the chair, and I apologise again to Mrs Fisher as chatter resumes around the table. When I join Morgan outside, his expression is one I can't read.

"Morgan, I'm really sorry about the plate."

He jerks his hands to his hips. "What were you thinking, turning up here drunk? In front of my family? They were really looking forward to getting to know you, and now this is their first impression?"

"I *wasn't* thinking. I'm sorry."

"You've been acting really strange these last few weeks. I can't get a handle on you – you're up and down like a yo-yo."

Unsure how to respond, I keep quiet. This seems to frustrate him more.

"I mean–" he folds his arms, "–I get the impression there's a lot you're not telling me."

I keep my eyes on the ground; I don't want to do this right now. I know I resolved to talk to Morgan about Sparrow and the carnival when the time was right, but this doesn't feel like it. My head's too fuzzy and I can barely keep my thoughts straight.

"People at school were talking," he says, "about Rachael's attack." I slide him a wary glance. "They said you had something to do with it. I mean, there's no way, right?"

Wincing, I think of Rachael's phone turning up in my backpack. "I came to Kimchi on the night she was hurt," I admit. "We argued on the pier."

"You were there? Why didn't you tell me?"

I shrug and steady myself against a verandah pole.

"What were you arguing about?" he asks.

"She knows about something I did as a kid. Something I'm ashamed of."

He moves closer and I have to fight the urge to run away. "What do you mean?"

No going back now. You have to tell him.

I grip the pole so tight my knuckles sting. "It's about what I told police on the day Mallory disappeared."

Morgan swallows. I catch the way his eyes give me a quick once-over, as though he's already seeing me differently.

"I told them I watched Sparrow lead Mallory away from the carnival."

Morgan's lips part. There's a pause before he speaks. "Sparrow? Your *bogeyman* Sparrow?"

"I thought it was real. I thought he was playing a game."

"Wait. So, you actually *saw* someone take Mallory from the carnival's toilet block?"

"Yes. I mean no, not really. I don't know. He was imaginary."

Morgan stares at me a beat too long. I can sense alarm bells clanging inside his head. "Why would you do that?"

"I'm sorry," I say, moving closer. He takes a subtle step back. "I don't know what was wrong with me. Nobody believed me anyway."

"Because you made up stories," he says, his voice rising. "You lied—"

"I was eight—"

"And, what? That makes it okay?"

"No, I just mean—"

"That was the worst day of our lives, Tash," he says. "And you were making shit up about it for kicks?"

I suck my lips into my mouth and bite down hard. I have no excuse. I have no better explanation.

"Ever since we moved back here, you've been all over us like a rash," he says. "Do you have some kind of sick obsession with my family or something?"

"Of course not!"

"How can I believe anything you say?"

My mouth opens before I realise I don't have a clue how to answer that. I close it again and Morgan turns away from me.

I know I should leave now because Morgan wants nothing else to do with me. Only, something he said is gnawing at me. Maybe guilt is making me desperate for someone else to blame, but I feel like I can't let it go.

Ever since we moved back here.

My mind sifts through suspicions I've filed away and haven't let myself properly dissect.

Ever since we moved back here.

Everything started when the Fishers came back to town.

Morgan trapped me in his laundry when he knew the door was faulty. He was at the shopping centre on the day Tim disappeared. He suddenly appeared inside Ally's house after Benny was injured even though I knew I'd locked the front door. Morgan dropped me off at my house the day a box of dead sparrows turned up on my doorstep, and he was also at Rachael and Christopher's party. It could have been Morgan who snuck up on Rachael and stole her phone so he could plant it on me.

Is Morgan capable of that? Such cruel things to torment me, punish me. Is it revenge? If he blames me for his sister's disappearance he could be capable of anything at all.

"You've known all along?" I manage.

Morgan frowns. "What do you mean?" He moves a step closer, catlike, watching me a bit too closely. It feels like some kind of game.

Crushing my hands into fists, I press them to my temples. Can this be right? Is it Morgan I should be afraid of? What about my suspicions regarding Ally?

What about my suspicions about myself?

"I–I need to go," I say, turning quickly and stumbling. I need to sober up so I can think straight and figure this out, away from here, away from Morgan. I wobble my way back to the front door. It's cracked open a few inches and a small figure is silhouetted against the light from inside.

She pushes the door open wider to let me through.

"Mal–" Morgan starts, just as his sister hurries away. Who knows how much she overheard? I want to apologise to her, plead my case, but a frantic voice inside me insists, *Get out, get out, get out.*

I keep my head down as I duck past the dining area and into the kitchen. I retrieve my bag from the sideboard just as Mrs Fisher appears in the doorway.

"Tash, honey? What's wrong?" She moves to touch my arm and I back away. "Did you and Morgan have a fight?"

Only now do I realise that my eyes are wet. I rummage quickly through my bag for a tissue, and it slips from my grip, tumbling facedown onto the floor. I drop to my knees to gather up its contents.

Mrs Fisher hitches her satin skirt to kneel beside me. "Everything will be all right, sweetheart," she says, rubbing my back. "You've just had a little bit to drink. Everything will be right as rain in the morning."

I give her a sniffly nod, but I don't believe that for a second. Mr Fisher slips into the kitchen and hovers around us, his forehead wrinkled with concern. An uncertain look passes between him and his wife.

"You can't go back to your aunt's house in this state," says Mrs Fisher. "What will she think?"

"I'm okay," I manage, although the idea of going back to that dark, empty house is almost as dreadful as staying here.

Mrs Fisher reaches up and wipes hair from my damp cheek, tucking it behind my ear. "You should stay the night here, sweetheart."

I draw in a shuddery breath and shake my head. "Thank you for dinner." I haul myself to my feet. "And I'm just so sorry. For everything."

"Oh, Tash–" Mrs Fisher smiles sadly, "–it was just a broken plate."

Mr Fisher insists on driving me home and dashes off to find his car keys. As his wife has one more stab at coaxing me to stay, she's distracted by something over my shoulder.

"You'll look after her tonight?" she says, her brow softening. "Are you sure?"

My pulse kicks up a notch. I don't want to be alone with Morgan – I'm too confused. I need to call Sadie. I need to call my parents.

I spin around to tell Morgan no, but it's not him in the doorway clutching a backpack and pillow. It's Mallory.

She doesn't look at me as she nods once for her mother.

34

THEN

20 DECEMBER 2016

TRANSCRIPT FROM THE OFFICE OF DR INGRID BALLANTINE, PHD

CHILD AND ADOLESCENT PSYCHIATRY,

NEWCASTLE CHILDREN'S CLINIC

PATIENT: NATASHA CARMODY, 17 YEARS OLD

IB: You'll be starting your final year of high school soon.

NC: Mm-hmm.

IB: How do you feel about that?

NC: Great.

IB: That "great" sounded a bit flat.

NC: Did it?

IB: It did. Do you have some reservations?

NC: Nope.

IB: Have you been feeling anxious about it?

NC: Nope.

IB: Your body language is interesting to me.

NC: Is it?

IB: You seem very guarded today. Closed off. Do you not want to be here?

NC: Not really.

IB: Why's that?

NC: I don't think I need to come here any more.

IB: I see.

NC: ...

IB: You feel you're coping well with your anxiety?

NC: Yep.

IB: And there have been no recent incidents?

NC: Of ...?

IB: Bad dreams. Claustrophobia. Panic attacks.

NC: All one hundred per cent under control.

IB: I'm not sure you really believe that.

NC: Here's the thing, though — no one's ever really tried to understand what I believe.

IB: Can you explain what you mean?

NC: I'm tired of explaining. Let's label me cured and call it a day.

35

NOW

Mr Fisher insists on switching off the car and walking us to the door of Ally's house. Any faint hopes I had of my aunt materialising while I was out are dashed by the empty driveway and dark windows. I hadn't left the verandah light on for myself earlier, and in my dishevelled state it takes me three tries to get the key into the lock. Mr Fisher offers to come inside and help us get a fire started; I assure him we'll be fine with the oil heater. He smiles and says, "I'll stop fussing and leave you to it."

He lingers in the hall until we've drawn the curtains, stipulating that Mallory keep him and her mother informed via text that everything's okay. I assure him that Ally will be home soon, although I don't really believe it. But I don't want to be alone. Mallory and I barely know each other and yet her presence is already a comfort.

"Don't worry about that son of mine," says Mr Fisher as he's leaving. "He'll get over himself and apologise for whatever he's said to upset you. I've never seen him happier than these last few months." While I know he's trying to cheer me up, instead I feel crushed.

After Mr Fisher leaves, I feel the full weight of Mallory's wide-eyed appraisal. I'm glad she's here, but why did she offer to come? Should I feel wary of her too?

There's something about the way I felt connected to her across the Fishers' dining table that makes me think Mallory is here because she knows I need someone in my corner. If her brother *has* been enacting some kind of revenge these last few months, my gut feeling tells me Mallory's in the dark about it all.

I lead her into the kitchen. "Do you want tea? Hot chocolate?"

She ponders this, then spies the red wine bottle sitting on the table. She moves to the sink where two glass tumblers are upended on the draining board.

"Really?" I say. "After my classy performance in front of your parents?"

Mallory shrugs and plonks the tumblers on the table in front of me. I almost laugh as I pour two generous glasses. I mean, what the hell, right? Things are a complete mess – may as well get messier

We both take a large sip at the same time, and it occurs to me this could be Mallory's first taste of alcohol. I suddenly feel big-sisterly and responsible for her. As much as I'd welcome oblivion right now, I need to slow Mallory down.

"Pyjamas?" I say. She places her glass down and gives me a thumbs up.

Upstairs, I offer her the bedroom I slept in last night, and insist we flip the sheets and use the pillow she brought with her. I choose Ally's room to sleep in because the only other upstairs bedroom is missing a mattress. We take our time getting changed, and I double-check all the windows and doors, trying not to be obvious about it. Mallory taps my shoulder when I bypass the downstairs guestroom, and I feel the blood drain from my face.

She frowns at my hesitation before throwing the door open and marching across the room to check the window herself, pretending not to notice the way I grimace at the moonlit window seat like it's a monster.

I find us two of Gran's crocheted blankets, and we take our drinks into the living room. I select an old nineties rom-com on TV while Mallory texts her parents goodnight.

"Thanks for keeping me company," I tell her, and once again I feel like I'm on the verge of tears. Mallory nods and gives me a curious half-smile. She leans over and grabs my phone from the coffee table, tossing it lightly into my lap. She types something on her phone and mine chimes in response.

What happened tonight? Why are you so upset?

When I glance over, her upturned eyebrows echo the concern of her text message. At this moment, I know nobody could understand me better than Mallory. How can I put this into words, though? And how can I voice suspicions about her brother?

Long story, I text back. *It's complicated.*

Why don't you start with tonight? she asks. *What did you and Morgan fight about?*

Sliding her a guilty look, I take a large swallow of wine. "He's upset with me because of what I told police on the day you disappeared."

And next thing the words are spilling out of me like a sickness, like a demon needing to be purged. I explain about the two weeks I spent here when I was eight, inventing Sparrow, my ensuing troubled childhood and years of therapy. I go into detail about what I recall from the carnival.

"I didn't know Sparrow was imaginary until later," I tell her. "I didn't know that no one else could see him. I swear, when I watched him lure you away from that toilet block, it seemed as real as the nose on my face."

Mallory considers this. She frowns into her glass as she takes another sip.

"I just don't want you to think your disappearance was some kind of joke to me," I say. "I didn't mean to waste police time. I told my parents and the police what I truly believed had happened. I really wanted to find you."

Mallory picks up her phone.

At least you tried to tell them something.

Tilting my head, I consider this. There are so many questions I've wanted to ask for years, and now I have my opportunity.

"Why couldn't you tell anyone anything?" I say. "Why did you stop speaking?"

I sip from my glass while Mallory composes her reply.

My therapist calls it traumatic mutism. Mum said whenever

police tried to question me about what happened, I'd seize up. Ever since then it's like my brain just doesn't know how to do it any more. I block on words and end up gaping like a goldfish. Kind of a mess, tbh.

"What about that stuff in the newspaper?" I say, glancing up from my phone. "I read in an article that you told police you thought you'd been asleep for most of the time you were missing."

Mallory nods as she types a response.

Felt like I'd been asleep coz there were so many blanks between leaving the carnival and waking up in the national park. Police psychologist had me draw what I could remember – apparently lots of pictures of me lying down with my eyes closed. Then a whole bunch of the bush.

I shift on the couch. "Like the trees in your journal?" I ask, before remembering I'm not supposed to know about those. "I'm sorry, I glanced through it when it fell off your bed that day you threw the lamp at me."

Mallory chuckles at the memory and I find myself sniggering too. I don't know why it seems so amusing now – it certainly wasn't at the time.

"So what about the vintage wardrobe drawings?" I ask. "Is that a memory too?"

She shakes her head as she types her reply.

It's weird. I have this picture of it in my mind but don't know how it got there. I keep refining the details. Can't get it down on paper the way I see it in my head.

"Maybe you want to be a furniture designer," I joke. Mallory smiles and shrugs. She eases back in her chair and sips from her glass again. "You can't remember anything else about those missing days?"

Mallory considers this for a moment before wedging her glass between her knees to text with both thumbs. Halfway through her message she pauses, her cheeks aflame.

Only snippets. Certain smells. Dozing inside a moving vehicle with a radio playing. This is gross, but I think I remember wetting my pants a few times. Maybe even crapping them once. Don't know what state I was found in and I'm too embarrassed to ask Mum if that's the case.

I muster a sympathetic smile. "I wet the bed too as a kid. I even had an accident at Rachael Tan's birthday sleepover, if you want to talk about embarrassing. Be thankful your memory's sparing you the details." As soon as I say it I realise how insensitive that sounds. "Sorry. I don't mean that. It must be so frustrating not being able to remember things that have happened to you."

Mallory drains her glass. She sits cross-legged as she types her next message, squinting at the screen as though she's having trouble reading her words.

Doctors say I have dissosssive ammeesia.

"What?" I say, looking up from her message. She re-reads what she typed and we both erupt into giggles. She tries again, taking her time with every character.

Dissociative amnesia. Linked to my speech issues too.

"Wait," I say, fumbling with my phone. I almost drop it. "I've heard of this. My shrink brought it up with my parents when they were worried I was making up stories to block out a traumatic event."

Mallory nods and continues typing. It takes her a long time to compose the message, her thumbs more sluggish than before.

Been told I still have memories of what happened but deeply buried. Every now and then a small detail comes to me, usually triggered by a sound or smell.

"Like what?"

Like when you leaned over my bed that day I threw the lamp. No idea why I was scared. Just knew I should be.

I shift in my seat. Mallory's already typing another line.

Couldn't see your face. Something to do with the hood?

"The hood?" I say. "You think it could be a memory?"

My mouth doesn't seem to cooperate and my words run into one another. Mallory shrugs. She leans over to place her empty glass on the coffee table, missing by several inches. It thumps onto the rug. She blinks at it slowly, mildly amused.

"That's funny," I tell her, yawning. "Sparrow always wore a hood. He was wearing it when I watched him take you away."

In my head this feels significant, but the words come out sounding slurred and silly. I know we've had a serious conversation about something, and right now I can't put my finger on exactly what we discussed. Mallory smiles lazily like I've told a joke, her eyelids heavy. All of a sudden, sleep seems like the best idea in the world.

We manage to haul ourselves up the staircase, propping each other up for support. I feel a different kind of drunk to earlier, less warm and floaty, more sluggish and heavy. I feel like everything I've consumed tonight is churning in my stomach like gruel.

As I wait for Mallory to use the bathroom, I break into a cold sweat. I stumble into Ally's bedroom to search her wardrobe for a knitted cardigan. Ally's smoke-infused gardenia scent engulfs me and I'm hit with a wave of nausea. I manage to swallow the rising acid in the back of my throat long enough to ensure Mallory makes it safely to her bedroom.

She's practically asleep on her feet – I shouldn't have let her drink. She's only fifteen and so tiny. I didn't realise one glass would have this effect.

"Thanks for being here," I tell her, feeling an impulse to hug her. She's like a rag doll in my arms, swaying limply and allowing Ally's cardigan to swamp her.

I'm just about to release her when she stiffens, her whole body as rigid as a board.

I let go of her. "You okay?"

Mallory doesn't move. Her bleary eyes travel from my head to my feet and all the way back up again. She's looking at me like she's never seen me before, like she's wondering how she even got here.

"You need to sleep," I tell her, nodding towards the bed beside the window. Something about the way she's looking at me makes my stomach fold over itself. My mouth floods with saliva and I hurry towards the door.

"'Night," I manage, before stumbling into the bathroom just in time to throw up.

36

THEN

It's as black as night inside the wooden box. Blacker. I can't even see my hand in front of my face. It smells like damp towels and onions and sweaty socks. And what about all those costumes piled up on the muddy ground outside? Colourful shirts and fancy jackets, curly wigs and feathers. They're probably ruined now. It's going to look like my fault.

This was a bad idea. I shouldn't have said yes.

"Ten seconds is up," I tell him, banging my fist against the lid of the trunk. "I did it! Let me out."

The box tips on an angle and I slide towards one end. I get all bunched up and my forehead hits the end of the trunk. White dots ping around in front of my eyes.

"Ow!" I yell, thumping the box's side with my arm. "Stop it." My knees feel bruised where they press into the wood. "I want to get out!"

Everything jolts and I hit my head again. There's a sharp pain in my neck like a pinch. I jerk back and forth like the box is being dragged. Where is he taking me? He never said anything about this.

This isn't part of the game.

"Open it!" I yell, except it doesn't come out very loud. My head is on a weird angle and it's hard to get any air in.

The box jolts again. He's ignoring me.

I can't breathe in here.

What if I'm running out of air?

He told me he'd do this. He said if I didn't play in the cellar he'd lock me in a box and I'd starve to death.

"Please! I've changed my mind. Let me out!"

The box stops suddenly and drops onto the ground. I can't hear anything except a pounding noise in my ears and my breath bouncing off the wood. My arm feels weak as I raise it one last time to bang on the box's lid. The side of my hand hurts and my throat is sore like I might cry.

"Please let me out!"

Too dark, too dark. Don't run out of air.

Be small.

Breathe small.

"Please."

I can't hear anything. What's happening? Is he ever coming back?

I don't want to starve to death.

I want to tell Mum and Dad about the things Sparrow's done.

I want to meet my new baby brother.

There's a muffled voice outside the box. Somebody swearing.

Is that—? Can that be—?

"Dad?"

Maybe all that shifting and bumping was me travelling through time and space! Maybe Sparrow kept his promise after all. Maybe he really is magic. I'm finally home and the two weeks at Aunty Ally's house was all a bad dream.

"Dad!"

The trunk's lid is yanked open. There's blue sky above me and I squint at the sunshine.

"Git the hell outta there!" *a voice growls.*

I blink at the bear-like shadow leaning over me. Not Dad. Definitely not Sparrow.

"I'm sick of you kids playing hide-and-seek back here," *the voice says, as I push myself to my knees.* "This is not a play area, you hear me? Performers only. Git outta there and run on back to your folks."

A large red glove appears in front of my face. I grab it and it helps me out of the trunk. A man with a painted clown face and curly wig tuts at me as I stare around feeling dizzy. Sparrow was dragging me somewhere.

Any minute now he could come back.

"Sorry," *I say, backing away from the clown. He flicks a hand at me as though he's wafting away a fly.*

I run away from the big tent and into the crowd of people along sideshow alley. I don't want to be here any more. I need to find Morgan Fisher and everything will be okay. I saw him earlier at the dodgem cars with his parents and sister. They live in Port Bellamy too, and if I ask nicely they might take me home with them.

I hold in my tears as I hurry back towards the food trucks. I try not to think about my sore knees and that stinky dark trunk.

I keep one thought in my head to help me run faster.

Find Morgan.

Find Morgan.

Find Morgan.

And find him before Sparrow finds you.

37

NOW

I wake up stiff, my shoulders aching, and for one horrifying moment I fear I'm back inside the box. The surface beneath my right side is unrelenting, my cheek mashed against something cold and rigid. I crack one eye open. It's not the suffocating pitch black of the trunk that greets me, but the sombre light of dawn. I shake off the remnants of my dream and realise I made last night's bed out of the bathroom floor.

Attempting to sit up, my head hollers in protest. My mouth feels like sandpaper, my stomach, empty and delicate. Did I really drink enough last night to warrant this kind of a hangover? The memory of being hunched over the toilet bowl comes flooding back and it's enough to encourage a repeat visit. Whatever was in my belly last night has already come up; I manage only a shaky dry-wretch.

I stagger to the sink to swill out my mouth, rubbing some of Ally's toothpaste along my teeth with my finger. Peering at my reflection in the mirror, I appear almost ghoulish in the dim light. I'm pretty sure I stink like wine and vomit and god knows what else, but I need to check on Mallory before I shower. If she's feeling even half as rough as I am, she's going to wake up in a bad way and may need my help.

As I move towards the door, I instinctively reach for the light switch, and it only now occurs to me that I don't remember turning it off last night. Grey dawn seeps in through a squat window near the ceiling and the frosted glass panel above the bathroom door. I close a hand around the brass doorknob, giving it a tug. The door doesn't budge. I twist the handle in the opposite direction, yanking more firmly now. The door creaks and clunks in the doorjamb and remains stuck fast.

Crouching on my haunches, I peer through the keyhole to the hallway on the other side. If this door has a key, it's not sitting in the lock, and it's not inside here with me. Maybe Ally mentioned something about the door lock being dodgy. Maybe it likes to stick on chilly mornings.

Seriously? Why the hell is this house always working against me?

The familiar thump of my heart protests about the confined space. I release a steady breath and rap a knuckle against the door.

"Mallory? Are you there?" I knock harder. "Mallory, you awake?"

I crouch and peer through the keyhole again, not detecting

any movement on the other side. I'm about to stand up again when I notice a small red smear on the white floor tiles beneath my feet. I lift up one foot to inspect it, finding tiny scrape marks on the side of my ankle. The skin is broken in places, one scratch dotted with pinpricks of blood. I check my other ankle; there are matching scrape marks on that one too.

Baffled, I glance around the bathroom.

What on earth have I been doing in my sleep?

I really need to get out of here. *Now*. The tiny painted-in window is somehow more unnerving than if there'd been no window at all.

"Mallory!" I yell, tugging on the doorhandle again. "Mallory, can you please come and help?"

I pace up and down behind the door. What are my options here? Sit and wait for Mallory to wake up? Or try to bust my way out? I glance up at the frosted glass panel that Gran installed above the door to help prevent damp and mould.

Come on, Tash! Think.

My eyes scour the room and land on a ceramic toilet brush holder beside the cistern. I grab a handtowel from the sink and wrap it around my fist. Hoisting myself up onto the bathroom vanity, I send a silent apology to my late grandmother as I swing the ceramic pot into the window panel.

The glass shatters, raining down onto the floorboards on the other side. I use my towel-covered hand to knock out any remaining glass teeth still clinging to the doorframe. Plucking two bath towels from hooks on the wall, I drape them over the window base then pause, listening for Mallory's quick footsteps. I'm both deflated and confused when I hear none.

Is it possible Mallory locked me in here?

Or was it me who chose to lock her out?

I grip the padded windowsill, fear and adrenaline driving me as I swing my body up and over the window frame. Momentarily dangling half in and half out, I wiggle just enough until I'm able to squeeze a knee up into the gap beside me, then unwittingly tip forwards, somersaulting out into the hall.

I land hard on my hip and rump, broken glass crunching beneath me. I quickly inspect my arms and legs for shards, plucking a few small pieces from my pyjamas and skin. It could have been much worse, and for that I'm thankful; even more thankful to be out of that pokey bathroom.

"Mallory?" I say again, yanking off Ally's knitted cardigan that I vaguely remember borrowing last night. I drape it across the broken glass and tiptoe my bare feet out of the danger zone. Moving quickly to the bedroom Mallory slept in, I find the bed rumpled, sheets strewn sideways to the floor.

On the staircase, I listen out for breakfast noises. There's no bubbling kettle, no rustling cereal box. When I enter the kitchen, it's as murky and silent as a tomb.

I try again, louder this time. "Mallory? Come on! Where are you?"

I check rooms systematically, moving towards the front of the house, legs growing weaker with every step. I have to force myself to check the guestroom I'd rather steer clear of, coming away feeling queasy.

This house has done it again. It's trapped me here alone.

I carry a weak hope Mallory sleepwalks. Maybe she ended up in some other bedroom by mistake. I bolt upstairs again, running in and out of rooms like a child playing hide-and-seek. Arriving back in the room Mallory slept in, I notice her phone is on the bedside table. Her shoes are upended by her backpack near the foot of the bed.

I peer out of the window into the garden below and notice the grass is coated with an uninterrupted layer of frost. Scurrying downstairs, I dash to the back door and peek through the small window before reaching for the door bolt. Logic stops me. Mallory can't be on the back verandah if the door is still bolted from the inside.

At the front door, both the deadbolt and security chain are still in place as well. I move from room to room checking windows, to find them all still firmly locked. Only when I've done a complete circuit of the house, checking every walk-in wardrobe, underneath every bed, the pantry, the laundry and behind the shower curtain, do I let myself succumb to rising panic.

Mallory's disappeared on my watch.

From a house that's still locked from the inside.

I grab my phone and sit at the kitchen table, almost calling Mallory's phone until I remember it's upstairs. Out of desperation, I dial Morgan's instead. He's either still asleep or screening calls because I get his voicemail.

"Morgan, please call me as soon as you get this," I say. "It's urgent. It's about Mallory."

Tossing my phone aside, I stare around the empty kitchen feeling helpless. I think of all those years ago when Ally sat here reassuring me it was okay to be different, how concerned she was that my parents would find out something was glitchy inside my head. I saw things that didn't exist and invented situations that won me attention.

Am I still doing it?

Am I obsessed with the Fisher family like Morgan accused me of?

And if so … could I have done something to Mallory?

I place my head in my hands and struggle to get air into my lungs. Sadie's words come back to me: *What's the common denominator here, Tash?* I thought all of these disturbing things were happening *to* me, but what if they were orchestrated by my own hand? What if I've designed all of this to garner sympathy and attention, like those parents with mental illness who poison their kids?

What if I was the one who hurt Benny?

What if I've hurt people too?

My whole body trembles. So many things don't make sense to me. Now I wonder if they ever did, whether I've ever been able to distinguish truth from fantasy. No wonder my parents are overprotective – they probably understand me better than I understand myself.

I'm shaking so much it feels like my bones are splintering. I reach for my phone and dial the only person who's able to negotiate me down off my self-imposed ledge.

Sadie answers after the third ring. "Hey. It's early – you okay?"

"Sadie," I whisper.

"Tash? What's wrong?"

313

"I–I think I've done something, Dee. Something bad."

"Tash, speak up. I can barely hear you. Where are you?"

"At my aunt's house in Willow Creek."

"Okay," she says. "What's going on?"

Shifting in my chair, I bring an unsteady hand to my forehead. "I might've done something to Mallory."

"Mallory *Fisher*? What are you talking about? Where's your aunt?"

"Ally's not here," I say. "And Mallory's just … v–vanished."

Sadie releases a low breath. "Okay, Tashie? I can hear how upset you are. I need you to calm down and explain to me exactly what's going on."

My grip is vice-like around the phone. "Mallory stayed here with me last night. This morning I can't find her."

"Maybe she went for a walk," Sadie says. "Did she borrow your keys?"

"No. They're right here. She can't bolt the doors behind her anyway. That can only be done from the inside."

"What about a window? Maybe she panicked when she couldn't get a door open."

"The windows are all still locked from the inside too."

"Well, what do you possibly think *you* could have done to her?"

"I–I don't know. I think I'm sick. I think I've done stuff and blocked it from memory."

"Like what?" Sadie says, trepidation in her voice.

"Attacking Rachael at the pier. I think I took her phone because she recorded what I said about Sparrow at the sailing club."

Sadie's voice is firm. "You didn't attack Rachael."

"How do you know?"

"Because I know *you*, Tash. You wouldn't hurt her even though we all know she deserves a good smack over the head sometimes."

"Dee, I'm not joking."

"Neither am I! There's no way you did it. You'd remember."

"I'm not sure, though. I'm not sure I trust my memory ..."

"*I'm* sure."

"What about that stuff you said about me being the common denominator in all the weird things that've been happening?"

Sadie sighs, her breath a sharp blast down the phone. "I think we've both said some things we don't really mean."

"It's still true, right? The common denominator?"

"Yes. But obviously someone *else* is a common denominator too. There's got to be some other explanation."

"Apart from me being crazy?"

"Tash," she says, "you're the sanest crazy person I know."

I hang my head. "I'm really scared. I feel like I'm losing it."

"Look, you're not alone in this – you know that I always have your back. I'm going to borrow Mum's van and drive up there. We'll figure it out together, okay? What's the address?"

As I give her directions, I squeeze the phone so hard I might break it.

"I'm leaving now," Sadie says. "Eat some breakfast and take a shower. Just sit tight. Nothing bad is going to happen if you don't leave the house."

That's the thing, though – it's this house that's the problem.

This is where it all started, so it stands to reason that this is where it all must end.

*

Taking Sadie's advice, I try fixing some dry toast for breakfast, the only thing I can think of that might stave off more nausea. Without thinking I flip open the breadbin, which contains nothing but Rachael's hastily stashed phone. My chest tightens as I pull it out, turning it over and over in my hands. I switch it on and it doesn't prompt me for a passcode.

I scroll through her photo folder and find a few short videos of her at the beach and at school, some mucking around with her parents and Christopher at home. The most recent one is three minutes of birthday party footage at Kimchi. There's nothing from the sailing club, no recording of my confession about Sparrow. Rachael was bluffing all along.

Or I've already deleted the evidence.

Pushing the phone away from me across the table, my gaze drifts around the kitchen. I stare at Margaret's fridge magnet, mulling over what she said about not hearing a peep from Ally. So, that's now two people I'm connected with that have gone missing.

I storm upstairs to Ally's bedroom, tearing through her wardrobe and drawers for some kind of clue about where she could be. I don't even know what I'm looking for when

I stumble across a suitcase in the back of her wardrobe. It appears to be the same battered brown one she packed for last month's yoga retreat. I remember it sitting by the front door.

I drag the suitcase into the middle of the floor to unzip it. Inside are Ally's long floral skirts and earthy T-shirts, black yoga pants, a toothbrush and a packet of cigarettes.

Did Ally even make it to the yoga retreat? Or did she just not bother unpacking when she returned?

Staggering to my feet, I head into Ally's study at the end of the hall. This was one of the rooms that remained locked and off-limits nine years ago. Today I throw open the door and sift through the junk on Ally's desk without giving her privacy a second thought.

I leaf through Post-its and notepads, hunting for anything that might explain her current whereabouts. Underneath a pile of unopened mail is a spiral-bound weekly planner. A satin ribbon marks a weekend in March with my name written in ballpoint pen on three consecutive days. On the Saturday of that weekend, Ally's written *Life and Mind, Byron* and circled it. I search for a scrap of paper to write that down, then change my mind and scoop up the whole book to take downstairs.

In the kitchen, I use my phone to google *Life and Mind, Byron Bay*. A business listing comes up as the first search result. I dial the phone number in the listing, relieved when someone actually answers considering it's not yet eight o'clock on Easter Monday.

"Hello. My aunt attended your yoga retreat in March," I tell the receptionist, citing the dates in the planner in front of me. "At least, she planned to attend. I just need to check if she actually turned up."

"You can't just ask her this question yourself?" comes her snippy reply.

Doing my best impersonation of Sadie's polite-but-no-bullshit approach, I say, "My aunt is missing and I'm asking you for help. Are you able to tell me or not?"

The woman sighs. "Just one moment."

She puts me on hold and I spend several minutes listening to pan flutes and trickling water. When she comes back on the line I hear the shuffle of papers.

"Okay," she says. "I'm obligated to tell you we do not give refunds for no-shows."

I sink into the nearest chair. "Are you telling me there's no record of Ally Carmody attending?"

"That's correct. However, we did try contacting her several times and we can't be held responsible if she didn't return our calls. It's a prepaid event and refunds are only provi—"

I hang up and flip through Ally's planner in the weeks leading up to my March visit. Her scribbles are either illegible or so brief I can't make any sense of them. I go all the way back to the day she arrived on our doorstep in Port Bellamy, a whirlwind of bohemian fabric and animosity. There are two sentences scribbled on an angle across the page.

The first reads: *GET KEYS BACK FROM RICH!!*

And underneath it: *PJ – 9 am. Corner Mavis and Lindsay Street, Cessnock.*

The obvious thing screaming for my attention is the mention of PJ. As in Ally's high school sweetheart? Peter or Patrick something? I'd assumed he was no longer in the picture. It seems he's alive and well and living in Cessnock, if this is indeed the same person. When I was eavesdropping on Mum and Dad talking in the kitchen that day, Dad mentioned Ally was passing through on her way home from the Hunter Valley. So, was PJ the reason Ally was there?

Maybe he knows where Ally is.

She might be in Cessnock with him right now.

I snatch up my phone and google the street address, hoping for a residential directory listing with a phone number. If Ally won't answer her phone, maybe PJ will answer his. The first search result is a grey Google Maps box with the address listed underneath. An arrow pinpoints a location.

Cessnock Correctional Centre.

Frowning at the screen, I hit the backspace button and key in the address again. The same result comes up.

Ally was at a prison at nine in the morning on the same day she turned up at our house? When she marched through our front door, I distinctly remember a person smoking in the cab of her truck. It seems like a distracting tangent complicating my search for Ally, which in turn doesn't ease my concern about where Mallory is. But my instincts tell me this scrap of information is important.

I scour my memory for details about Ally's former boyfriend, things she told me right here in this kitchen. He was a runner or something. On the school athletics team –

the Pocket Rocket. Peter Jones? Patrick Jones? Patrick Jonas? Yes! *Patrick Jonas.*

I google "Patrick Jonas" and "Cessnock Correctional Centre". The first search result is a newspaper article.

Holding my breath, I click open the link.

38

THEN

The Shore Observer | Archives

Section: News

Date: 28 February 2008

GLOUCESTER, NSW – Gloucester man sentenced to eleven years for methamphetamine trafficking.

Patrick Michael Jonas of Gloucester on the New South Wales mid north coast was sentenced to eleven years in prison on Wednesday for the commercial supply of methamphetamine, commonly known as ice.

Jonas, 36, was arrested on 16 January after the NSW Police drug squad executed a search warrant at his Roberts Road unit based on an anonymous tip. Police seized a set of digital scales, $825 in cash and multiple clip seal baggies containing a total of 215 grams of a clear crystal substance. The substance was tested and found to be methamphetamine.

Jonas will serve eleven years at Cessnock Correctional Centre in New South Wales with a non-parole period of nine years.

39

NOW

Nine years.

The last two words of the newspaper article are like beacons in a black mist.

Nine years since my disastrous summer at Willow Creek. Nine years since Mallory disappeared. Nine years since Sparrow flew through my window in the dead of night and asked me to play a game.

I double-check the date Patrick Jonas was arrested – 16 January 2008. Four days after Mallory went missing from the carnival, and three days before she was found. It's thought she wandered alone in Barrington Tops National Park for up to forty-eight hours by herself. Patrick Jonas lived in the vicinity of Greenwillow at the time of his arrest.

It's like jigsaw puzzle pieces of my childhood are scattered all over the floor and I just need to pick them up in the right order to form a picture that makes sense.

I google "Patrick Jonas ice arrest" hoping for a photo from his trial. I click the *Images* tab and my screen fills with dozens of mugshot thumbnails. Scrolling through pages of faces, I enlarge the photos of any men that could be a similar age to Ally back in 2008. None of them are Patrick Jonas though, according to the file names and accompanying web links. They are frighteningly familiar nonetheless.

Gaunt faces. Sallow skin. Some with sores on their foreheads and noses. Scabs dotting their cheeks and trailing down their necks. One man is smiling for the camera revealing a mouth of rotten teeth, most reduced to black nubs receding into diseased gums. A few images show multiple arrests of the same person on different occasions, each subsequent mugshot capturing the rapid deterioration and premature ageing of the addict. It's impossible to pinpoint how old they actually were when the photos were taken.

Further clicks take me to a site about ice addiction, to an embedded YouTube video recorded by a bystander as police intercept an ice-affected man on a train. The addict is jittery and aggravated, unable to keep his hands still as he digs at the skin on his arms. He wheedles and begs and bargains with police, before turning on them the next moment, his hollow eyes flashing with rage.

I'm almost breathless with a soaring rush of recognition. Validation.

This man, these mugshots, remind me of Sparrow.

I place my phone down and drag fingers through my hair, trying to connect the dots.

Me, Mallory, Sparrow. Patrick Jonas and Ally. That summer afternoon at the carnival.

My headache surges as theories knock against the inside of my skull, echoed by the rhythmic clang of the old water heater refilling after my shower. If Benny were here, he'd be down the hall and outside that cellar door giving it a piece of his mind.

I glance up from my phone, my fingers finding the collar of my vomit-speckled pyjama top.

I haven't showered yet.

Whatever that sound is, it's not coming from the water heater.

*

In all my circuits of the house looking for Mallory, I never checked the cellar. Why would I? It's a dank, dark dead end. Nothing down there and nowhere to go. Being on this side of the cellar door is bad enough, without whatever claustrophobic underground horrors await me on the other side.

I only ever ventured into the cellar once when Gran was still alive, the time Dad helped her move some antique furniture out a year before she died. I tagged along to explore while Dad and Gran carried a set of walnut dining chairs out to her truck. I lasted less than three minutes down there before the water heater hissed, sending me running for the stairs convinced the ghost of a dead Scotsman was on my heels.

What I do remember is this: there are no doors leading outside. Not even so much as a window. If Mallory went down there voluntarily, it was to hide.

And if it wasn't voluntarily …

Drawing in a breath, I turn the cellar doorhandle, closing my eyes briefly as I release it from my hand. Wooden steps descend into the shadows below. I grope for a light switch, a musty scent rising to greet me. Chilly tendrils coil around my face and shoulders, drawing me down.

There are several lightbulbs dotted across the low ceiling beams, revealing crude walls of stone and render. At some point a concrete floor has been poured, and some of the structural beams replaced with newer wood. Tucked beside the stairs is an old workbench piled high with broken appliances, an old fridge with the door removed. The water heater stands in the opposite corner, rusty and innocuous, water dribbling down one side into a puddle on the floor. It's like some poor incontinent old soul, and I feel a weird sense of pity.

Funny how, when in the face of real danger, those things we once feared seem so trivial.

The other half of the long room is a mess of second-hand furniture, a haphazard arrangement of mid-century nesting tables, art deco bar stools and floral winged armchairs. A country-style buffet unit is pulled away from one wall on an angle. In one dimly lit corner, a makeshift bed is set up on top of an antique dining table, topped with a mattress and bedding I assume was pilfered from the bedroom upstairs. There are food scraps and empty packets, the stench of

326

decaying fruit skins. Empty water bottles are lined up against the wall like a game of skittles.

Someone's been staying down here?

The hairs on my arms stand on end.

"Mallory?" I say cautiously. I stop in my tracks and still my breath. There's a single second of pure silence as I cock my ear to listen. It's quickly interrupted by a series of muffled clangs. I spin around to face the water heater, my pulse spiking.

"Mallory?" I say again, louder this time. The clanging noise responds to my voice. I sweep the room scouring for its origin. It sounds like it's coming from inside the walls.

When I reach the pine buffet unit, the noise grows louder. I slip into the wedge of space behind it and press my ear up to the wall. It takes me a second to realise it's not stonework here. I shove the buffet unit aside so more light can fall behind it, uncovering a basic wooden door.

What the hell is this?

Backing away from the door, I search for something to arm myself with – there's no telling what I might find on the other side. On a small table in the corner is a pair of foot-high pillar candlesticks. I snatch one up. The turned hardwood feels robust and formidable in my hand.

I press my ear against the door again. The clanging noise has stopped, replaced by an urgent humming sound like somebody trying to hit the high notes of a song.

Raising the candlestick with my right hand and turning the handle with my left, I flick the door open and take a step back. Glaring daylight hits me in the face and I throw a hand up in front of my eyes.

Two horizontal windows near the ceiling flood the storage room with light. My mind tries to reconcile exactly where I am in relation to the house's floorplan. How did I not notice these windows from outside?

But, of course, I *have* noticed them before. The weekend I looked after Benny. I found him outside barking at these very windows, tucked away at ground level on the lower left side of the house.

I blink as my eyes adjust, registering more antique furniture: a mahogany bedhead, matching bedside tables, an empty bookcase reaching ladder-like up to the windows. A smell hits me, ripe and unclean, like a service station toilet. The familiar smell of urine-soaked clothing I know all too well from my childhood.

Somebody's been in here.

Somebody could be in here right now.

To my right is the back of a large cabinet, blocking my view into the other half of the room. I take a hesitant step, then another, all the while holding my candlestick high enough to strike. The tuneless humming sound starts up again, louder now that I'm inside the room. There's a shuffle and scrape of something against the concrete floor in a corner I can't see. I want to call Mallory's name again, but my instincts warn me to stay silent.

I'm only a few steps past the large cabinet when I see it: the wire dog cage that disappeared from Ally's garden shed last time I was here.

Mallory is crammed inside.

I lurch forwards, my first impulse to run to her. Then I

hear the scraping sound again and realise it's not Mallory who's moving. Something else is in here with us.

Creeping the last few steps, I peer around the front of the cabinet. A few metres away from the cage, somebody is hunched against the wall. Her back is to me as she works away at something in front of her, but I recognise the patterned fabric of her skirt, now soiled along the edges. Her hair hangs in long greasy strips across her shoulders.

"Ally?"

My aunt's head whips around at my voice, eyes wide with fear. Grey duct tape covers the place where her mouth should be. Her attempts to talk are reduced to urgent hums, her nostrils flaring with effort. I rush to her side as she flexes her whole body in communication, one filthy foot kicking out sideways to clang the water pipe running down the wall.

"Oh my god. What is this?" My fingers tremble as I gingerly peel at the corner of the duct tape. "*What's going on?*" I barely have a grip when Ally yanks her face sideways, pulling the tape off in one swift motion. Her skin is raw underneath, her lips flaky and cracked. She gags on a wad of gauze still stuck inside her mouth. I quickly pull it out for her.

"He's coming back!" she says, her voice like gravel. "He's coming *back!*" Her chest heaves and she's racked by a fit of dry coughing.

"Who?" I say. "Who did this?"

Ally winces. "PJ."

"Your high school sweetheart?" I think of the article about his arrest. "What? Why?" I glance at Mallory scrunched inside the wire cage, her head tucked into the corner as though she's napping.

"Hurry. He could be back any minute," Ally says, jerking her arms back and forth. Her hands are tied with orange plastic cord, the kind my dad uses in his whipper snipper at home. It's looped around each wrist several times, and then round and round the water pipe, finished with an impossible twist of knots. "You need to find something to cut me free."

Dropping the candlestick, I look around for something sharp. My eyes fall on the wire cage again, a chrome padlock secured on the door. "Mallory? Can you hear me?"

"She's out of it," Ally says. "He drugged her. He drugged you both."

"Drugged? What do you—?" Then I think of how wasted Mallory and I both felt after that single glass of red wine last night. We left our glasses on the kitchen table while we went upstairs to change into pyjamas and check the locks. "He spiked our drinks?"

"Don't know how you're even awake," Ally says. "I lost about fifteen hours when he did it to me."

I touch the collar of my pyjama top again, the sour smell lingering. "I puked my guts up before bed. I must have got some of it out of my system."

"Thank god." She jerks her head towards the cage. "He brought her down here last night. I've been waiting for him to drag you in here too."

I think of my achy shoulders, the mystery scratches on my ankles. "He dragged me somewhere. I woke up locked in the bathroom."

"Too heavy," Ally says, looking me over. "Too hard. Probably clicked you and I are the same size. Be thankful you didn't get bumped and dragged down two flights of stairs. I woke up black and blue."

I glance at Mallory, her petite frame in floral pyjamas. The idea of him carrying her, touching her–

"*Come on!*" Ally says, making me flinch. "You need to hurry! Find something to cut with. *Now.*"

I turn to search behind me. The floor here reeks of urine and faeces, and I spot a soiled bucket in the corner I have no intention of getting anywhere near. There are more food scraps here too, scattered water bottles and empty toilet roll cores.

Against the wall, beneath the windows, there's a large wooden chest full of vintage kitchenware. I rummage through rusted baking trays and painted cookie tins, hoping for scissors or a large knife.

"How long have you been down here?" I say.

"Weeks." Ally grunts, trying to loosen her shoulders. "Since that weekend you came to look after Benny."

I jerk my head to look at her. "But you've been texting me since then. You asked me to come here for Easter."

"That wasn't *me.*" She jiggles her bound hands as evidence. "It was *him.* He needed to get you back here."

"Me?" I say, gaping. "Why?"

"Things didn't go as planned that first weekend you stayed. He dragged me down here on the first night, and he was going to bring you down the following night once he got that cage in place." She nods in Mallory's direction. "He

331

couldn't get to you, though, because someone else was here."

"Morgan," I murmur. I can't believe I entertained the idea Morgan was dangerous. He actually prevented any harm coming to me that night. "He stayed with me because I was upset about Benny."

Ally strains against her binds to look at me. "Tash," she says. "I haven't heard Benny since the day I woke up down here. What did PJ do?" Her voice cracks. "What did he do to my dog?"

"No, no, Benny's fine." I feel distracted and frantic as my brain struggles to keep up. Benny had been barking at the cellar windows and scratching at the cellar door. He must've been in the way. "He was injured – we got the vet out here. He's being fostered and we can bring him home any time you like."

A look passes between us: there'll be no homecoming for Benny if we don't make it out of this cellar.

Giving up my search of the wooden chest, I move to a walnut dresser in the corner. I yank open the top drawer and riffle through it, shoving aside pens and elastic bands, rolls of duct tape, piles of paper that flutter to the floor. The middle drawer contains nothing but musty board games, a pink cardigan, grubby sandshoes, all useless junk that makes me swear under my breath. When I reach the bottom drawer I'm rewarded with the jangle of cutlery. I dig among cake forks and soup spoons until my fingers close around a large silver breadknife.

Pushing myself to a stand, my foot slips on some of the debris from my search I peel a Ziploc bag from the sole of my foot and almost fling it aside before something catches my eye. Scrawled across the top in wobbly ballpoint are the words 11 BORONIA AVE.

The Fishers' old address in Port Bellamy?

The handwriting is familiar. The letter "O"s have diagonal lines in the middle like zeroes.

Curled inside are a few lengths of creamy-coloured ribbon. I hold the clear plastic bag up to the window, the shimmery organza catching the light.

No, not ribbon.

I squint at the bag.

Is that …?

I glance at Mallory's head pressed into the corner of the cage.

"That'll do," Ally says. "Quick. Hurry. *Hurry!*"

I blink at her. She's nodding at the serrated breadknife in my hand.

Bundling the Ziploc bag into the pocket of my pyjama pants, I scurry back to the water pipe, dropping to my knees on the filthy floor beside Ally. I glance uncertainly at the knife's blade. It might cut through the plastic cord around Ally's wrists but I have no idea how to remove the padlock from Mallory's cage.

I swallow panic rising in the back of my throat.

Breathe, Tash. One thing at a time.

"Who is he?" I say, working the knife like a hacksaw over the cord between Ally's wrist and the pipe. "Who is he *really?*"

She sags against the wall. The skin on her wrists is rubbed

333

raw where she's struggled to get free. "My soulmate," she says, shaking her head like it's a hopeless joke. "Full of bullshit and promises. We've been splitting up and getting back together since high school. I told you about him last time I saw you. His name is Patrick Jonas. You …" She exhales, long and low. "You know him by another name."

I stiffen, the knife hovering over the cord.

Ally looks away from me. "Sparrow. Patrick is your Sparrow."

My throat tightens. I almost can't get any words out. "*My* Sparrow?"

She says it like he's mine and mine only, a figment of my imagination that no one else can see. That's not true, though, is it? It never was. And Ally's just admitted it.

I yank her by the shoulder so she has to look at me. "You knew?"

Ally stares at the wall, her voice oddly detached. "It was a delicate situation and—"

"You *knew*?" I toss the knife aside and stagger to a stand. "All along you knew what he was doing and you said nothing?"

"He didn't really *do* anything, though, did he?"

Gasping, I say, "He taunted me, Ally. He terrified me. He nearly drowned me in the creek!"

"I didn't know he—"

"I told you! I *told* you. You let people accuse me of lying and attention-seeking. I had nightmares for years because nobody believed me. My own *parents* didn't believe me."

Ally hangs her head, avoiding my eye. "I know. I felt sick about the whole thing. It was better for everyone to forget about it all. PJ was in prison anyway, far from being able to harm anyone."

"Harm anyone? He broke me, Ally. I was never the same after that summer."

"But you're okay now, see? You got over it."

"Do I look like I'm over it?" My voice cracks. "You know nothing about my life."

"Look, Tash—"

"God, I *trusted* you." It's impossible to keep the tremble from my voice. "You made out like I was different. You said we were alike. But I am nothing like you. I would never want to be."

Ally yanks at the cord, growling in frustration. "Look, he's coming back, you get that? Once we get out of here you can tell the whole world what an evil bitch I am—"

"Well, it won't come as any surprise to my parents."

"Yeah? No shit."

I turn away from her, biting back things I'd love to say. My anger is dizzying. I'm choking on tears I don't want her to see. I place a hand against the large cabinet to steady myself, my fingers finding a delicate rosette carved into the door. I stare at the rosewood grain beneath my splayed fingers, letting my gaze trail upwards along a decorative border. It curls its way around an inlaid keyhole, a brass key nestled in the lock, before finishing near the top of the cabinet's elegant arch.

Stepping back, I look at the piece of furniture in its entirety.

It's the Victorian wardrobe from Mallory's drawings.

I spin around to face the dog cage on the floor behind me.

Mallory stirs in her sleep, her pale cheek pressed up against the wire bars. Another piece of this sickening puzzle slots into place: Mallory's been held captive in this cellar before. I've seen her notebook. I've seen her memories.

"This is where he kept her," I whisper. I see Ally watching me from the corner of my eye. I march over to her. "Why did Patrick Jonas abduct Mallory from the carnival?"

Ally turns her face to the ceiling and groans. "We don't have time for this."

"You've dodged explanations for nine years, Ally. You'd better start talking right now."

Ally gives me a dark look loaded with the kind of contempt she usually reserves for my father. She nods at the knife on the floor between us. "You cut and I'll talk."

40

THEN

20 DECEMBER 2016

TRANSCRIPT FROM THE OFFICE OF DR INGRID BALLANTINE, PHD

CHILD AND ADOLESCENT PSYCHIATRY,

NEWCASTLE CHILDREN'S CLINIC

PATIENT: NATASHA CARMODY, 17 YEARS OLD

NC: I read a quote the other day.

IB: A quote?

NC: Somebody reblogged it on Tumblr.

IB: Okay.

NC: Ever since then the words have stuck in my head.

IB: What is the quote?

NC: "A bird sitting on a tree is never afraid of the branch breaking, because its trust is not on the branch but on its own wings."

IB: I see. What do you think it means?

NC: Well, it's a self-belief thing, isn't it?

IB: Go on.

NC: Like, am I relying too much on others? Do I have enough faith in my own abilities to save myself?

IB: And do you?

NC: Well, that's the thing. We'll have to wait until the branch breaks to find out.

41

NOW

I pick up the breadknife and resume my assault on the plastic cord. It's looped so many times it's like hacking through inch-thick rope. Mallory stirs in her cage again and the sight of her frail body stuffed inside there fuels the fire within me. It's so degrading. I wish I could take her place, now *and* nine years ago.

My aunt hisses as I yank the cord a little rougher than I need to. "You picked PJ up from prison?" I ask her.

"About three months ago. How do you know that?"

"Figured it out, no thanks to you. He's an ice dealer?"

"An ice *addict*."

I glance up. "I read a newspaper article about all that stuff they found in his unit. He was charged with trafficking."

Ally stares at the knife and stays silent.

"Wait, *you* were the anonymous tip that got him caught?"

"I had to do something! He was using way too much and getting violent. Things were out of control."

"If he was an addict and not a dealer, where did so much ice come from?"

I manage to sever the last loop of cord on one side of the pipe. Ally yanks her arm free while I move to her other side. She loosens the cord around her free wrist using her teeth.

"Ally?" I say.

She shoots me an impatient look. "I planted my supply at his place and called the cops."

"*What?*"

"It was mine, okay? My business. PJ helped me. Or helped himself, as it turns out."

The phone calls and deliveries, the locked rooms I wasn't allowed into. Ally had drugs in there? Wads of cash? *Jesus.* I was an eight year old in her care. My parents trusted her. *I* trusted her.

"I've never sold it since. Just weed now. A few pills." She glances at my knife paused mid-cut and rolls her eyes at my shocked face. "Oh, spare me the sanctimonious crap. I get enough of that from my brother."

You supply people with poison, I want to say. *You practically put it in their veins.* Ally criticises my father because he's a conservative tie-wearing desk jockey, yet she's made a living off other people's misery. I wonder if she can even hear herself. All that yoga and organic eating … what a joke.

"PJ was using all the time," she says. "He was losing weight and his skin was grey. Even his gums were grey – he'd lost teeth. His body was rotting from the inside." She shifts on the floor using her free hand to rub the spot between her shoulderblades. I'm hit with a whiff of pungent body odour. "I knew he had to be taking from our stash. The numbers didn't add up. Carl – our supplier – he expected payment. We *owed* him. I had to lock doors. I had to start doing all of our deliveries myself. I couldn't risk PJ blowing through any more of our stuff."

"So, you let a drug addict come and go as he pleased while I was staying here?"

"I told him to keep away," Ally snaps, "but he was hanging around outside and sneaking in at night." She juts her chin towards the windows above the bookcase. "He was getting in and out through the windows."

I think of the guestroom I stayed in, Sparrow perched on the window seat. He didn't flutter in like a little bird wanting to befriend a lonely eight-year-old girl. He broke in like the drug-addled criminal he was.

"Why would you let him anywhere near me?"

"I didn't. He stumbled across you in the downstairs bedroom that second night you stayed. He came up with a plan to extort money from my brother to pay back the drug debt."

"What do you–?"

"Then he screwed it all up. He kept trying to get you down here to the cellar. I mean, it's insane – this house is the first place the cops would search for you."

I can't possibly have heard her right. "The two of you were going to fake my *abduction*? Is this some kind of joke?"

"I mean, you saw PJ's face! He had to know you'd tell the cops everything afterwards. About this cellar, about where he'd been keeping you. It doesn't take a genius to figure out …" She glances at me, wincing.

"Figure out what?"

She swallows and looks away. "PJ wasn't planning on giving you back once we'd received the money."

Her words can't possibly apply to me.

"I got scared," she says, her bloodshot eyes pleading. "I told him I wouldn't go through with it."

Bile rises in the back of my throat. "Ally …"

"So I pulled the plug and told him to leave. He went and did it anyway." She nods in Mallory's direction. "He took that Fisher girl instead of you."

I roll onto my haunches, dazed, the knife slipping from my hand. It barely registers when Ally snatches it up and continues cutting herself free.

"He only told me afterwards," she says, her face pink with effort. "He brought me down here and showed me the cage. I told him he had to return her but he was too wasted to see sense. I had to put an end to it myself."

"Mallory …"

"PJ kept her sedated. She'd wake up and he'd feed her more food laced with something and she'd be out again like a light."

"How did she end up at Barrington Tops?"

Ally sighs. "I had to wait until after your dad came to collect you before I could get her out of this cellar and into my truck."

Realisation stuns me: Mallory was held captive right underneath my feet. And then my own aunt discarded her in the bush like a bag of garbage. I now understand why Mallory stiffened last night when I gave her a hug before bed. Ally's cardigan isn't the only thing infused with her sweet, smoky scent. It's all over her truck.

"*You* dumped her in the national park?" I say, breathless. "She was six years old ..."

Ally continues sawing at the cord, pretending she hasn't heard me.

I think about how Sparrow tried to lure me into the cellar, almost drowning me so I'd black out and he could drag me down here. He nearly had me that day at the carnival, hidden in a costume trunk, ready to load into a car and whisk me away.

Would I have been crammed into this cage instead of Mallory? Would I have ended up in the national park, starving and alone, tearing out chunks of my own hair?

Glancing at Mallory's blonde locks spilling out of the wire cage, a memory flashes into my head of Sparrow splayed across the back verandah, rambling about games and magic.

I can turn a fistful of hair into a pot of gold.

My breath catches. I touch a hand to the Ziploc bag in my pocket with the words 11 BORONIA AVE scrawled across it.

"Sparrow pulled out her hair," I say. I don't even need Ally's confirmation. "For the ransom."

It was supposed to be my hair. It was supposed to be me.

Ally grunts as she works on the last few loops of cord tethering her left wrist to the pipe. "He was going to send it to her parents to prove he really had her."

She says it in such an offhand way it nearly unravels me. Mallory and I were nothing but currency to a couple of debt-ridden drug dealers.

I tug at the door of the dog cage, yanking so hard it rattles the hinges. The padlock tumbles back and forth, unscathed and steadfast.

"Where's the key?" I bark over my shoulder.

Ally remains focused on freeing herself.

"*Where's the key?*" My hands are shaking so much I want to march over there and shake Ally instead.

Her head snaps up. "There is no key! Don't you get it? We're not supposed to get out of here."

Crawling around the cage, I hunt for a weak spot. "Why me and Mallory? *We* didn't dob him in to the cops!"

Ally makes the final cut through her binds and the cord falls away. "He's setting something up with guys he met inside," she says. "Some meth lab down in Victoria. They told him to get his shit in order and sit tight until he gets the call."

"What the hell does that mean?"

She tosses the knife aside and uses the pipe to pull herself upright. Her legs are weak and almost fail her. "Tie up loose ends, Tash," she says. "Which is why we need to get out of here."

It hits me: *we* are the loose ends. The remaining witnesses to his former crimes.

"But he got out of prison months ago," I say. "Why hasn't he done something before now?"

Ally grimaces in her second attempt to stand. "He had to track *her* down for starters." She gestures dismissively at Mallory. "He's been following you around. Looking for opportunities."

Opportunities for what?

Shuddering, I recall the day I spotted him at Watergardens, the sightings of Ally's ute around Port Bellamy, that feeling of being followed on my way to the Fishers' party. Ally led Sparrow to me the day he was released from prison, and then I unwittingly led him to Mallory just like I did at the carnival when we were kids. Mallory was always safe at home; there were no opportunities for him to get to her.

Until last night when I let her come here to comfort me.

"But I've been alone so many times. He could have grabbed me," I say, thinking about my mornings at the beach, the hours after I argued with Rachael at the pier. "He attacked my friend Rachael instead of me." It takes me a split second to realise I just referred to Rachael as my friend.

"The girl with the phone? Yeah. He heard her that night threatening you about some voice recording. It would implicate him in the abduction so he had to get rid of it."

"He didn't get rid of it," I say. "I found the phone in my bag yesterday."

"There was nothing on it anyway."

"So why give it to me? He could throw it away, smash it to pieces."

"Nowhere near as fun as messing with your head, is it? How'd you like all those dead sparrows?"

I'm stunned for a moment and Ally shakes her head.

"Don't you get it, Tash?" she says. "You're his little plaything. You were back then and you are again now. He gets off on making you afraid."

I swallow hard, embarrassed. If that's true then I've been giving him everything he wants. "How do *you* know?"

She snorts. "You kidding me? The drugs make him ramble; he never shuts up. I've been down here for weeks, Tash! You think I'm not asking questions, searching for weaknesses, trying to talk my way out of here?"

"If it's been weeks, why hasn't he tried to abduct me before now? Or Mallory–"

"Too soon." Ally staggers past me. "Too messy. He had to get you both here at Willow Creek."

"Why?"

"It's less suspicious to get rid of us this way than three separate disappearances."

"What way?" I scoff. "Triple homicide?"

"House fire," Ally says. "Tragic accident."

"*What?*"

"It's so damned neat. There's no way he came up with this by himself."

"I don't–"

"It's an insurance scam," she says, like she can't believe I'm not getting it. "Bastard sweet-talked me from prison, and the whole time he was plotting revenge."

I groan. Patrick Jonas is the "somebody else" Ally made beneficiary of her estate instead of my dad.

"His new associates will claim he moved straight to Victoria after being released," Ally says. "So he won't even be in the same state when this house burns down with us inside."

"It'll still be suspicious," I say, gesturing towards Mallory.

"Don't you think fire investigators will be suss about a body in a *cage*?"

Ally hobbles towards the door. "Who cares? You think PJ's thinking clearly? When you brought her home last night he hit the jackpot – all three under the same roof. He's scrambling around town trying to get what he needs to put his plan into action *today*."

She turns her back on me and starts shuffling away.

"Wait! You need to help me with Mallory!"

She ignores me.

"Help me!" I plead. "It will take both of us to carry her out of here. You owe her that much!"

Ally pauses underneath the windows, tilting her head. I think I might've actually got through to her but she shooshes me, glancing up. "You hear that? It's the sound of my truck on Cowpasture Road." She throws me a stricken look. "He's coming. We need to leave *now*."

Flicking the breadknife aside, I grope for the candlestick behind me on the floor. "Help me with her then!"

"If you're smart you'll leave with me right now."

"Not without Mallory." I whack the candlestick against the padlock, sending a tremor through the wire cage.

"I'll run to the neighbours," Ally says. "I'll send the police."

"They won't make it in time if he sets this place on fire!"

I look over my shoulder and realise I'm talking to thin air. I don't quite believe it until I hear Ally's feet thumping up the cellar steps.

"At least throw me my phone," I call after her. "It's on the kitchen table. *Ally*." I hear the front door being thrown open, then the screen door clattering closed. Ally's doing what she does best: looking after number one.

I thump at the padlock again and again, chips of candlestick flying off in all directions. The jarring sound rouses Mallory awake. She blinks at me, groggy and confused, raising a palm to touch the cage.

"Mallory." I shove my hand through a gap in the wire to grip her fingers. "It's okay. You're okay. I'm going to get you out of here."

She tries to sit up as I tug on the cage's door again. I've managed to bend some of the wire. Not enough for it to give way, though.

"Sparrow did this," I tell her. "He's real. He came back here for us."

Mallory spots the rosewood wardrobe and her eyes widen. I can only imagine the panic coursing through her, the familiarity of this cruel scenario.

Moving in front of her, I cut off her view of the wardrobe. "I'm going to get you out of this, okay? I will *not* leave you here alone."

Her eyes lock with mine and she nods, trying to hide the tremble in her lips. I'm about to ask her if she can kick the cage door from the inside when I'm interrupted by the sound of squealing brakes. The ute has pulled up alongside the house. I glance at the windows above the bookcase; from this angle I can see one is cracked open an inch.

Mallory whimpers. I bring a finger to my lips and move silently across the room. Can I sprint upstairs for my phone and make it back down here with enough time to barricade the door? I can't get Mallory out, but I can stop Sparrow from getting in. I just need to keep him at bay long enough for police to arrive.

From here, all I can see through the windows are a few tall weeds growing outside at ground level. I place my foot on the lowest shelf, assessing it for sturdiness. Mallory rattles her hand against the cage, shaking her head for me not to climb.

"It's okay," I whisper, reaching for a high shelf with my hand. "I'm just going to lock the window."

I freeze at the sound of a car door slamming. Footsteps crunch across gravel and I strain to determine if they're heading towards me or the verandah. I begin climbing again just as legs appear right outside the window – grubby cargo pants, steel-capped boots – and I drop from the bookcase to crouch low against the floor.

The window swings up and out, a red plastic jerry can shoved at one corner to prop it open. Another one is dumped beside it before the black boots move away from the window.

I don't need to see the spillage down the side of the jerry cans to know they are full – I can already smell the petrol from here. I glance around me at all the wooden furniture, realising how effectively it will work as kindling. Mallory rattles the cage to gain my attention, and I crawl to the wire door and tug at the hinges. They're buckling a little, yet still holding fast. She shoves a hand through the wire and grips my wrist, making me look at her.

"I know," I say, my voice strained. "I *know*."

She squeezes my hand again, her mouth open wide. Her throat lurches like she's gagging. It takes me a second to realise she's attempting to speak.

Her mouth allows one desperate wisp of a syllable, her haunted eyes expressing perfectly what she's trying to communicate.

Hide.

42

THEN

I hide.

Crouching and shivering, I watch him from behind the popcorn stand. He hovers just outside the toilet block like a shiny black crow. He's waiting for me to come out, but I'm not in there; I'm hiding.

I won't play his games any more.

It feels like I've won.

He ignores the tilt and whirl of the mechanical octopus, the bouncy organ music from the carousel. A group of noisy teenagers swerve around him and one spills popcorn on the ground at his feet. He doesn't move, though, still as a statue. Waiting for me.

But I'm waiting for Morgan. His parents will take me home. The Fisher family will look after me.

Morgan's little sister appears in the doorway of the toilet

block, her blonde hair bright in the sunshine. Two balloons are tied to her wrist — one pink and one yellow — bobbing and bumping behind her and making her giggle. She looks around for her brother and her eyes find me peeking out from behind the popcorn stand.

I almost raise my hand to wave.

Then Sparrow swoops in, dark hood low over his face, and swallows her up with his shadow.

Mallory Fisher? What does Sparrow want with her?

She looks up at him.

Mallory can see him too!

He bends in front of her, his lips moving quickly, pointing towards the path leading down the hill to the car park. Mallory nods, letting him take her hand. He yanks the balloons from her wrist and sets them free, like a magic trick.

He told me he can make things disappear.

Sparrow glances over his shoulder at the popcorn stand, at my hiding spot that isn't a hiding spot at all.

He knows I'm here.

He knows I'm letting him take another girl instead of me.

Grinning at me with his black and yellow teeth, I know he's daring me to stop him. He wants me to come out and take Mallory's place.

But it's just another trick.

I keep hiding as my Sparrow flies away.

43

NOW

Hide!

Mallory mouths it again, more urgently this time. I follow her line of sight to the high windows across the room. His footsteps are close by again, his shadow looming just outside. He places two more jerry cans beside the others and then he's crouching on his knees.

My eyes scour every wall and piece of furniture. I don't want to leave Mallory exposed and alone. It's too late to duck past into the cellar; Sparrow's already manoeuvring his legs through the window.

Mallory forces her arm through a gap in the wire cage and whacks my thigh for my attention. She points at the wardrobe, the brass key nestled in the lock. I slide across the floor as Sparrow clambers on the bookcase. I'm hidden from view here but reach for the key delicately, easing it clockwise till it clicks. The varnished door releases beneath my hand and I coax it open just wide enough to fit through. I'm met with the cool mustiness of hungry shadows.

My skin ripples with goosebumps as I crush my hands into fists. I try to convince my brain to go against every instinct it's ever had.

I can't do it.

I can't willingly climb into that small space inside.

Around the other side of the wardrobe is the thump and slosh of jerry cans being dragged through the window. Behind me, Mallory's resumed a sleeping position on the floor of her cage. She watches me hesitate too long at the wardrobe's door, and something in her face changes: a slight parting of the lips, a slackening of the muscles around her eyes.

A silent exchange passes between us, of inevitability.

Of giving up.

"I'm sorry," I mouth at her, shaking my head. It's like she senses how much I despise myself at this moment, my frustration that I can't control my fear enough to give us a fighting chance. She blinks once slowly, graciously, as if to assure me: *It's okay, Tash. It's not your fault.*

No, it's not my fault we're down here, or that we were targeted as kids. It's not my fault we were stalked and drugged, insignificant pawns in a much larger game. But I've let myself become all-consumed by Sparrow and the cruel things he did to me. I'm letting Sparrow define who I am.

The bookcase creaks under his weight as he lowers himself to the floor. I snatch up the pillar candlestick and slide Mallory a look of reassurance.

We're doing this. We're getting out of here, together.

Sucking in a breath, I squeeze through the narrow door gap, pinching the lock casing on the inside to pull it closed. The door won't seal properly unless it's locked from the outside. For this I'm grateful – the half-inch slit of light from the storage room is a lifeline. While it's a space large enough to accommodate extravagant dresses and tail coats, it might as well be a coffin. My breath and pulse are already galloping away from me. My whole body flushes hot as though even my blood is desperate to find its way out.

As I strain to pinpoint Sparrow's position, every tiny movement I make is amplified, bouncing back at me from the cupboard's panels. I peer through the crack. All I can see from here is the wall pipe Ally was tethered to.

I think I must have revealed my position when Sparrow spews a string of expletives on the other side of the door. Maybe it's the sound of his voice, or the fear he'll lock me in here, that makes my bladder weaken. I press my legs together so hard my thigh muscles burn.

He appears right in front of me – a sliver of Sparrow – a glimpse of his gaunt profile as he crouches near the pipe. After so many years of being told differently, it's almost inconceivable he actually exists in the real world and not just inside my head.

He retrieves a piece of plastic cord from the floor and growls another swearword. I flinch as he tosses it aside and stalks out of my line of sight. I hear him kick Mallory's cage and have to bite my lip, count to five, to hold it together. He prowls the room. The cage rattles again and I pray Mallory's still faking unconsciousness.

Clutching the candlestick in one hand, I place the other flat against the door.

I have the element of surprise on my side. As long as I don't blow it.

My whole body pulsates. I wait for my moment. His shadow moves across the gap and I throw my full weight against the door. It connects with some part of his body and he's knocked off balance as I tumble out of the wardrobe on top of him. I swing the candlestick as he's turning to face me, missing his head and finding his shoulder. In a blink, he's clutching my throat with one hand and yanking the candlestick away with the other.

He steers me to the wall and slams me into the stonework. Things go black for a second. I blink to clear my vision and find Sparrow's face within inches of mine.

His skin is waxy and pockmarked. Deep crow's feet fan out beneath his eyes. Absurd thoughts zip in and out: *He's getting old. He's not the ageless pixie creature I thought he was.*

"Somebody's awake," he says, a nerve in his eyelid twitching. His pupils are inky and dilated. "Did we help aunty get away?"

His forearm is zigzagged with ropy veins, his hand a metal bar across my windpipe. I try to prize his fingers from my throat but they're locked onto me like a bear trap. I wriggle my body against the wall – it only makes him apply more pressure. White dots dance in front of my eyes.

As his lips peel back, mouth open wide, he releases a guttural roar into my face.

Flinching against his hot breath and rage, my body stiffens. I hear Mallory's terrified thumping and kicking at her cage.

"This time you're mine, you little bitch." He flicks and spins the heavy candlestick in his hand like a tennis player getting ready to serve. "We play things *my* way."

He drives the end of the candlestick into my stomach. Air shoots from my lungs and I double over, gagging. He lets me collapse onto all fours. From the corner of my eye I see his leg swing up and there's no way of preparing. The crack of his boot is like an axe splitting my ribs.

I collapse onto my side. I can't even catch my breath to cry out. Sparrow's fist jerks towards my head and I shrink away from the blow. It's my hair he wants. He grabs a handful and uses it to drag me to the water pipe.

Dumping me against the wall, he snatches up one limp arm to loop plastic cord around my wrist. I rally some strength and attempt to shove him away. He responds with an elbow to my face. The blow releases a warm river from my nose and a keening wail through my eardrums. I'm so out of it for a moment I almost think I hear someone calling my name.

I turn to look at Mallory. She's staring back at me, wide-eyed and ashen.

Mallory can speak now?

I hear my name again and Mallory's lips aren't moving.

"Where are you?" the voice calls from upstairs. "Front door was open. Tash?"

Sadie.

Shit, shit, shit!

"Don't," I gargle, gagging on blood at the back of my throat. "Sadie, *run*."

My ribs ache with every word. Sparrow rams me into the wall again and takes off across the room. He grabs two jerry cans and runs flat out for the cellar stairs.

"Sadie, *run!*" I yell again, hauling myself upright. "*Get out of the house! Get to your van!*" I unravel the cord on my wrist and stagger over to Mallory's cage. Somewhere underneath the pain, my adrenaline is surging. "Mal, you've got to kick the hinges, okay? Do it now. *Hurry*."

She nods, then bunches up her leg and kicks the wire door until the top hinge buckles. She keeps it up until the metal casing splits and falls away.

"Nearly there!" I pull the wire, skewing the door on its axis. This new gap is almost large enough for her to squeeze through. She tries, but her head gets caught halfway.

She kicks it some more and attempts it a second time. I bounce the door on its remaining hinges and it bends further. Another tug or two and Mallory can—

I'm yanked backwards by my hair.

Mallory gasps a silent scream and scuttles into the corner of her cage. Sparrow swings me into a headlock and forces me to my knees. His sleeve is wet and reeks of petrol. Upstairs, a smoke alarm comes to life.

Sparrow drags me to the water pipe, loosens the headlock, clamps a hand around the back of my neck. He forces me to lean forwards on my hands as he scrounges for orange cord on the ground.

Suddenly, I'm eight years old again, my face thrust into

the creek, at Sparrow's mercy. I fought him off that day.

I just have to do it again.

Mallory reaches an arm through the wire bars, and for a second I think it's to comfort me. Then I spot what she's straining for: the pillar candlestick is half a metre from the cage tucked up against the wall. I hold my breath as her fingertips brush the round base, almost pushing it further out of her reach. Her fingernails catch the edge and she flicks it towards her. It's barely in her hand before she sends it skidding across the concrete towards me.

If Sparrow sees it coming, he has no time to react. The candlestick is in my hand and swinging up to his face in one fluid motion. I feel it crack against his jawbone, his face flying sideways. He drops to his knees and I crash-tackle him to the ground.

"Now, Mallory!" I scream, climbing on top of Sparrow's back. "Get out of there!"

It's like a starter gun at a swimming carnival – Mallory is moving. She pushes at the cage door with every ounce of her strength.

I smell smoke. I picture flames licking up the walls and eating Ally's furniture. I don't know how much longer we can safely get out. Sparrow groans beneath me and I know he'll only stay down for a short time. He has too much at stake, too much capacity to bounce back and keep fighting.

Throwing my whole weight against Sparrow's upper back, I hook my arm around his neck. Mallory tries to squeeze her head out again but the gap is still too small. She spins around, bracing her upper body against one end of the cage

359

to kick the door with both feet. Sparrow buckles underneath me, trying to throw me off.

It's like a switch flips inside my brain. *Don't you dare!* White-hot fury shoots through my veins.

After all of this, he can't have us.

After everything he's put us through, he can't win.

Mallory tries to squeeze her head through the gap so violently, the wire cuts into her temple. She sobs as she strains for freedom. It's so painful to watch, I start crying too.

I tighten my arm around Sparrow's throat. He flails his arms, slapping at my thighs.

"You're not playing it right," I hiss into his ear. "Stop struggling."

I should know by now – *I should know* – that Sparrow's wiry frame disguises his strength. He rolls like a crocodile, flipping me over with him. I crash into the wardrobe so hard the door flies open, knocking the remaining wind out of me.

Sparrow scrambles to his feet. I curl up in anticipation of his boot or a fist. Instead, he moves with a singular mission: the red jerry cans on the opposite side of the room. He has the lid off one in seconds. I wait for him to kick it on its side, letting it glug and pool on the floor at my ankles. Instead, he lifts it by the handle. He's taking it somewhere. Maybe back upstairs. Maybe we have another chance to climb up the bookcase and get away.

It's like slow motion when he tips it over the dog cage.

"No, no, no, no, no, no, NO, NO, NO!"

Mallory squawks and crushes into a ball as liquid splatters through the bars to soak her. I lunge towards the cage and slam my body on top of it, my ribs shrieking out in pain. The remaining petrol splashes all over my back, into my hair, trickling down my neck and into my mouth.

How is this happening?

We're supposed to get out.

Jerking upright, I'm ready to run at him, pummel him, with whatever I have left. He's holding a silver Zippo lighter in his hand.

"Uh, uh, u–uh," he singsongs, carefully stepping out of the puddle of petrol spreading from beneath the cage.

The fumes burn my eyes. My breath is wheezy. I'm so exhausted I can barely think of what I should do next.

I shove my hand through the bars of the cage and clutch Mallory's wrist. She slides her hand into mine and our fingers intertwine.

We are tethered, Mallory. Like sisters holding hands.

"You don't look at him," I tell her, as I sense Sparrow backing away from us towards the cellar. She nods, her ice-blue eyes locked on my face. "You just look at me, Mal. Only me."

Sparrow says nothing, no poignant parting words. No justifications or empty apologies.

We mean nothing to him. We are pawn pieces.

Inconvenient loose ends.

Still my mind scours for possible weapons and escape routes, how I can get us out of this cellar. Even if we're burning. Even if the whole house collapses on top of us, I'll find a way.

The lighter *clinks* open. I keep my eyes locked with Mallory's.

"I'm right here," I assure her.

I don't know what to do.

I haven't given up but I don't know – *I don't know!* – how to help us.

Do I have the energy to rush him? Trick him? Drag Mallory's cage across the room? One flick of the lighter and our clothes will be up in flames.

Mallory's sobbing now. A lock of hair falls across her eyes and sticks to a tear track on her cheek. I almost reach into the cage to brush it away. Instead, it encourages an idea.

A tiny spark of hope.

"Wait!" I tell Sparrow, spinning to face him. I squeeze Mallory's hand and straighten to a stand, lining myself up with the open wardrobe. "You've won fair and square. It's only right you should have a memento."

Whether it's his drug-eaten brain or twisted enjoyment at prolonging our torture, something makes him pause. I dig in my pocket for the Ziploc bag. I tip out Mallory's hair and hold it up in the palm of my hand.

He edges closer. Still, it's not close enough. I wrap a finger around a lock of my own hair and yank it roughly from my head. That draws him nearer, reeled in by his sick sense of pleasure. I drape my brown strands across Mallory's blonde ones and hold them up like a sacrificial offering.

Sparrow advances slowly, brandishing his lighter like a pistol. My muscles tighten as I ready myself to launch. He moves in front of the wardrobe and I spring forwards, growling a desperate battle cry. I sink my shoulder into his chest. His boots skid backwards across the concrete until they hit the foot of the wardrobe.

I slap him, punch him, kick and scratch him, until he loses balance and topples inside.

"It's a magic trick," I scream. "I know how to make you *disappear."*

I swing the door closed but one of his ankles hangs out onto the floor. I crunch the door against it over and over again until he cries out and retracts it inside.

The door slams shut and I throw my weight against it as I fumble with the key, almost collapsing with relief when it clunks securely into place.

Sparrow thrashes inside the wardrobe. His voice is a shriek. *"I'm gonna kill you. I'm gonna rip you apart!"*

He launches himself at the door with such force the wardrobe rocks. He does it again, even harder. He must be breaking bones in there.

"It's game over, you sick bastard!" I say, thumping my fist against the door. "And I won." I almost laugh at the absurdity of my words. I think I must be in shock.

The wardrobe is robust and he won't have much room for leverage, but that doesn't mean he won't find a way out. I dash to the corner and clumsily drag the walnut dresser into the middle of the room. I line it up an arm's length from the wardrobe and tip it backwards on an angle to brace the door.

Sparrow roars again but his thuds are not as effective now the door is braced. "You're gonna burn. *You bitches are all gonna burn!"*

The smoke is getting thicker. The storage room has taken

on a bluish haze. I don't want to imagine flames tearing along the hallway and advancing down the cellar steps. My skin is hot and itchy from the petrol and Mallory is covered in angry red patches too.

"Right," I tell her. "It's time to kick your way out of here. Pretend this cage door is that arsehole's face."

This elicits a wisp of a smile, and then she's all business. Our small victory has renewed Mallory's energy stores. She attacks the cage door with a vengeance, and in five kicks the bottom hinge splits. I wrench the door towards me, and Mallory scrambles through the gap and into my arms. She hugs me so tightly, I can barely breathe, but I don't tell her to let go.

Something thumps on the floorboards above us. Another smoke alarm joins the chorus. I hear a crackling noise in the cellar that's far too close for comfort. I pull at Mallory's petrol-soaked pyjamas.

"Can you climb?" I ask, nodding at the bookcase. She props me up and we shuffle towards it together. Above Sparrow's incessant banging, I hear a male voice calling Mallory's name.

"Morgan?" I yell. *"Morgan!"*

In seconds he appears at the window above our heads.

"They're here!" he calls over his shoulder. He flattens onto his stomach as a pair of purple Chucks skid up to the window beside him. I'd recognise them anywhere. I'm so relieved I want to cry.

"Sadie?" I call out. "Are you okay?"

Morgan leans his upper body through the window as

Mallory starts her climb to freedom. I steady her from underneath.

"Sadie's fine," he says, reaching for his sister. "She heard you screaming and saw the flames. She called emergency services."

"Thank god. He didn't hurt her?"

Mallory's between us so I can't see the question on his face. "Who?" Morgan says. "She didn't see anyone."

I almost laugh. *Story of my life.*

Smoke and heat are billowing into the storage room now. I spot an ominous orange glow from the cellar beyond. Sparrow is still pounding at the wardrobe, although with less gusto than before.

As Morgan helps Mallory through the window, I start my ascent. I'm hindered by the choking smoke and my tender ribs. Morgan leans back inside and reaches a hand down to me. As I glance up to take it, he gasps. "Tash …"

My heart lurches.

Sparrow's got out. He's standing right behind me.

But I hear the persistent thump against the wardrobe and I know I'm safe. It's just the blood on my chin that's surprised Morgan, the way my eyes have started to swell.

Locking both hands around my lower arm, he pulls me to him. Sadie hovers outside the window and gathers me up as soon as I'm clear.

"Jesus, kid," she says, a tremble in her voice. She squeezes me so tight I wince. "The things you'll do for attention."

My snigger turns into tears and I slump against her as she helps me away from the house. Smoke is pouring from the windows now, the living room ferociously aflame. I hear the distant wail of sirens and wonder if they'll get here before the blaze devours the storage room too.

We shuffle past Ally's brown truck where two more red jerry cans sit in the truck's tray. Sadie directs Mallory to her mum's catering van where she has spare polo shirts to replace our toxic clothing. Mallory's already shivering under the hose as she washes our ordeal from her limbs and hair.

"Tash?" Morgan calls, still crouched by the side of the house. Thick smoke plumes out of the window now, and Morgan backs away rubbing his eyes. "That banging in there. What is it?"

I lift my face to the sky with its dusting of fairy floss clouds. The sun warms my skin and I close my eyes.

I don't hear the knocking from here.

I no longer hear him at all.

"The bogeyman," I reply.

44

THEN

Dad finds me near the rusty old gate at the back of Gran's garden, except it's not Gran's garden any more – it belongs to Aunty Ally now and her bouncy puppy who digs holes. The grass is a lot spikier than I remember, and the passionfruit vine along the fence is all crispy and shrivelled. Dad sighed earlier when he kicked at a lumpy square of dirt where Gran used to grow lettuce and tomatoes.

"She doesn't bother taking care of it," he said, glancing around.

Maybe some people just aren't good at taking care of things that aren't themselves.

I've collected some white daisies and a few pieces of tree bark, some twigs and two pocketfuls of pebbles. Dad crouches in front of me and picks up a smooth grey stone, rubbing it between his fingertips like a lucky charm. I hold up my hand and he places it right in the middle of my palm.

"I'm going to make the baby a present," I say, spreading everything out in a patch of dirt. "Something for his bedroom to welcome him home."

"Like a fairy house?" Dad says.

"Da–ad." I roll my eyes at him. "I'm eight. I don't believe in fairies."

He pretends to be shocked. "Why not?"

"They're not real."

"Is that so?" He scratches his stubbly chin. "Well, I have it on good authority that kids can see all kinds of magical creatures grown-ups can't. Maybe you just haven't been looking hard enough."

I flick his knee with a twig because he's always teasing. But I don't really mind. I kind of like the idea that magical creatures could be real. If one ever visits me, Dad will be the first person I tell.

"It's time for me to get going," he says. "We'll call you as soon as the baby's here. Okay, sweetheart?" He leans over to kiss the top of my head.

"Okay, Dad."

He hangs around for a minute instead of walking to the car, and I think maybe he's changed his mind. He might want me to go to the hospital with him and Mum after all.

Then he jangles his keys. "Okay, then. Wish us luck."

"Good luck!" I say, and I give him a super big smile because he looks a bit worried about the new baby coming. And I'm a bit worried too because lots of things are going to change.

Things will be pretty different when we all get home.
  But different is okay.
  Different will feel normal after a while.

45

NOW

Dr Ingrid's therapy room has had a makeover since I was last here: new pale green walls, smart mid-century style couches. There's a colourful geometric rug that probably screams out for a little too much attention. The revamp could have happened any time in the last six months, yet it feels fitting that this appointment with her is a turning point into something new.

I'm distracted by a trio of vintage ceramic birds on the wall and almost miss her next question.

She blinks at me slowly, her pencilled eyebrows arched just enough to show interest but not judgement. She hasn't aged much in all the years I've known her. Maybe she wrinkles up when she smiles; I've only ever seen her smooth mask of passivity.

"Your aunt," she repeats politely. "Do you plan on having contact with her?"

I readjust myself in the armchair and glance out the window across Newcastle's leafy city streets. Bloated clouds sag low over the terrace houses and church spires.

"Not until I have to," I tell her. "Not until her trial. That's probably months away."

Dr Ingrid knows all about Ally's arrest. I had to give police permission to access transcripts of our previous therapy sessions as part of their investigation. Mallory's original abduction case has been reopened, and Ally's facing charges of being an accessory after the fact. I'll probably be called as a witness for both the prosecution *and* the defence. Dad assures me this is nothing to worry about because all I need to do is get up on the stand and tell the truth.

Believe me, the irony of his words is not lost on any of us.

"How do you feel about your aunt?"

I shrug. "I suppose I feel sorry for her. She managed to mess up her life pretty badly."

Dr Ingrid tilts her head like she knows I'm just saying what she wants to hear. I don't want to say what I'm really thinking: I don't forgive Ally. Not yet. Probably not ever. I know forgiving her is supposed to be more about helping me move forward than making her feel better, especially since, in the end, she became a victim of Patrick Jonas too. But regardless of whether I try to understand why she chose to protect her unstable boyfriend and betray her own niece, I will never get past her dumping a drugged and defenceless six year old alone in the bush.

"And how do you feel about Patrick Jonas?" asks Dr Ingrid.

"How do I feel about his death?"

"Well, if you like ..."

"I don't know how to feel about it." I sigh. "I don't like that I was involved in another person's death, if that's what you're asking."

"Do you feel responsible?"

"Should I?" I counter.

Dr Ingrid's pen pauses over her notebook. "Would you like to talk about it?"

I glance out the window again. "Not really."

"Something for a future session perhaps," she says, scribbling a few lines.

I suddenly feel compelled to pummel *her* with questions.

How do you *feel about Patrick Jonas, Dr Ingrid? How do* you *feel knowing Sparrow was actually real all along?*

Instead, I look down at my hands and stay silent. It's all too easy for bitterness to creep in. I've spent so many years resenting people for not believing me, I can't spend any more time or energy resenting those same people now that they do.

Smiling mildly, I glance at the wall clock: five minutes left of the session. I agreed to do this as a favour to Mum as part of our new agreement to be more understanding of each other's concerns. She's loosened the apron strings enough to let me come here today by myself and spend the evening in Newcastle with my friends.

"So, what's next for you, do you think?" asks Dr Ingrid. "Last time we met you mentioned university applications."

"Yeah. I'll start applying in a few months. I'm working on getting my photography folio ready for interviews."

"Are you still interested in a Melbourne-based university?"

"That's my first preference. I'm also looking at options closer to home. I need to talk things through with my parents before I make any big decisions."

"You mentioned something about a boyfriend when you arrived …"

I glance out the window again, knowing Morgan is waiting for me in the cafe on the corner. He's barely left my side since the fire three weeks ago. It's more of a close companionship right now, and each day the physical tension between us is growing. I know he's giving me the mental space I need to process everything that's happened, but I secretly wish he'd stop being such a gentleman. I miss him. I miss where our fledgling relationship was headed.

"It's been sort of a bumpy start for us," I say, "so we're taking things slowly."

"Sounds very wise." She glances up at the clock and recaps her pen. "Now, at your last appointment you indicated you'd like to 'call it a day' with your psychiatric care. Do you still feel that way after everything that's happened?"

"I'm going to continue with therapy for now," I tell her. "Obviously, I need to work through some trust issues. Not just because of Ally and Patrick Jonas, but also because of how I wasn't believed by those I turned to for help."

Dr Ingrid nods knowingly. "Of course. I think continuing therapy would be a good idea." She swivels in her chair and reaches across the desk for her appointment planner.

"That said, Dr Ballantine–" I rise from my seat and slip my bag over my shoulder, "–I'm really going to need a referral for a new psychiatrist."

I'm waiting to cross at the traffic lights when I remember to switch my phone back on after my session. There's a lengthy voicemail from Tim complaining about some kind of haircut-and-family-portrait scenario Mum's threatening for tomorrow. I call home and Tim pounces on it the moment it rings.

"I don't wanna get a haircut," he whines, after airing his grievances all over again. "Plus, photos with Mum and Dad aren't cool. What if the kids from school find out?"

"You shouldn't worry so much about what the kids from school think."

"They'll laugh at me."

"Who cares? Let them laugh if they've got nothing better to do," I say. "They can laugh at me too."

"Are you coming?" Tim asks hopefully.

"Absolutely! I'll even come for a haircut too." I tuck a wispy strand behind my ear, more than ready to try something new. "You know they allow furry family members in the photos as well? I mean, Mouse won't be into it, but Benny will pose like a champion. And there's nothing uncool about that, is there?"

I smile at the relief and excitement in Tim's voice as he calls out to Mum, informing her of our updated plans. At some point he places the phone down and forgets to disconnect. I'm in front of the cafe now. Morgan, Christopher and Sadie are sitting by the window having an animated discussion so enthralling they haven't seen me. Sadie's girlfriend, Alice, wends her way to the table clutching a fistful of teaspoons and a sugar bowl. She spots me and grins. I give her a wave.

"Tash?" Mum says, finding the abandoned phone. "You still there?"

"Yep."

"I'm glad you're coming with us tomorrow," she says. "I wasn't sure if … Well, I wanted to give you your space."

"Wouldn't miss it, Mum. Just tell Tim he has to give Benny a bath first. He rolled in fish guts on the pier this morning."

Mum laughs. "Will do. Enjoy yourself tonight."

"We won't be back too late," I assure her. "I can text you later if you like. So you know I'm okay."

"Tash, it's fine," she says. "I trust you. Now go and have fun."

*

Light raindrops fall against the cafe's corrugated awning as I move to open the door. I'm almost inside when I hear rapid footsteps on the footpath behind me.

"Wait, wait, wait!" calls a familiar voice. "Hold the door."

I turn to find Rachael and Mallory scurrying to join me under the shop's awning. Draped across their forearms are two large rigid envelopes they're trying to protect from the rain.

"You got them?" I say eagerly, standing away from the doorway to let them through. "How do they look?"

"Brilliant," Rachael announces. "I'm telling you, this

printer is the best. That's why my mum uses them for all her real estate stuff. It's worth the hour's drive."

Mallory elbows her, holding up two fingers.

"Yeah, okay – the *two*-hour round trip," Rachael says. "No need to get technical, Little Miss Chatterbox."

Mallory snorts and flips up her middle finger instead. Rachael laughs and rolls her eyes. "Full of sass, this one."

"Ha!" I say. "Pot. Kettle. Black?"

Rachael allows me a small smile. We're still trying to work out the details of our ceasefire. It currently falls somewhere between polite communication for the completion of our school project, and tolerating each other socially for the sake of our mutual friends. We'll need to sit down and talk it out properly one day soon, but at least right now the stony wall between us is letting through a few cracks of sunshine.

While my own dealings with Rachael are slowly limping forwards, her new friendship with Mallory is blossoming quickly. They've completely hit it off since discovering they're both into creative journalling. I'd always noticed Rachael bent over a notebook in art class and I had no idea she was writing page after page of poetry. After our ordeal at Willow Creek, Rachael took flowers to the Fishers' house and found Mallory in the middle of her bedroom floor surrounded by sketchbooks. Since then, they've been swapping journals to critique each other's work.

In fact, it was Mallory who encouraged Rachael to share her writing with me – she knew Morgan and I felt our *Dreamscapes* project lacked something vital. Rachael turned up at my house one day clutching a Moleskine, and I knew within reading three pages exactly how we could incorporate it into our art project. Not only was Rachael cooperative about it, she actually negotiated a decent discount from the printer too.

"Put them here," I say, clearing space on an unoccupied table. Mallory slips away to join Sadie and Alice by the window. "I'm dying to see how they look."

Rachael takes both envelopes and places them delicately on the tabletop. She moves away to leave me to it, and I touch her lightly on the arm.

"Thanks, Rachael," I say, "for your poetry and the printing. You pretty much saved our arses on this one."

"Rumour has it you can save your own arse just fine." She gives me a guarded smile. "But I appreciate you saying it anyway."

"Project all finished then?" Christopher says, walking over to join us. "Thank *god*. Maybe you people will do *fun* stuff on weekends now, like the scooter park and Comic-Con and–"

"*Computer markets*," Rachael and I say at the same time. I laugh while Rachael rolls her eyes.

"Right. Just for that you're not having one of my sliders," he says.

"You can keep your hipster food," Rachael replies, following him to the counter. "I'm ordering a pizza."

Catching Morgan's eye, I beckon him over, wanting to do the big reveal with him by my side.

"Can you believe this is our work?" he says, leaning over my shoulder for a closer look. The large photo prints are spectacular, the colours vivid and crisp with a finish as glossy as liquid. "How did this even come together with so much other stuff going on?"

We've created four montages featuring photos of the abandoned carnival overlaid with Morgan's ethereal sketches, and finished with feverish scribblings from Rachael's journal. The images are eerie and haunting, simultaneously desperate and desolate. To me they represent us at our most vulnerable, in those moments before sleep when we are stretched out in the silence with only dark thoughts to keep us company.

Fear. Aching loneliness. The worry of being misunderstood.

I realise now it's what we all have in common, regardless of our circumstances. We all share the fundamental need to be heard, to know we matter. It's what tethers us to one another and reminds us we are never truly alone.

"So, what should we do now?" I say, slipping the prints back inside their envelopes. "Check out that karaoke place? Or maybe catch an early movie?"

"Nah," Morgan says, nodding at the steady rain outside. "How about we park here for a little while instead."

I glance over at our friends laughing and teasing and swapping stories, and realise this is exactly where I want to be. With my new photography work under one arm, and an evening of freedom stretching out in front of me, I slide my hand into Morgan's, feeling my small space expand with possibility.

ACKNOWLEDGEMENTS

Firstly, my gratitude goes to the team at Walker Books for plucking me out of the slush pile and believing in my writing, especially my editor, Nicola Santilli, and my publisher, Linsay Knight. They both understood everything I was trying to achieve with this story and I'm so fortunate to have gone through this debut experience with them by my side. Thank you to everyone at Walker for their enthusiasm about my creepy little novel, and to Amy Daoud for the cover and book design.

Heartfelt thanks to Fleur Ferris for her ongoing kindness and encouragement, and for providing so many lovely blurbs to choose from for the cover; I would have gladly used them all if I could! Also to Ellie Marney and Rachael Craw, whose words I'm honoured to have gracing my book as well.

To my extraordinary critique partners, Erika David,

Janelle Weiner, Ingrid Alexandra and Rebekah Beddoe, who have encouraged, advised and reassured me in this journey to publication, as well as brainstormed and commiserated with me over various manuscripts, revisions and rejections – thank you for your wisdom, support and friendship. It has helped me more than you know.

Also, a debt of gratitude to Emily Mead and Emily Marquart for critiquing assorted chapters, query letters and manuscripts over the years and for making this long road so much more enjoyable with their friendship. Much love to Abigail Henderson, Georgina Kinkade and my sister, Vicky Watson, for being my earliest readers and encouraging me to think of myself as a "real writer".

Thank you to my kidlit buddies on Twitter and in Jen Storer's Duck Pond who make the sometimes lonely task of novel writing so much more fun and inspiring. And to the readers, reviewers, librarians, booksellers, book bloggers and bookstagrammers who celebrate their passion for stories so tirelessly and enthusiastically – you are absolute treasures and so very appreciated.

To my parents, Pat and Roy Bolton, and my in-laws, Pat and Rob Epstein, thank you for always being my unwavering cheer squad.

Finally, and most importantly, thank you to Anthony Epstein, the most patient and supportive partner in crime I could ever ask for, and our boys, Hugo and Harvey, who make me proud every single day. Without your love and encouragement I would never have got this far. Look, kids – Mum finally made it onto a bookshelf!

SARAH EPSTEIN spent her childhood drawing, daydreaming and cobbling together books at the kitchen table. A writer, illustrator and designer, she grew up in suburban Sydney and now lives in Melbourne with her husband and two sons. She is passionate about YA, especially the thriller genre, which is her favourite to read. *Small Spaces* is her first novel.

When Gwendolyn Bloom realizes that her father has been kidnapped, she is the only one with the will and determination to find him. As she tracks him across the dark underbelly of Europe, Gwendolyn takes on a new identity to survive in a world of brutal criminal masterminds and has to learn a terrifying truth about herself: to overcome the cruelty she encounters, she must also embrace it.

"Bergstorm is a mastermind." *Goodreads*

"Raises the bar for the thriller genre." *Amazon*

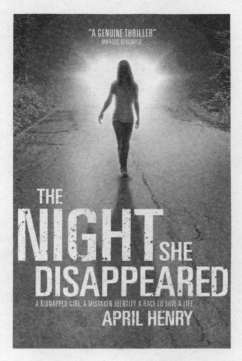

"A GENUINE THRILLER"
MARCUS SEDGWICK

THE NIGHT SHE DISAPPEARED

A KIDNAPPED GIRL. A MISTAKEN IDENTITY. A RACE TO SAVE A LIFE.

APRIL HENRY

Gaby delivers pizzas part-time. She also drives a Mini Cooper.

One night, Kayla, another delivery girl at Pete's Pizza, goes out with an order and never returns. Gaby learns that the man who called in the fake pizza order had asked for the girl in the Mini Cooper. Was Kayla's fate really meant for Gaby? She is determined to find the missing girl, prove that Kayla isn't dead – and to find her before she is.

"A genuine thriller that races along from first page to last!"
Marcus Sedgwick